I0726303

By The Same Author

Grand Openings Can Be Murder

70% Dark Intentions

Out of Temper

Free Chocolate

Pure Chocolate

Fake Chocolate

Story Like a Journalist

There Are Herbs in My Chocolate

AMBER ROYER

A SHOT IN THE 80% DARK

GOLDEN TIP
PRESS

GOLDEN TIP PRESS

A Golden Tip Press paperback original 2022

Cover by Jon Bravo

Distributed in the United States by Ingram, Tennessee

ISBN 978-1-952854-14-9

Ebook ISBN 978-1-952854-15-6

Printed in the United States of America

To Jake, for getting over his fears and trying SCUBA with me.
We've been through a lot together, and you're still always willing
to learn and grow, and always up for a new adventure.

The bird looks me straight in the eye and says, "If you do that, I'll kill you."

I freeze, my hand halfway out to touch the edge of the sculpture the big white bird is perched on. The sculpture is of a pirate ship, roughly seven feet tall, plus the mast. I hadn't noticed the bird perched at the mast's bottom tier --until it had moved, startling me. Now, it makes a sudden dip forward, like it might fly. I jump, and pull my long brown hair back from my face.

The bird says, "Hey!"

"Pardon?" I ask, feeling stupid for talking to a bird like it's a person. It's a cockatoo, I think, and I'm not sure what it's doing in an art museum.

"If you do that," the cockatoo repeats, stretching so that its yellow crest arcs upwards, "I'll kill you." It looks deathly serious, with round black eyes focused in on me. I'm in my early thirties, with freckled cheeks and pale skin that goes red in the sun – or when I'm embarrassed. My cheeks are probably crimson right now.

"I wasn't going to touch the sculpture," I tell the bird, though I totally was. I've been offered a commission to re-create this hodgepodge of iron and brass and marine salvage – out of chocolate. I'm here to consider what I'm getting myself into before I say yes, and some of the salvaged pieces that have been used to make up the mosaic that is the body of the ship are fascinating – especially the shiny telegraph disk marked with different engine speeds, part of a dial about the size of my splayed-out hand.

I'm wondering if that instrument, recreated out of chocolate, could have as much crisp detail as the real thing. I think with the right technique, it could. Though, honestly – I've never done anything like this before. I'm a craft chocolate maker, which means I focus more on coaxing flavor out of fermented cacao beans. My work is similar to that of a winemaker or a coffee roaster. And like a wine maker, I source each batch of beans from a specific farm or collective, to celebrate the unique qualities – from fruity to smoky – that make the chocolate grown in that place special.

My shop does do bean-to-bonbon, so I do have a few cute molds to work with. But the scale of this sculpture is beyond what could be created from a single mold. Parts of it would likely have to be 3-D printed, just to get it done in time. And, after all, the main issue I have with this project is the timeline this museum already has in place. My addition was an impulsive whim on the part of the museum director, and she doesn't seem to understand the term *last minute*. The gala where I would be presenting the sculpture – along with chocolate bonbons and 2,000 chocolate desserts – is in two weeks. Which means I would be asking a lot from my shop's staff and my business partner if we take this project on.

I hold up my phone and tell the bird, "I'm just going to take pictures of the details."

The cockatoo raises a foot and says, "Pieces of eight." Like it's been watching pirate movies. And thinking about money.

"Tell me about it," I say, as I start taking close-up pictures of the different salvage pieces that have been used, focusing in on each one separately. 3-D printing is expensive. I'd recently done a three-foot-tall sculpture of Knightley, my lop-eared bunny, as part of a display for my shop. Knightley is the mascot for Greetings and Felicitations, and his picture is on the wrappers for most of my bars, which are printed with space where people can write a message, making the bar double as a greeting card. I have a neon sign up on the wall with the bunny outline that I've used as a logo from the beginning. But I had wanted something more realistic, to draw people in and show what can really be done with chocolate. I'd had a disagreement with Logan, my business partner, over whether the Knightley sculpture was worth the outlay of cash, and he had only deferred because the shop was my original vision.

But if I get this commission—in part because someone had seen the Knightley sculpture and recommended me—the fee the shop will be paid will justify my original decision. And Logan will have to admit it. That's a little petty, I know, but the relationship between me and Logan is complex. I need his respect, but there's also a playful banter thing between us that's been stressed by the disagreement, and I want to get that back.

"If you do that," the cockatoo says. This time it doesn't finish the sentence.

Mrs. Cook, the director of the Lily Museum, located not far from my shop in the historic district on Galveston Island, bustles back into the gallery space, carrying a manila folder jammed with papers. She's wearing a lavender power suit that projects that vibe. She has bright blue eyes, brown skin and long dark hair pulled back into a severe bun.

I also have long hair, but that's where the comparison ends. Mine is a mousier-brown, and I also have brown eyes and the aforementioned freckles. And today, I dressed up by wearing black slacks and a colorful blouse. Now I feel underdressed, unfocused, and at a disadvantage in this exchange. Plus, I'm talking to someone who introduced herself by her last name. I lower my phone. I hadn't asked for permission to photograph in here.

Mrs. Cook gives me a tight smile, and I can't tell whether or not she's upset about me taking pictures. She just says, "Don't mind Renoir. He has no idea what he's saying."

"Does he live at the museum?" I ask.

"Oh yes, he's our artist in residence. He literally works for peanuts. And the occasional coconut." Mrs. Cook's eyes crinkle at the edges, as she waits for me to laugh at her joke. But the cockatoo's words had been too unsettling. And I'm not sure what she means.

I ask, "Your bird is an artist?"

Mrs. Cook ushers me over to a different part of the museum, through a partially open door, into a small gallery where there is an enormous bird cage taking up half of one wall. The wall space around it features canvases done by splatter painting, and images that look like a wing was dragged through paint. There's even one that looks like the bird walked across the canvas after stepping in lime green paint – with a big paint splat in the corner. Mrs. Cook sounds excited when she says, "Renny's paintings are our biggest fundraising project. Some of them are actually done in food, which we lacquer over. People love to watch him work and want to take home a souvenir. He makes money for the museum – and for bird conservation in the local area – so they get to feel good about the donations, too."

I blink at the canvases. This isn't anything I would define as art. But to each her own, I guess. I say, "He must be a talented bird."

I take out my phone again and pull up my notes program. This is my opportunity to ask questions, and make sure I can deliver on what I'm promising, if I accept the commission. Since I've never taken on a project like the one Mrs. Cook has proposed, I'm not really sure of everything I need to know.

Trying to sound confident, I ask, "What kind of chocolate do you want this sculpture to be made out of? Greetings and Felicitations specializes in craft chocolate from single-origin beans from around the world. I've visited some of the farms personally. I can show you some images of the cacao trees that grew the chocolate you'd-"

Mrs. Cook holds up a hand to interrupt me. "That sounds expensive. No one is actually going to eat the sculpture. I'd prefer if you used the cheapest junk chocolate you can find for the sculpting. Then we can do the mini desserts and bonbons with the good stuff. That's all people will care about at the exhibit opening."

"Right," I say. I guess I should have seen that coming. And it makes sense. But I feel heat rising into my face. I should have thought things through more before opening my mouth.

And yet, Mrs. Cook looks intrigued. "How many images would you say you have of these cacao trees?"

I shrug. "Hundreds? I take a ton of pictures each time I travel. A lot of them wind up on my social media, but I have a whole archive I've never even used."

Mrs. Cook takes me back into the gallery with the boat sculpture and gestures around at the high-ceilinged walls, which have a few paintings hung on them already. There's a large watercolor of Pleasure Pier, and a couple of different studies of palm trees. There's also a disturbing image of soldiers fighting and dying up against a dock – one even falling into the water – which claims to be a woodcut of a period illustration from the Battle of Galveston. She says, "There will be other pieces in this space when the exhibit opens. The goal is to highlight different aspects of the history and uniqueness of Galveston Island. But . . ." Mrs. Cook tilts her head and gestures with her chin towards a small room connected to this one through a wide doorway on the other side of the gallery. The smaller room is bathed in moving blue light, making patterns on the walls and floor. "That space isn't spoken for, and I'm always looking for little bonuses that would be an extra draw to get people into the museum. I think it might be fun to have an immersive cacao tree exhibit. People could eat bits of chocolate while standing in the middle of images of the trees, and we could show process of how you made the sculpture. We could charge them an extra fee, to cover materials for all the samples." She hesitates and chews at her bottom lip. "Assuming your photos are up to our standards." She laughs. "I've never taken on an artist sight unseen."

I start to say, *I'm not an artist.* But I bite back the words. After all, Mrs. Cook seems to think the cockatoo is an artist. And I'm pretty sure I can do better than that. I stammer out, "I can send you a link to some pictures."

She waves a hand at me again. "No. I'll send you a trial for some software. You send back the finished presentation, then we'll see if it works."

I can feel my frustrated heartbeat in my fingertips. I want to tell her that's a lot of work for something she hasn't said yes to. Especially given the time frame, and all the other work she's asking for. And I'm no expert when it comes to graphics software. But maybe I can get my nephew's friend Miles to help out with it, now that he's started working at the shop on days when he's not in school or at football practice. Because if there's one thing we Texans take seriously, it's college football. Miles was able to help when I needed to 3-D print chocolate molds for a project aboard a cruise ship where I'd been invited to do demos. I'm sure formatting some pictures must be easy compared to that. Though I'm going to have to ask him to help with the molds for the sculpture too. I should probably see how much time he has before I commit him to tasks no one else knows how to do. And I should tell Mrs. Cook that she needs to look at sample photos before I ask Miles for that much paid time.

But I've always had trouble saying no to projects, and especially now that I'm working for myself.

"Okay," I say, forcing myself to sound light and excited. "That sounds fun."

Mrs. Cook says, "There's an artist's studio in the back. You will be able to do assembly of the sculpture there, so you won't have to arrange to move the completed piece. And you can use the equipment. There's a lathe, and sculpting tools, and we have a food-safe 3-D Printer. If you need it, there's some heavier equipment. You have to do a safety training, then I can give you an access key for the duration of your contract."

"Really?" I say, not even trying to hide my excitement. "That-"

There's a clatter somewhere in the back of the museum. Renoir lets out a screech and flies towards the noise. Mrs. Cook follows, so I go along with them. A girl is sitting awkwardly on the floor in what must be the museum library. She's petite, pale, with curly brown hair and gold-brown eyes with a helpless look in them. She's surrounded by books, some of them splayed open, and she is rubbing at her elbow. A book cart is on its side, one wheel rolling forlornly to a stop.

"What happened in here, Tracie?" Mrs. Cook says in a clipped voice.

Instantly, Tracie's face goes crimson, and her hand moves away from her injured arm. "Nothing, Mrs. Cook. I was just trying to turn the cart, and I had all the books on one side, and it overbalanced."

Mrs. Cook sighs, and I find myself coming to Tracie's defense. "That sounds like an easy mistake to make. if you get in a hurry."

Tracie says, "I'm always in a hurry. I need to finish up here so I can get to my other job."

Mrs. Cook says, "You need to focus while you're here, if you want to keep *this* job."

"I'm sorry, Mrs. Cook," Tracie says as she looks down at the floor.

A door opens somewhere down the hall, and then rushing footsteps head towards us. A Latino guy comes in, about Tracie's age. He's tall and bald, wearing a dress shirt paired with a tie printed with melting clocks. He sees Tracie and goes to her, helping pick up some of the books.

Mrs. Cook says under her breath, "You've met Tweedle Dee, now here's Tweedle Dum."

That's harsh. I feel a lurch of embarrassment on behalf of the two docents or assistants. I would never speak about employees like that – let alone right in front of them.

The guy apparently feels the same way. He straightens his shoulders and says, "Look, Delores. I've been considered gifted since preschool. My artwork has won awards and been exhibited. You can't just-"

Mrs. Cook sighs loudly. "And yet, Hernan, you need to work here, so that there's something concrete on your resume when you graduate."

Hernan gives Mrs. Cook a dirty look. And I can't help but think, if somebody gets murdered around here, it's bound to be her. The thought raises goosepimples along my arms. Because – since when did I start thinking that way?

I'm a chocolate maker, not a detective. Yet because of circumstances I've found myself caught up in, I've had to face down three desperate killers. The media has taken to calling me a murder magnet, and at least one person in my life has encouraged me to start carrying a gun, though I'm quite happy with the pepper spray in my purse, thank you very much. But the first murder happened at Greetings and Felicitations' grand opening party, and the shop has had notoriety surrounding it ever since. I realize that's bound to change anyone's perspective.

But I don't want to be the type of person who walks around looking for murders – or for potential murder victims. I've only been a chocolate maker for a bit over a year. I'd left my previous job as a physical therapist because I wanted to make people happy. No, not just wanted – I *needed* to see happy people. There had been a lot of personal pain that had gone into the decision. I had just lost my husband to an accident, and had been dealing with the roughest parts of grief, so I'd come home to Galveston Island and started my own business.

It hadn't been my fault that there'd been a murder just when I'd opened the shop, or that other troubles had followed since. Recently, Felicitations has started to become a gathering place for the community. My chocolate – and my pastry chef's creations, made with said chocolate – have been making our customers happy. And taking on Logan as a business partner has expanded my vision of what Greetings and Felicitations really can be.

Things might be a bit complicated between me and Logan personally, since I'd kissed him – and then later kissed Arlo, the cop who had been my first boyfriend. Even so, things in my life in general have been much more optimistic, and I'm finally moving forward.

I don't need to go borrowing trouble by thinking about murder.

I bend down and retrieve some of the books. One landed face down, bending some of the pages. I flip the book over to straighten the paper out, and I find three faces scowling up at me from the page, roughhewn men with loose white shirts and orange sashes at their waists. A pirate flag centers the image behind them.

I close the book and look at the cover. Robert Louis Stevenson's *Treasure Island*, with illustrations by N.C. Wyeth.

"That's the 1911 edition," Hernan says. "Wyeth did illustrated editions for many of the classics, from *Robin Hood* to *Rip Van Winkle*. The *Treasure Island* paintings are considered to be his best collection. He's actually one of my favorite illustrators, even though he came to hate the commercial nature of his own work. He couldn't seem to understand that he was bringing to life the words of such amazing adventure stories. Instead, he felt limited by the needs of the book industry over absolute artistic freedom."

"That's fascinating," I say as I move to put all the books I had picked up back on the cart. "My late husband always liked those old adventure stories. He was a voracious reader."

Mrs. Cook takes the copy of *Treasure Island* back off the cart and holds it out to me. "Take it."

"Excuse me?" I ask.

She shakes the book. "It's damaged now, due to *someone* being in a hurry." She emphasizes the word someone and give Tracie a pointed look. "That means it has lost much of its value. Since it seems sentimental to you, you should take it."

From the look on her face, I get a feeling that she just wants to take the book away from Hernan. What's up between those two?

I look down at the book in her hand, her perfectly manicured fingernails a lavender that matches her suit. Unexpectedly, my heart goes cold, but the beat speeds up at the same time – in a rhythm of sudden anxiety. The last time someone gave me a rare book, it had been tied up with a murder. And I'm feeling a strong sense of déjà vu. I look up at Mrs. Cook. She isn't the most pleasant person, but I don't want to see anything happen to her, and it feels like if I take another rare book, something bad is bound to follow. I know there's no real logic to that, but I can't help the way I feel.

I shake my hands in a *no*. "I couldn't possibly."

"I insist," Mrs. Cook says. "You're going to be sculpting us a chocolate pirate ship. This could well provide some inspiration."

I take the book, because it's easier than trying to explain why I don't want it. Instead, I tell Mrs. Cook, "You take care of yourself, all right?"

She gives me an odd look and says, "I always do."

"Good," I say. "You should be really careful." I sound like an idiot. But I can't tell her I'm paranoid on her behalf.

Hernan says, "You're the one working on the chocolate sculpture? I would love to learn to work in that medium. Let me know if you're hiring help."

"Me too," Tracie says. "I would love to actually get paid for doing art for once instead of waiting tables, or filing things around here."

I hesitate. It would be nice to have trained help with the artistic side of the project, instead of relying entirely on Miles. But I don't know anything about either of these potential employees. Finally, I say, "I'll have to price out a few things before I will know if extra help is in the budget. And I have to consult my business partner on hiring."

That last part isn't strictly true. Logan and I don't really have rules like that about the business, and he lets me take the lead on major decisions. But consulting with him not only gives me time to make a more reasoned decision – it gives him time to do background checks. Logan used to be in law enforcement, and after that he spent time as a body guard, and who knows what else, before coming to Galveston to start a small business of his own. So I tend to leave the background check kind of thing up to him.

Hernan and Tracie both give me cards that have QR codes on them, along with original art. Apparently, it's the modern equivalent of handing over a portfolio and a resume. Hernan's card features a detailed image of an impossible tree, with multiple kinds of fruit and flowers. Tracie's is more subdued, and somehow even more surreal, a black-and-white image of a teapot with a staircase leading inside it.

Mrs. Cook gives me the manila folder which contains information on the project and a contract for me to sign. I'll obviously need to look over it, so I take it with me unsigned and head for the museum's lobby.

As I'm leaving that gallery, Renoir squawks and declares, "You don't love me anymore!"

Mrs. Cook waves a dismissive hand at the bird. She tells me, "That's just his way of saying goodbye."

Chapter Two

I'm sitting at a table near one of my shop's plate glass windows. Said window that looks out onto Galveston's Historic Strand. It's one of the main shopping areas on the island, not far from the cruise terminal, with restaurants and kitschy tourist shops and real antique stores jumbled all up together. It's also one of my favorite spots here. I like to people-watch while I work, and I've been crunching numbers about the museum commission, so I need the relief.

In the back, on the other side of the wall from me, I can hear Logan bringing in the bags of cacao beans that he picked up from the storage facility where we rent space. There's the noise of him setting the heavy bags down in the chocolate processing area, where the cargo door is located. After a few more trips with more bags, that door slams shut.

The shop has a room for roasting and winnowing the beans. Winnowing means removing the husks, so the resulting chocolate can be smooth. That room has a lot of heat and dust. The bean room is also where the supplies get stored. There's a separate room where we conch the chocolate and make the finished bars, bonbons, and truffles. Past that, a hallway leads to our restrooms and my office, but I rarely use the office space anymore – in part because a killer had once trapped me inside it and I now prefer to be able to see people approaching my workspace.

We also have an industrial kitchen, which I use for making fillings for the bon-bons and ganache for the truffles. But Carmen, my pastry chef, spends more time there than I do, so I wind up keeping things organized for her convenience. Miles comes in to help with special projects. We all take turns running the register and acting as baristas for the coffee and horchata bar that helps keep customers here long enough to get to know us. After all, it doesn't take that long to look at a few different chocolate bars, and we want people to feel welcome to hang out, or study or do work at the shop's tables.

There's also a small section of travel books and unusual literary finds that I've collected over the last year. On that same side of the shop, but close to the register so we can keep an eye on it, is the secured case with what people like to call my "murder books."

The "murder books" are actually one of the shop's biggest draws. The volumes of *Sense and Sensibility* that had helped me solve the first murder I'd been involved with. The copy of *The Invisible Man* that I'd gotten when Mateo had disappeared. The signed copy of *Murder on the Orient Express* that I'd won in the raffle on that cruise ship, after the mystery author had been killed.

Ash Diaz, local blogger and sometimes pest, had featured the books in one of his many articles about my *exploits*, as he calls them. His readers – and others – had taken to visiting the shop for the macabre aspect of it all. I still get people wanting to eat my chocolate on a dare, convinced that if they eat my 100% dark cacao bar, someone might try to murder them. It still bothers me that that's my business's reputation, especially since I had gone through so much trouble to give my shop a comfortable shabby chic vibe. But those customers tend to spend a lot of money in the shop, so I can't exactly ask them to leave.

There had been a whole van worth of true crime fans in here when I'd gotten back from the museum, and they'd had me autograph their chocolate bars. They'd each bought thirteen bars. I'm not certain what they expect to get from that, but it made for a good sale.

Logan comes through into the seating area where I am. He walks up behind me and catches me looking at cheap bulk chocolate on my laptop. I can feel his skepticism before I even turn around. He clears his throat and quips, "We changing our business model? I expect the customers might notice."

I scrunch up my nose at him. "Do I tell you what kind of fuel to put in your airplanes?"

Logan is a puddle jump pilot, when he's not checking in at the chocolate shop. He has his own successful charter business. He doesn't respond to my playfulness. He crosses his arms over his chest and asks, "Is that something you're likely to do in the future?"

I can't help but feel a little skip in my chest over how hot he looks when he does that. He's wearing his usual leather pilot's jacket and black tee combo. Sometimes he mixes it up with a gray tee, or a dark green one, but I can only imagine that half his closet is black tees and jeans. Logan has intense green eyes, dark hair and a chiseled jaw. And very kissable-looking lips, even when they're narrowed into a line.

I tell him, "We would use bulk chocolate for the museum sculpture. I'm pricing out everything to make sure we can do this with the budget the museum is offering and make enough profit for it to be worth all the work." Our hands brush when I give him the manila folder. He opens the folder and starts reading, though I'm still focused on that brief touch. He's backed way off since I'd kissed Arlo. He said it's because I need to find closure with Arlo and decide what I want in life. But he's made it clear that he's open to pursuing a relationship after I've done that, if I'm still interested. But sometimes I think maybe he's turned off by the fact that I'm taking such a long time to make a decision.

I don't know. Maybe I'm reading too much into his reactions, and he really is trying to focus on work while we're at work. He seems to be reading the contract information very carefully. Logan doesn't even look up when the shop door opens, and a woman comes in, wafting a strong sent of myrrh and patchouli around her. I can tell by the way his jaw tenses that he notices, though, and is observing. She's wearing a bright flowy tunic top and bell bottom jeans. Her look is very much 1970s, but she's carrying a modern cell phone.

Carmen, who has been working in the kitchen, comes to the counter, ready to assist this new customer, but the woman sees me sitting at the table and makes a beeline over. Carmen raises a skeptical eyebrow, then goes back to the kitchen. Carmen is in her twenties, and dresses athletically – with her dark hair in a sleek ponytail, and a surf-company tee – except for her collection of ruffled aprons. The one she's got on now is neon pink polka dots trimmed out in lace. She's in one of her recipe creation modes, so the kitchen is where she really wants to be. It's that slow part of the afternoon, and we aren't getting many people in aside from that one van full of customers, so it hasn't been a problem.

"Mrs. Koerber?" The woman asks.

"That's me," I tell her. "But you can call me Felicity."

She says, "Oh, thank goodness. I was afraid you were going to be another Mrs. Cook when she introduced you like that."

Apparently, Mrs. Cook has been talking about me working on her project to other people – before I've even accepted.

"Are you with the museum?" I ask.

The woman says, "I'm Amálie Timbers. For the last several years I have been working with local salvage companies to create art including maritime items, celebrating Texas. And I've been doing a separate series of sculptures repurposing metal from cars and buildings damaged by recent hurricanes into something meaningful. This new sculpture incorporates elements from both. You should know that, if you're recreating my work."

Logan and I look at each other and blink.

Logan says, "That's quite an introduction."

Amálie frowns at him. "How do you introduce yourself?"

"Logan," he tells her. "Just Logan."

"Well, Just Logan, I hope you have the art skills I think I see in your sensitive hands and world-weary eyes." She touches the back of Logan's hand.

"I'm more of a craftsman," Logan says. "And a mechanic. I repair my own planes."

"I think it's a bit early to worry about art styles," I tell her, not sure I want someone that insightful and intense anywhere near Logan – even though I officially have no claim on him. I know he's attracted to strong women, and Amálie is actually quite beautiful. I emphasize, "We haven't actually accepted the contract yet."

"But you will," she says. "You must. And I want to make sure there is something I can actually eat at the reception."

"Are you allergic to something?" I ask. That's not an uncommon issue in any food-related business. If she says nuts, that could be a problem, since we process gianduja in one of our melangers, and some people who are allergic to nuts can be extremely sensitive to cross-contamination.

She says, "I can't do gluten or dairy. And I am deathly allergic to strawberries."

That's much less of a problem. I get up and move over to the shelf that holds our chocolate bars. I select a few appropriate dairy-free ones, and offer them to her. "These are some of our two-ingredient chocolate bars. Nothing but sugar and cacao. They are processed in the same equipment as our milk chocolate, but everything is thoroughly cleaned between products."

She takes the bars. "That should work. But the museum is promising desserts as well as chocolates."

"That would be Carmen's department," I tell her. "She does all our baking. Let me go see if she has a minute to talk preliminary ideas. Assuming we accept the contract."

I get her together with Carmen, and they're talking excitedly, already bouncing ideas, by the time I get back to the table. I sit down again and close the browser on my laptop.

Logan is still flipping through the contract, reading each page closely. Without looking up, he says, "I was thinking. I was looking at the country stamps on the bags of beans you sent me to get today. I still haven't been on a sourcing trip. And if I do eventually make my own specialty bar for the shop, I want it to be from somewhere where I've actually seen the farms. Maybe after this project is over – and after Autumn's wedding – we could go to Brazil."

My mouth slides open in shock. I close it. I can feel my heartbeat in my fingertips again. "Logan."

He holds up a hand, "I don't want you thinking I'm asking you to shirk on any of your matron of honor duties. And I know the timeline for her wedding is pretty short."

"It's not that," I protest. I'm not ready to go on a solo trip with Logan, and he should know that. We've danced around the idea of having a romance, even kissed once. But after Arlo, who had been my first love, had confessed he still has feelings for me, Logan had backed off and left me confused. Things have been awkward all around. And I'm no closer to making any decisions between the two guys in my life than I was when he'd told me that. "Logan, I can't-"

"Breathe, Fee," he tells me, giving me a wry grin. "I wasn't suggesting a romantic weekend in Rio." He shrugs. "Though maybe someday." While I'm still trying to decide exactly what he means by that – and if it implies that he's potentially considering marriage, when we haven't even been on a proper date – he adds, "I have a plane that can fly six people comfortably. It would be perfect for a trip with friends. We could even bring Arlo along, just to keep it fair."

Fair. As though there's anything fair about being stuck in a love triangle, afraid to make any decision because it might be the wrong one. As though spending equal amounts of time with both guys makes anything fair. "I guess," I say.

He shrugs again, "Just think about it. Arraial do Cabo isn't far from Rio, and it has some great diving spots for beginners. We could plan far enough out that you could get dive certified, if you wanted – and if your doctor approves."

Logan and Arlo are both into diving, have even done some local rig diving together. It's weird that they've become friends. But maybe it says something about the type of people I'm attracted to – affable and generous-hearted. Though in most ways, they couldn't be more different.

"I've never even thought about diving," I say. My late husband and I had spent plenty of time near and on the water. But I've always suffered from asthma. I've undergone a new experimental treatment which seems to have worked, and I haven't had an attack in months. And I know that some asthmatics dive anyway. But what if I get scared about breathing underwater, and that triggers an attack?

Logan is looking at me so hopefully I can't just say no without at least considering the idea.

Fortunately, before I have to say anything, the door opens again and a chattering family comes into the shop. I do a double take as I recognize them. "Tam Binh!" I jump up and run across the shop to embrace my friend – who I mostly chat with online, since she doesn't live anywhere near Galveston. When we break the hug, I ask, "What are you doing here?"

She and her family are digital nomads, bloggers who travel the world sampling food for their Mixed Plate blog. Tam Binh has Vietnamese heritage, and Stewart's very Anglo grandparents live in Cornwall, so as bloggers the couple are all about celebrating their children's mixed genetics and global palates. Last I'd heard, they were in Iceland, trying some questionable delicacies.

"Blame her for inviting me." Tam Binh points at Carmen, who waves over at us excitedly, despite still talking with Amálie. Tam Binh says, "The plan is to spend some time in the kitchen talking about Carmen's cooking philosophy, while we're baking, so that I can do a series of blog posts leading up to the release of the cookbook. There's going to be some podcasts too, if you want to sit in."

"The cookbook is mostly Carmen," I say. "I just did a chapter in the back on making truffles and bonbons. Which are more my specialty."

"But you make the chocolate Carmen is using in the recipes," Tam Binh says. "And it is called the *Greetings and*

Felicitations Cookbook, after all. You're the Felicitations. Listeners will want to hear your personal story. Especially if you talk about sourcing trips and people you've learned from."

"I could do that," I say. I know that Tam Binh would ask questions in a way to make sure I'm comfortable, and if there's two things I love talking about, that would be travel and chocolate.

Amálie heads back towards us. She says, "See you at the gala. Or at the studio, if we're both working at the same time."

I don't even try to remind her that I haven't officially said yes. As excited as Carmen looks right now after talking to her, and as confident as Logan had sounded, I'm pretty sure I'll be signing the contract.

Now I just have to talk to Logan about potentially hiring the two artists I had talked to at the museum, to help us get this done on time.

Logan stands and shakes hands with Stewart, asking him, "What are your plans, while your wife is busy with all these interviews?"

Stewart gestures down at his three young daughters. "We're going to explore, and do our own posts documenting it. I thought I'd arrange a fishing charter. Sarah here loves fishing. She caught a striped marlin off the coast of New Zealand two years ago, when she was only eight."

Sarah, the tallest of the three girls, blushes and pulls at the end of her straight dark hair. She says, "Only because you helped me reel it in, Dad."

"Well, what are dads for?" Stewart says. He gives her a very cheesy *dad* wink. "I still think you'd have got it without me."

"What about him?" Logan asks, pointing to Stewart Jr., who has crossed the shop to the pastry case and has his hands pressed flat against the glass so he can get a better look at the pan dulce and other treats inside. "He a fisherman too?"

"Oh Stewart Jr.? He's a baker. He'll help Carmen and me out," Tam Binh says. Then she realizes he's smudging the case and rushes over. "Stu, what have I said about touching displays?"

I hear Stewart Jr. mumble, "Sorry Mom," as he takes two steps back.

It's all a little bittersweet for me to watch. I love kids, but Kevin and I had never been able to have any. Even if I *were* to get married again – not that I'm seriously entertaining the idea, no matter what Logan's earlier statement might have put into my head – I probably couldn't. But I'm happy that I have this family in my life – even if I mostly get to see their antics and adventures from a distance, on their blog and in videos.

Carmen moves back behind the counter and asks Stewart Jr., "Do you want a cochinito – that's the piggy cookies – it's spiced like gingerbread, and mine are special because I add a chocolate glaze. Or do you want a piece of cheesecake with a chocolate swirl? That's basically all we have left, unless you want to wait."

Those both sound like amazing options to me. Our customers here have gotten used to trying whatever Carmen has baked, because it's all delicious. She doesn't bake anything to a schedule, and there are no regular menu items, just whatever she's in the mood to do that morning – or the morning before, since some days she still manages to go out early to surf. She's had fewer surfing days since she started working on the cookbook, but I'm sure she'll get back to her regular schedule soon.

I hadn't really intended for the chocolate shop to have a big bakery component – just a few samples of what could be done with the chocolate I'm selling, and to complement the coffee and horchata bar. I had initially hired Carmen as a barista and shop assistant – what Miles is doing now. But I think the fact that Carmen bakes whatever she wants, and people never know what to expect, is part of what draws our regular customers back.

Stewart Jr. doesn't hesitate to choose a piggy cookie, but once he has it, he doesn't eat it right away. Instead, he turns towards his mom and poses, and Tam Binh takes a picture of him holding the treat and grinning for the camera. She takes a few steps back and takes another picture, probably to get Carmen in the background. But the second Tam Binh puts her phone down, Stewart Jr. devours the cookie.

"What about you?" I ask Charlotte, who is about eight. "Do you like to bake or do you like to fish?"

She scrunches up her nose and says, "Nope."

I'd meant it as an either-or question, but apparently she likes neither.

Stewart says, "Char there is all about birds right now. She's decided she's going to grow up to be a parrot trainer like the one we saw in Florida. She hasn't been eating chicken since then, and some of the food we saw in Iceland was a little intense. She's going vegetarian for a while."

"But you're taking her fishing?" Logan asks.

Charlotte says, "I want to see the birds follow the boat. I don't care if birds eat fish. That's just what they do. As long as *I* don't have to eat it."

I can't argue with her logic. And it gives me an idea. "You want to go see a bird who's an artist? The museum I'm doing a project for has a bird that paints with his wings."

Charlotte's eyes go big. "I can see that?"

"Well, I'm not sure if he will actually be painting while we're there. But you can definitely meet Renoir the cockatoo and see paintings he's done. I have to go by and drop off some papers anyway." I give Logan a look, and he nods. That means he thinks everything is okay with the contract, and from what I can tell the budget and payment are generous, so our first foray into serious chocolate art is a go. Even if I'm still afraid we may be getting in over our heads.

"Should we go to the museum now?" Stewart asks. "I'm sure Tam Binh's going to want to take pictures in your kitchen for a while, for the initial blog post."

Carmen says, "We can take care of the customers, too, if you're not back by the after-work rush. Miles is supposed to be in later to work on the order for that hotel that wants the custom one-ounce bars, so if it gets too crazy, we have backup."

I love that I have someone competent that I can leave in charge, and friends that feel comfortable coming into the kitchen to create, or to hang out – or at this point just to take photographs. I've come a long way from being possessive of this business, the way I had been when I had first opened it and had been dealing with the rawest parts of grief. As a widow, it had been hard letting people into my life again, but I'm much happier now that I have. I still have my rough moments, but they're a lot fewer and farther between. I've had a lot of healing moments, too, over the past few months.

"That sounds great." I find myself smiling, despite the ominous feeling I'd had earlier when Mrs. Cook had handed me that copy of *Treasure Island*. Which is currently locked in the filing cabinet in my office, lest it wind up anywhere near the case displaying the murder books. I know it's silly. Because logically, there's no reason that I should ever wind up involved with another murder. Statistically, I am way over the estimate for how many one person should have to deal with in a lifetime. It was just an odd blip of circumstance that all these things happened at once, and now it's over.

As we're heading out of the shop, Charlotte tugs on my sleeve. She stage whispers, "I love your giant chocolate rabbit."

She points at the sculpture, which is behind the counter, on an elevated pedestal up against the wall. It shows a three-foot-tall white chocolate lop reaching up to nibble at chocolate lavender bushes. I had covered the bushes with edible paint, but left parts of the chocolate showing through, so you can see what the product underneath really is. I've been watching sculpture demos, and sometimes there's so much paint and decoration that you can't even tell the piece is made out of chocolate. It's a cool look – but not really what I was going for.

I smile even bigger. "That's a sculpture of my pet lop Knightley. He inspired the images on all my chocolate bars, and he's always been there for me, especially when I was first getting my business off the ground. He really did nibble a couple of lavender bushes, even though he likes parsley and cilantro even better. But he doesn't like to go places, so he's at the hotel where I live. If you're in town long enough, you might get to meet him too."

Charlotte's eyes get big again, and she says, "You live at a hotel?"

I think of the best way to explain to a kid that my aunt is a house-flipper, and that we're both living at the hotel while it gets renovated. I say, "Yes, but it's not open for people to stay at yet. My aunt and I – along with some friends – are making it pretty, then she is going to sell it to someone who wants to run it."

Charlotte nods. "I've seen house-flip shows on TV. Sounds like a lot of work."

I laugh. I think I'm underestimating these kiddos. "Those lavender bushes I recreated in the sculpture are from the garden we're doing out back. The garden has been my main contribution to the whole hotel flip project."

She looks at me, considering. "It sounds like you're busy enough here. Did you say you're making a chocolate boat?"

"I am," I tell her. "And it is going to be amazing."

We head to the museum. Logan and I take his car, and the Saveur family – minus the mom and Stewart Jr. – follows us in their rented SUV. When we get to the museum building, there's a cop car out front. Which is alarming, but the place is still open, so maybe it's just a coincidence. Police officers like art too. Maybe the officers just stopped by to say hi to Renoir. Right?

When we get inside though, I don't recognize the girl sitting at the reception station, and she tells us that Mrs. Cook is unavailable. When I explain who I am, and that I've brought the contract, she says that Mrs. Cook will probably be available soon. She adds, "Of course you're welcome to visit the galleries, without charge. Or to watch Renoir create his latest masterpiece. I'm about to give him an orange, and you should see what he does with it."

Even though we're not being charged admission, she still makes us sign in on a paper log, on a clipboard she takes from beneath the counter.

Of course, the bird's performance captures the kids' attention, and we spend a few minutes watching the cockatoo bite into an orange, getting the juices all over his feathers, especially his chest, where it starts running down onto the canvas he is standing on. There are three other small canvases arranged in front of and to the sides of him. When he's done eating the orange, he drops what's left of the rind and then shakes out his feathers, splattering the canvases. He declares, "Put that back! It's for the history, not the glory!"

Which makes no sense, as none of us have touched anything.

The girl laughs and says, "Birds often repeat things they hear out of context. That's become one of his favorite phrases. It's also one of the most complex."

I can't help but wonder who's been talking to – or near – this bird. Renoir comes up with such random phrases. Maybe there's a television in here somewhere. I haven't seen one yet, but it's the only thing that makes sense.

Renoir then hops around on the big canvas. The girl offers him some purple paint that he can step in, and he's in the process of signing his work when I decide to take a glance at the ship exhibit and see if I can get any other ideas on how to make sure the sculpture is capable of supporting its own weight. I've watched a number of demos and shows where people make chocolate art, and that seems to be the biggest problem I'm likely to run into. The exhibit isn't open, but it's down a hallway that doesn't have a door to close it off, so maybe I can just peek around the edge, which might actually help me think about this from another angle.

The gallery looks the same as when I was here earlier, with the exception of a line of Wet Floor signs further isolating the area. Even from this side of the barrier, I can see that Mrs. Cook is standing off to one side, literally wringing her hands.

Tracie and Hernan are each talking separately to a police officer. I don't recognize either of the cops.

Mrs. Cook sees me and waves me into the space. I make my way carefully between the signs. As I move towards her, the other side of the ship sculpture comes into view – and there's a gaping hole big enough to walk through, into the sculpture's hollow interior.

"What happened?" I stammer.

Mrs. Cook says, "We close every day for an hour for lunch, from one until two. When we got back, the sculpture was like this." She gestures wildly with her hands at the side of the hodgepodge ship, where it looks like a six-foot oval-ish part of it was burned off with a blow torch. Pieces of metal are lying inside the sculpture – but I don't see the section with the brass dial, and whatever else had been surrounding it. Mrs. Cook sounds uncharacteristically flustered when she says, "The power was off. It looks like the breaker was thrown on purpose, so our cameras didn't even catch anything. I looked at the footage from before we lost power, but there's no feed that would have shown someone throwing the breaker, or of anything near the maintenance closet. What a silly place not to have a camera. Not that I ever would have thought that would be important."

"That's terrible," I say consolingly. I have to stop myself from asking if that means the gala and the project will be cancelled. After all, asking about that when she's this upset would be a bit insensitive.

Mrs. Cook says, "Amálie is on her way over to see if the sculpture can be repaired, but much of what she uses is marine salvage, so even if she can put it back together before the gala, it won't likely be exactly the same." Mrs. Cook plucks the folder with the signed contract out from under my arm. "Which means you will have to work with her to make everything match. Even if your sculpture has to have a giant hole in it."

She starts flipping through the papers to make sure everything is in order.

"I'm not sure that's going to work very well. The internal structure of a chocolate sculpture this size will have to be braced and-" I say, but Mrs. Cook brushes me away as one of the cops approaches.

She pats my hand. "I'm sure whatever you need to do will work out fine."

The officer, a black woman in her early thirties, nods in my direction and asks, "Who's this?"

Mrs. Cook introduces me, and explains that I was in the building previously.

The officer turns to me and asks, "Did you see anything out of the ordinary?"

"Not really," I say. I'm assuming she doesn't care about talking birds giving people side-eye.

Chapter Three

Things start coming together quickly over the next couple of days. Hernan and Tracie are programming in and 3-D printing lightweight structural pieces to go under the chocolate layers of the sculpture. Miles is putting the photos I selected into the software for the immersive slideshow. Logan is building frames for us to temper oversized sheets of chocolate. And Carmen and Tam Binh are baking. So much baking, they've had to make multiple runs for supplies.

I'm working on all the bonbons for the gala, which are going to be on a display that will make them look like they are spilling out of a giant treasure chest. The overall theme of the event is celebrating Galveston's past, so in addition to the maritime salvage sculpture paying homage to Galveston's history as a port, Mrs. Cook has decided she wants to highlight the piratical elements of the island's history. After all, the pirate Jean Lafitte was known for his participation in the Battle of Galveston during the Civil War – the very event pictured in one of her prize images for the exhibit.

"Hey Lis," Arlo says as he comes into my work area. He's Cuban, dark haired and well built, without the trace of an accent. He's a cop, but he's off duty, so he's wearing a soft-looking blue shirt that compliments his warm brown eyes. Arlo and I have a history. He was hot back when we dated as teenagers. He's even more handsome now that he's all grown up. Having him here unexpectedly sets me off balance – in kind of a good way. He picks up one of the special boxes of truffles that will be on sale at the museum gift shop. "What's this?"

I feel a bit embarrassed to say it. "It's a treasure map. Which supposedly leads to pirate Jean Lafitte's treasure."

"Privateer," Arlo says automatically.

"That's debatable," I say. After all, Jean Lafitte, who spent time in both Galveston and New Orleans had trouble with concepts like loyalty. While he may have held privateer contracts, he changed which country he was backing based on who was most likely to win the most recent conflict. He also engaged in some of the most morally reprehensible of illegal activities. And yet, he was considered a gentleman pirate because he always released the crews he captured instead of ransoming them, and because he was handsome and rakish and full of panache. Some believe he wasn't even French, and had probably changed his name and invented the persona of Lafitte to hide from previous crimes. I tell Arlo, "I took a commission to provide chocolates and desserts for a gala at the Lily, along with an art piece. The museum wants something fun for families, and kids like the idea of pirate ships and swords and cannons, even if they wouldn't like actual pirates. So the box is a treasure map, but it takes people to landmarks around Galveston. If they mark them all off, they can take the box back to the museum and get a little plastic treasure chest."

Arlo says, "Remember that time we all went looking for real pirate treasure? Autumn was convinced that she knew which park it was buried under."

Autumn and I have been best friends since our middle school years – though we had to reconnect a bit after I'd moved back to Texas after years in Seattle. Now I'm about to be matron of honor for Autumn's upcoming wedding.

I'd started dating Arlo towards the middle of high school, so we'd all hung out together a lot.

I grimace, remembering how much of a fiasco our attempted treasure hunt had been. We'd been lucky not to have gotten arrested for vandalism that night – which had only reinforced my belief that not following the rules usually causes more trouble than it is worth, a belief that still influences my life, though hanging out with Logan has led to me bending the rules a couple of times to investigate clues.

We'd had a metal detector and a couple of shovels, and there may have been a couple of azalea bushes that were shovel-related casualties. I say, "None of us had taken into account the sea wall, or the fact that they raised the island by multiple feet after the 1900 hurricane, so if there had ever been any treasure, it had gotten buried under all that sand."

"Well, that old guy told us all that." Arlo laughs. "Remember his little dog?"

That dog had peed on Arlo's metal detector. I'm pretty sure the guy told it to. But not before he lectured us on the improbability of there actually being treasure buried on the island, because there was only one historically confirmed incident of a pirate actually burying anything other than bodies. More likely, that treasure had sailed away on a galleon, or had been lost in the ocean.

I think we had probably all seen Goonies with a few too many times. And we had drunk a few wine coolers from Arlo's grandmother's stash in their second garage fridge.

Arlo says, "You know my abuelita counted the wine coolers and figured it out? But all she did was make me pay back twice what they had cost. She never even lectured me about drinking."

I tell him, "I think she knew deep down you were always a good guy."

Arlo comes over and takes my hand in his. "Thank you for saying that."

"It doesn't make up for me missing her funeral," I say. That had happened after Arlo and I had broken up, but I still should have been there. It's part of the conflict that still hangs between us. Though maybe Arlo's over it, because even when I bring it up, he doesn't pull away.

Instead, he holds onto my hand, and I have to admit the familiarity of it *is* nice. But I am beyond busy. And Logan could walk in here at any minute. I don't want to make things any more awkward than they already are.

"Arlo," I say, "I need to finish all this work."

"What can I do to help out?" he asks. "Today's my day off, and I want to spend time with you. If that means making chocolates, then so be it."

As far as I know, Arlo still doesn't cook. And he's not exactly the artistic type. But at this point, I'm willing to take whatever help I can get.

"Fine," I tell him. "Wash up and grab an apron. We're making ginger lime coconut bonbons, and all I need you to do is spoon in the filling."

Arlo comes back wearing one of our new black aprons, which Logan ordered. It has Greetings and Felicitations embroidered in white on the top. Arlo says, "Let's do this!"

I show him how much filling goes into each chocolate-lined cavity in the mold, and how to add it without getting filling on the edge. Messy edges make it difficult to get the chocolate layer across the top of the mold – which, when you flip it over, creates the bottom of the bonbon – to seal. He actually does a pretty good job.

Logan comes in. He nods at Arlo, like he's not surprised to see a cop spooning souped-up lime curd into chocolate molds. Logan looks at me, though, when he says, "I've got the next set of frames built, and Hernan says that the ones we did earlier have set up nicely. The wood print from the frames transferred to the chocolate just like you thought it would. We can bring the new frames over to the museum whenever you're ready. Hernan and Tracie are going to start assembly with what they have."

Arlo's brown eyes light with curiosity. "What exactly are you making? It sounds complex."

I tell him, "The art piece I was telling you about is a giant pirate ship. Out of chocolate."

Arlo grins. "Why didn't you say so? You have that going on, and we're stuck here making these?" He gestures down at the bonbons.

"You want to help build a pirate ship?" Logan asks skeptically.

"I've always loved model boats," Arlo says. "My grandfather died when I was nine, but before that he used to let me help him do ships in a bottle. The best part was always the sails."

"How did I not know that about you?" I ask. After all, I had dated the guy for multiple years.

Arlo looks at me seriously. "There was a lot of stuff we never talked about when we were dating. We were too busy being nervous and trying to impress each other, and just plain trying to figure out what love even was."

"I guess so," I say. We had been so young, then.

There's a beat of silence. I can't think of a way to break it.

Logan says, "I had an awkward first love too. She wound up married to my best friend, because he had love figured out way before I did."

Arlo gives Logan a look I can't really read. Is he upset about Logan directing the conversation away from mine and Arlo's shared past? Or is he thinking Logan's issuing a challenge relating to my affections in the present day?

I can't tell what Logan is thinking either, and I just want to back away from the whole situation. But I can't tell either of these guys that I don't need their help. I've been blowing off too many things with friends and family already, trying to get this project done. I've already cancelled my usual lunch with Autumn this week.

I'm supposed to squeeze in a few minutes to try on bridesmaid dresses later today. The bridesmaids are going for drinks and Mexican food first at Chalupa's, and I'm supposed to meet up with them at the dress shop. It's not ideal matron of honor behavior, especially considering how reluctant I have been about the whole wedding. But Autumn knows about the sculpture – and she says she's okay with me skipping a few things now, as long as I do a custom sculpture for her for the wedding. She hasn't decided what she wants the design to be, and knowing her it could be anything from a white chocolate castle to a dark chocolate blues saxophone.

But for the museum project, Logan and Arlo are exactly the strong hands I need for hauling giant quantities of chocolate, which will then need to be melted and carefully transferred into the frames that Logan built. Logan has everything already loaded into the catering van, so it's just a matter of unloading on the other end. The van only seats two, unless someone wants to use the pull-down seat in the back, but it's uncomfortable, plus the whole back is full of supplies, so Arlo follows in his car.

When we get to the museum, we park near the studio entrance at the back. The door has been propped open, which makes things easier as we start bringing in our stuff. I can carry some of the smaller frames, and the equipment for melting and tempering large quantities of chocolate is already here, so unloading shouldn't take too long.

Arlo keeps pausing to look around at things in the studio, getting distracted by some of the other artists' projects, watching over their shoulders as they work. It makes sense – Logan and I have been in here multiple times over the past few days, so now it is all familiar. Unlike the main part of the museum, which is open and airy, with lots of windows, this place is closed in, with a roof made partly of corrugated metal. There's zero natural light. Instead, there are shop lights hanging from the ceiling, making the decor feel industrial. Some of the artists have set up their own lighting, probably to get a more consistent result with their colors. To make better use of the cubic footage, one half of the room has been converted into a loft, dividing the giant vaulted space partially into two floors. From what I've seen, the loft is mainly full of supplies and equipment and abandoned projects, but it's too musty and crowded up there for me to have explored much. Not after I felt the tickle of a cough forming from all the dust.

Even I stop to watch one artist who is painting a cat sitting in a bed of flowers. He has brought said cat with him, though the flowers are purely imaginary, spirally purple gossamer things. The cat has fallen asleep. The guy seems to have started the painting when the animal was awake.

We finally get everything unloaded. When we go to check on the progress Tracie and Hernan are making with assembly of the 3-D printed supports and the initial chocolate pieces, Amálie is there, down by the side of the base, directing the work. That sort of makes sense. After all, she's here repairing the damage to the original sculpture. But part of me is worried that she's going to want to take over my project too. And while part of me would be relieved, I don't want Logan to see me as incompetent compared to her.

I wave, and Amálie waves back and starts moving towards me. When we get closer to each other, she says, "I have photos on my phone of some replacement pieces I'm considering incorporating into the damaged side of my sculpture. I want your opinion on which ones will be the best match. We can sit down together, just as soon as we all get to a break point."

"That will be great," I tell her. And if that's all she wants, it is very kind of her to ask me.

I get the chocolate we had brought started melting, while Logan and Arlo set out the frames that have been created for the heavier pieces.

Tracie comes over to me. Today she has her hair back in a braid, and she is wearing a pink tee with paint stains on it, looking every bit the working artist. But she's holding a hard hat. She asks, "Did you ever decide what you're going to do with that copy of *Treasure Island*?"

I shake my head. "Not really."

The book is still in the filing cabinet at my shop. I'll probably get it appraised with the bent pages and see what it's worth.

Tracie says, "If you decide you don't want it, I would love to have it. Even if it's not worth much, any little bit helps when you're as behind on the finances as I am."

I make a noncommittal noise. I'm already paying Tracie well for her help with the project. And the way she's asking for the book so that she can sell it – knowing I sell books too – just makes me feel uncomfortable.

Hernan is up on a scaffold at the side of the room, his black jeans and white button-up shirt still looking spotless. He's skipped the tie today and made his look more casual with black-and-lime-green sneakers. He waves at us, but remains focused on his work. He is controlling a winch, which he is using to pull up the larger pieces into place. I glance up to see he's got one of the biggest pieces elevated to go into place as the top of the ship's side wall.

Tracie gestures with the hard hat and says, "I should get back over there. It's my job to glue that in place and put the supports into the joints."

"Okay." I turn back to my own work. I'm beginning to understand why Mrs. Cook had gotten so irritated with Tracie. But not why Mrs. Cook had been equally upset at Hernan, who so far is a conscientious worker.

Amálie is standing near the sculpture, shouting instructions to Hernan. I'm guessing whatever she's saying is probably more irritating to him than helpful. She moves to the center of the sculpture, waving her arms to get him to line things up exactly. That's not really a safe place to be, so Logan waves her back over to the side. Though I doubt she'll stay there.

I look down to check on my chocolate, which the tempering machine says is ready. I start filling cups with tempered chocolate from the spout, and I start moving in a rhythm as I get into my own work. Fill – fill – pour – pour. Fill – fill – Suddenly, the lights go out, dropping the room into pitch blackness. The exit lights don't even come on. There's a few noises of complaint from the half dozen people working here today, and I hear Hernan say, "Oye! What's the big idea?"

Then a bang echoes through this space, made jarring by the vaulted roof and corrugated metal pieces that both amplify sound. I jump, startled, no clue where the sound came from. My brain says that maybe that sound is whatever made the lights go out, but that's backwards, isn't it? Someone must have dropped their work in the dark. I look up, at first unable to sense anything, but with the light from the cracks between the doors on either side of the room I find my eyes have some light. There's a sense of motion and then a thud as Hernan crumples and falls from the scaffold to the floor. There's more motion as the winch he's been controlling goes loose, leaving the giant sheet of chocolate swinging wildly towards the constructed pieces of the sculpture – in conjunction with a heart-rending scream. It's hard to tell where the sound is coming from, let alone who it is.

Was Tracie standing by the sculpture? Or Amálie? I'd lost track of who was where before the lights went out.

Somebody gets a spotlight turned on – must be powered on batteries – swinging it wildly, blinding me for a moment then arcing past. There's little snatches of space and movement being lit up as the spotlight moves. And then it centers in on the chocolate sculpture, which is shattered. I'm horrified by the loss of all that work, but then as my panicked brain takes in the impact of what's just happened, I'm more horrified by the danger to the people. If someone really was standing between the sculpture and the heavy chocolate swinging on an industrial chain, they could have been seriously hurt.

And Hernan – he hasn't moved from where he fell. I drop the chocolate, cups and all, into the mold and wipe my hands on my pants as I race towards him. Even the shadows show he's sprawled at an angle that makes me want to pull away. Still, as a former physical therapist, I have medical training. I'm obligated to at least try to help. When I get in close to him, and I use my phone to put light on his face, and it's obvious he's not breathing. Could he have had a stroke up there, or a heart attack? He's so young . . . but it's still not impossible. I move towards his chest, mentally preparing to do CPR, but I stop when I realize that there's blood spreading over the front of his shirt. He's been shot. I touch him, and he moves limply like a ragdoll. I look back at his face. Even by my phone's light, his eyes look vacant. There's nothing I can do.

I stand up slowly, then turn to the pile of rubble that was my sculpture. It's obvious that someone really was under there. Logan and Arlo are already pulling pieces of chocolate away – revealing Amálie. She isn't moving either. They get her uncovered, and I can tell from the grim looks on the two men's faces that the news isn't good.

There's temporary light as the door leading from the studio to the parking lot opens and then bangs closed. Somebody is leaving in a hurry, but I only register that dimly.

"Stay there," Logan says, without hesitation, and somehow there's a gun in his hand as he runs for the door. Obviously he thinks whoever shot Hernan is trying to beat a quick retreat. Logan still has vague connections to his past in law enforcement, so him taking instant action isn't a surprise.

Arlo doesn't follow. The one more focused on logic, he's still studying the scene here, his attention on the loft with its shadows, and on the people left in the darkness. He calls loudly, "Is everyone else okay?"

There are a number of voices of assent. Not that anyone would be able to say if they *weren't* okay.

I ask Arlo, "What happened?"

He says, "I'm not forensics. But it looks like that chain started swinging free, and the carabiner holding everything together hit her in the head."

"Oh my God," Tracie says, looking down at the white hard hat in her hand. Somehow, she's standing at my side. In the dark, with my shocked focus elsewhere, I have no idea how she got there – or when. Tracie stares in horror down at the mess of the chocolate. "Oh my God. That was supposed to be me."

Meanwhile, I'm thinking about how I was jealous of Amálie, and of every thought that had gone through my head second guessing her motives both towards Logan and towards the project – when objectively she hadn't done anything. I feel like an awful person.

"Everyone stay where you are," Arlo says, more loudly. Arlo's on his phone requesting an ambulance – but more as an afterthought, than because he thinks either of the artists can be saved. Arlo moves quietly over to the stairs leading up to the loft, about to go up there and make sure there's no killer hiding up there in the shadows. He turns back, giving me a significant look. Is he asking me to make sure nobody else leaves? Or to keep an eye on the artists, to make sure nobody is trying to dispose of a gun?

Even if I'm reading too much into that look, I decide that it is smart to pay attention. I start taking an inventory of who is here, what they were doing when we came in, and what they're doing now – at least as far as I can tell by the light of my phone.

Whoever has the battery powered spotlight seems to be taking stock too, shining the light at the various workstations.

There's a girl standing not far from me. Eighties-style metal bangle bracelets that go halfway up her arm tinkle together gently as she raises a hand to shield her gray-ish eyes. She's a white girl with pale, curly hair that's been dyed an ombred teal. I've seen her here before, working on an intricate wooden relief sculpture, done in a style that makes it look antique – right up until you take a closer look and realize the figures she's carving are a hodgepodge of the characters you'd see in a bad sci-fi monster movie. Her name's Destiny, and she's seriously talented. But right now, she's just standing there, nowhere near where she was working. I watch her watching the proceedings until the light moves on.

The guy who had been painting his cat is now holding the cat in his arms. It's a big black-and-white tuxedo cat and when the spotlight flashes over him, it looks like the cat's clinging on for dear life. I doubt he could have left the cat in the dark amidst the chaos of the shooting and then found it again. Maybe he could have stuck it in a carrier, but I still don't see him as being a potential killer. He looks genuinely freaked out.

There's also a woman with pixie-cut blonde hair and a red tee. When the light hits her, she's sitting on the floor. She's on her phone, probably already texting friends or posting about what just happened. That's not ideal – the police always want to have some leads and a coherent response before the news hits the press. But there's nothing I can do to stop her.

Over in the corner, there's a skinny black guy wearing protective equipment and holding a pair of safety glasses. He's got a hat smashed down low on his head, and he is sitting, leaned back against the wall, not far from the base of the stairs. His eyes are closed, and he doesn't flinch back, even when the spotlight is turned on him. I gasp. Could there be a third victim? I rush over to him. Thank goodness, he's breathing. I touch his wrist to check his pulse, but at my touch he flinches away and lets out a groan. He shifts, and I can see that there's a gun in his other hand.

He opens his eyes and groans again. Then he asks, "What hit me?"

I say, "Put the gun down and we can talk about it."

"Gun?" he says confused. Then he looks down and sees the gun in his hand. He makes a half-strangled noise, then tosses the gun away on the floor. With that gun in his hand, if anyone here looks suspicious, it's him. Because even I have heard that if you commit a crime and you can't escape – then fake being a victim.

But I've met him before too, and he seems like a sweetheart. His name is Jonah, and he's actually a fan of mine, because I've solved real-life mysteries. He works in neon, and his current piece is a 3-D pink rose with a grouping of delicate butterflies. And if he was just faking about being knocked out – that was some of the most realistic acting I've ever seen.

"Let me look at your head," I say. I help him take his hat off, and there's an ugly welt going from his temple back into his hair, and the end of it is bleeding a little. From the shape, it could well have been caused by the gun he'd wound up holding. Head injuries are serious. He's definitely going to need to get checked out by the ambulance Arlo has coming.

I stand up and head over to where they keep the first aid kit, to find him a bandage in the meantime. And for no immediately identifiable reason, a chill runs down my spine. Maybe it is because in theory, any of the people I've just seen could be a coldblooded killer – along with whoever has that spotlight.

But that door being propped open when we got here complicates matters. Everyone here right now should have an access key, and if the door had been kept properly locked, then the only suspects would be people with those keys. So yes, it's possible that whoever shot Hernan came in with a legitimate key, committed the murders, then blended back in with the other artists in the studio. But it is equally possible that someone came in through that open door and then exited, chased by Logan.

Logan and Arlo look for the shooter in their respective directions, but both come back empty handed. And all my beleaguered brain can come up with is, well, at least the victim isn't Mrs. Cook.

The lights come back on, and about a minute later, Mrs. Cook herself comes in through the other door, the one from the hallway connecting to the main body of the museum. She looks angry. "All right, who blew the breaker? Am I really going to have to spend donated money that could go to getting visiting artists to put in more cameras to-"

But then she takes in the scene, screams, and then faints.

Chapter Four

I do what I always do in time of crisis: I make coffee. Arlo has taken over the museum's staff break room as a place to interview witnesses, and Logan and I followed him in here. There's a couple of giant coffee urns over in the corner, undoubtedly for events. It should be easy enough to make one giant pot for the cops and for all the witnesses waiting for Arlo to interview them – if I can figure out how this thing works. It's not like the ones we have at the shop.

I call Carmen and ask if she's ever used this type of coffee machine.

"Why are you making coffee?" she asks. "Can't you just ask Mrs. Cook how the machine works?"

I say, "There's been an accident. Well, a murder. A murder that caused an accident."

Carmen says, "Take a deep breath. You're not making any sense."

I explain briefly what happened. Carmen calmly explains how to use the coffee machine, and once the coffee is brewing, she says, "I'm on my way with snacks. Miles is here, and Tam Binh is saying she's happy to stay and cover the register."

I can hear Tam Binh saying something in the background, but it isn't clear what. It sounds suspiciously like, *really is a murder magnet.*

I suck in a breath. If that's what my friends are saying – it's really hard to deny. And Carmen hangs up before I even try.

I tell Arlo that Carmen is bringing goodies.

He says, "Lis, that's not necessary. My CSI guys don't expect you to cater every murder you come across."

"You telling me that they're going to say no to Carmen's baking?" I ask.

"Well, no," Arlo admits.

I give him a wan smile. "At least this time I didn't have to call you to tell you I found a body."

Arlo looks serious. "I don't think witnessing the crime makes it any better. Especially since we don't know if this crime has a connection with the break-in, and it was your work that got sabotaged. You just need to give your statement and go home."

"I've got no problem with that," I say. "This one really is none of my business."

I sit down and tell him everything I saw, and I share the notes I made in the aftermath of the crime.

Logan, who has been leaning against the counter, pushes away from it and tells me, "You will do fine as a credible witness. Nobody really saw much. You're wrong about one thing, though."

"What's that?" I ask. He looks serious, and troubled. Natural, given that there was just a murder. But anxiety floods my chest at the thought I'm messing up my statement.

Logan turns towards the counter and starts opening cabinets until he finds a container of sugar and one of powdered creamer. He puts them down next to the still-brewing coffee. He says, "You said there was a murder that caused an accident. I doubt that's what actually happened. The way it played out – I have a hunch that Amálie was actually the intended target. Poor Hernan was just a means to an end."

"I disagree," Arlo says. "That sounds convoluted. I mean, how would the shooter have known that the chain would hit Amálie? Or that there would be enough force to kill her? Or that she wouldn't be wearing Tracie's hard hat? They could have wound up killing Hernan for nothing. Why not just shoot Amálie directly, if that's the goal?"

Logan shrugs. "It's just a hunch." He thinks for a second, then adds, "Maybe there was a problem with the angle for a direct shot. Or maybe the shooter was just showing off. I've seen that kind of thing before."

I don't ask for details on that one. There are things I'm sure I still don't want to know about Logan's past. I don't even like guns, and I've had a hard time coming to terms with the fact that both of the guys I like carry them.

Arlo studies Logan. "Just for the record – you didn't discharge your weapon today, right?"

Logan unholsters his gun and puts it on the table. "Nope."

Arlo touches the gun with the back of his hand. I guess he's satisfied that if it isn't hot, it wasn't fired. Arlo says, "I know everyone in that studio saw you holding it. If I ask for a GSR test, you'd probably just give me an override note from the governor again."

There have been some sore points and rivalry between Logan and Arlo, because Logan had used his shadowy and potentially high-powered connections in the past to get Arlo to back off certain avenues of inquiry.

This time, though, Logan laughs. "Test me if you want. I understand wanting to dot your i's and cross your t's."

"Now that just takes all the fun out of it." Arlo gestures in the general direction of the studio. "They already tested the kid who had the gun in his hand. It's not the murder weapon and he didn't fire it. It was just another element of misdirection. This killer is laughing at us, maybe even daring us to solve this. I'm going to test everyone in there. We don't know where that shot came from, and I don't want to let a killer walk out of here just because they look innocent."

Considering that no one knows exactly what direction Hernan was facing when the shot was fired, there probably won't be a way to figure out where the shooter was. I may not be an expert in dealing with firearms, but logic tells me that.

"Didn't you see the killer run out the door?" I ask Logan.

He scowls. "I didn't actually see anything. I heard the door slam, so I assumed someone had gone through it. I checked all the cars in the lot, and circled the building. I never saw anyone. But it is likely I was just too far behind."

I ask Arlo, "Then why did you go up to the loft?"

Arlo frowns too, but for entirely different reasons. I can practically hear him getting ready to tell me that he can't discuss the case with a civilian. But I guess he figures since I was there, he might as well answer, because after a long pause, he says, "I thought I might have seen a muzzle flash. Logan had already followed whoever might have gone out the door, so he had that possibility covered. But once I got up in the loft, I couldn't find either a person or a discarded weapon. So either I imagined that flash, or the shooter somehow got back downstairs."

"That's frustrating," I say. The three of us had all been right there when the crime had happened – and it seems like we have less information than in the other murders I had helped solve. I stop myself. I shouldn't even be thinking *other murders I had helped with*. That's not an accurate statement, because I'm not getting involved this time – even if the puzzle of it all is darn intriguing. The other times, I had been personally involved, helping clear my friends. I have no such justification here. And a killer this bold – it feels more dangerous than the other cases. Therefore, I have no business being frustrated by the lack of clues.

Arlo reads a text on his phone and types a reply. Moments later, a uniformed officer leads Carmen through to the breakroom. She's not alone. Autumn comes in behind her, a jaunty bridal veil perched on her afro. She's a little curvy, and the gold and white dress she has on is flattering and suitable for a party. She's carrying a stack of bakery boxes.

I ask, "Did you blow off dress shopping to come here?"

"What kind of dress shopping would it be without the matron of honor?" Autumn says. She places the bakery boxes on the table in front of Logan, then she moves over to me and gives me a hug. "It felt like you needed moral support more than I did, so I went by your shop to see if you needed anything, and I ran into Carmen trying to carry too many bakery boxes out to her car.

The girls are still planning on meeting at Chalupa's in an hour. If we're done here by then, I can drive us over." She turns to Carmen. "That means you're coming with us."

Carmen grins at her, a sudden happy smile. "I'm cool with that."

I wonder if Carmen wants to be included more in my friends' group. She always seems to be busy doing her own thing – but maybe that's just because I haven't invited her places. It's difficult, because I rely on her so much to hold everything together at the shop when I can't be there. Maybe I really need to hire another full-time shop assistant. Most of my money is still tied up in the hotel I helped my aunt finance, but when Naomi flips it, I should be able to budget for new staff.

Carmen says, "Don't worry. I plan on getting to Felicitations super early tomorrow, so I can get a start on baking before the news rush."

"What's a news rush?" Arlo asks.

Carmen says, "As soon as the news breaks that Felicity was on site for another murder, we will get a crowd of people wanting to catch a glimpse of the chocolate maker detective. Last time, they bombarded the store even though the murder was on a cruise ship, so she couldn't possibly be there. If I don't make extra baked goods, we miss out on sales."

Arlo looks bemused. "I didn't realize murder was good for business."

I say, "Usually it's not. You can blame Ash and his blog stories, trying to turn me into a femme fatal folk hero. That's a lot of what has given the shop its morbid following. But this time, Ash is going to be out of luck, because I'm taking your advice, going dress shopping, and then going home."

Both Autumn and Carmen turn to stare at me, obvious shock on their faces.

"You're not going to help investigate?" Carmen asks.

"Why not?" Autumn asks.

I don't even dignify that with a serious answer. Instead, I quip, "Because I'm too busy being matron of honor. And once we can get some coffee and some sense back into Mrs. Cook, I may well have a job still to do for this museum."

"Right," Carmen says. "Where should we put out the desserts?"

There's a serving cart in the closet, alongside the industrial sized bags of chips and the chafing dishes. We pile everything onto the cart, including foam cups and the powdered creamer, which I tried to leave behind, but Arlo saw and put on the cart. Both him and Logan with the powdered creamer. Why do cops – and former cops – who can have good taste in food, insist on such bad coffee?

We take the cart into the studio, where the artists waiting to give their statements are looking anxious yet bored. The guy has put his cat in its carrier, and it has fallen asleep again. Which says something about the vibe.

There's an open stretch of counter where we put the bakery boxes, and then assemble everything for folks to prepare their coffee.

Carmen tells everyone, "You caught me on a day when my friend and I were working on Mexican-Vietnamese fusions desserts. You have pandan chocoflan, café de olla honeycomb cake, and cacao and red bean empanadas. You should have seen us in the kitchen, trying to one-up each other. I told Tam Binh that chocoflan is called magic cake, because as it bakes, the layers actually change order. So she said that was nothing. With honeycomb cake, you have to cool the pans upside down so the tapioca flour doesn't collapse on itself, which gives you all those long bubble areas."

There are some enthusiastic responses to this news, and I'm excited that I will get to come back and sample everything. But first, I need to check on Mrs. Cook.

I'm not sure how she takes her coffee, so I guess and mix up a cup with a little sugar and bring it to her office. I knock hesitantly on the door. I hear a weak grumbling noise, which I take as a sign of assent, so I go on into the office. There's a small leather sofa on one side of the room, the kind that is all modern, with large decorative buttons but zero padding. Mrs. Cook is lying on it, curled up and unmoving. She looks at me and blinks, which is a relief. I couldn't take another dead body today.

I have no idea why she's taking this so hard. Obviously, an incident like this won't be good for the museum's reputation. But Mrs. Cook didn't seem to be close to either Tracie or Hernan. So while I can see her being upset, this near catatonic state seems a bit overdramatic. Although, she really didn't like Hernan, so it's possible that she could have been the one who shot him, and now she's stuck in a loop of overwhelming remorse. She had come into the studio from the main part of the museum, but theoretically she could have run out the back door and gone around the building. Although, it is hard to see her being able to outrun Logan – especially in those shoes. She's wearing three-inch heels.

Most women would have taken the shoes off before curling up in the couch. I guess she's just in that much shock.

"I brought you some coffee, Mrs. Cook," I tell her.

"Call me Delores." She levers herself up into a sitting position, with some difficulty. Then she says, "Thank you."

"It's not great coffee," I clarify. "Delores."

Still, she takes it and takes a sip.

"Are you okay?" I ask. There's a little blanket on top of a lidded wicker basket in the corner. I pick it up and start to bring it to her.

She looks up at me. The mascara trails running down her cheeks stand out sharply. She says, "What am I supposed to tell my sister?"

"Pardon?" I'm confused, and the hand holding the blanket comes down to my side. Is her sister an investor in the museum? I thought these things were owned by foundations.

Delores leans forward and takes the blanket from me. "Hernan was my brother-in-law. He lost his job – which wasn't steady work anyway – so I took him on here. I mean, what else could I do? They're having a baby. Diapers aren't cheap."

"I thought you didn't get along with Hernan," I say. "Was that just for show, to avoid showing him favoritism at work?"

Delores lets out a weird barking laugh. "Hardly. I always found Hernan arrogant and self-centered. I opposed the wedding, and Rosa never forgave me for it. I've only just started repairing the relationship. I promised her I would look out for Hernan here. And now – her baby shower is tomorrow. How am I supposed to tell her that her husband is dead?"

Echoed pain arcs through me. I know from experience that there's no easy way to hear that news. Mrs. Cook's sister's life is about to be turned upside down, and she's not going to be quite the same person ever again. I identify with Rosa, and preemptively ache with her. But Delores is in pain too. I tell her, "Nothing about this is your fault. Just tell her what happened. I'm sure she won't blame you."

Delores nods. "That's probably what I should do. Still. I think I'm going to head out of town for a while. Go spend some time with my mom. Get a little distance from all of this."

I open my mouth to say how preposterous that is, this close to the gala opening, but then I realize how insensitive that sounds. Still. I can't just ignore the problems her leaving would cause. I ask, "What about the exhibit?"

She flutters a hand at me. "Obviously, that's going to be canceled. People won't come to the museum if there's still a murderer lurking around. They'll feel in danger."

Panic arcs through my chest. "But what about all the outlay of expense? The cost of the chocolate alone was significant, and we bought a new tempering machine to get the project done in time. I run a small business, and we don't exactly run that far ahead on our profit margin."

She tilts her head. "But you have nothing to show for it. You can't expect the museum to cover the cost for chunks of chocolate. I could have done that myself."

I cross my arms over my chest, but say nothing. She knows full well that I have bought literal tons of cheap chocolate that I can't use for anything else and probably can't return, since much of it has been opened and prepped for melting. I have a contract in my filing cabinet back at the shop, with a whole paragraph about good faith and cancellation of the commission on the museum's part. I'm still supposed to get a significant part of the commission. But to enforce that, I'd have to take the museum to court. Which would be expensive and time consuming.

Finally, I say, "There's still a week before the gala. If the killer gets caught by then, you could hold the exhibit opening as scheduled, right?"

"I guess," Delores says hesitantly. "But do you think that's likely to happen?"

"At least wait and give the police the chance to do their job before you cancel. Please." And if I happen to come across any information useful to the investigation – it could help things move faster.

Delores studies my face for an uncomfortably long time before she says, "I guess I could give it a few days. What difference will it really make, when I'm at my mom's?"

So right after telling Arlo that I'm going to stay out of his case this time, here I am making plans to get involved. I ask Delores, "How well did you know Amálie?"

Delores runs her hands down the side of her face. "Not well. I was intrigued by her art style, and she has enough followers on social media for her to draw a crowd. She had a reputation for being somewhat eccentric, but I never saw her behave in any way out of the ordinary."

"Eccentric in what way?" I ask. Because there's charming eccentric – like telling someone you can see art in their eyes – and then there's enemy-making eccentric.

Delores says, "She was apparently overly blunt at times. But Hernan said that she would just stare at things, sometimes for hours, and then after sitting still, she would go into overdrive, unable to stop moving or working or talking or whatever."

"So Hernan knew her," I prompt.

Delores shrugs. She wraps the blanket around her shoulders, seeming to get herself together a little. "Only as another member of the art community, as far as I know. Her name only came up because I asked him to make the fliers for the gala, and send out emails to our sponsors. Hernan had opinions of just about everybody. But, like I said, he was arrogant, so I always assumed his view was a little skewed. Mostly, I just ignored him."

"Or needled him a little," I say, "like when you called him Twedle Dum."

Delores winces. "I admit, that wasn't kind. I knew it would hit his ego. But he had started a big fight with Rosa, and she had called me to vent, so I was mad at him. How Hernan could be so book smart but completely miss what other people needed from him is just beyond me."

"Was it the kind of fight that could have made your sister snap?"

Delores narrows her eyes. "It wasn't like that. Don't you tell your police friends that it was like that."

"Okay." I hold out my hands in a placating gesture. "I'm sorry. Hernan obviously had an abrasive personality. Did any of the other artists in the studio today have reason to dislike him?"

"That sounds like a question the police would ask," Delores says. Her body language has closed, with her arms drawn in tight at her sides. I guess I pushed too much, and now she's shut down completely.

I shift the conversation back to the museum, but I don't get anything else useful. Finally, I tell her, "My friends brought some snacks for everyone who got stuck here. Let me know if you want me to bring you anything else. Or if you're feeling up to it, the food is all out in the studio."

Delores shudders. "I can't go back out there right now. I'll just see where they both were lying – and it will just break my heart."

So finally, I leave her in the office. I'm sure Arlo will talk to her soon enough and ask all the questions she didn't want to talk about with me.

Chapter Five

I take a bite of the chocoflan, making sure to get parts of both the chocolate cake and the creamy flan. The pandan flavor is pronounced, but there's also a subtle undertone of coconut, and it works well with the chocolate cake. Carmen said she used black cocoa powder, which isn't actually a product that we make. It is ultra-dutch processed, which uses alkaline to remove much of the acid from the cacao. It creates a different flavor – more like what you get with a chocolate sandwich cookie – which she wanted to pair with the pandan, and I think it was a good choice. Even if it's not doubling as an advertisement for my chocolate.

Pandan flavoring comes from the plant's blade-like leaves. The taste is complex, and the flavor notes are grassy and a little bitter, but with elements that remind me of both vanilla and rosemary. Trying to really understand the taste of such a complicated herb is like trying to unravel all the notes in a new cacao bean, which as a chocolate maker, is one of the most fascinating parts of the job – and one of the things that had drawn me to craft chocolate in the first place.

I've also got a piece of one of the red bean empanadas. The filling is studded with rehydrated cacao nibs, and Carmen and Tam Binh have sweetened it with piloncillo, unrefined sugar with a strong note of molasses. I pop the sample into my mouth. There is an element that is almost fermented, from the nibs, which makes it feel familiar – like a bean paste bun – but with an edge to it. I really like it, though.

"Well?" Carmen asks, coming up behind me, along with Autumn. "What do you think?"

"They're both delicious," I say, but I point to the empty tray. "But the honeycomb cake was such a hit that I didn't even get to try it."

Carmen looks disappointed. She says, "I wish you had. It was Tam Binh's idea, when she found out I needed to design a dairy free, gluten free dessert. It's made with coconut milk and tapioca and rice flour, so it fit the needs for the gala without even having to alter the recipe. Of course we mixed up the flavors-" Carmen stops mid-sentence. "If the gala is even happening."

I give her what I hope is a reassuring smile. "Hopefully it will. Mrs. Cook says she'll go ahead with the event if the murderer is caught by them."

Autumn scrunches up her nose, saying, "Are you sure that's not going to come across as insensitive?"

"Don't tell Mrs. Cook that," I say. "We've sunk too much money into this sculpture." I explain what Delores had said, and how Greetings and Felicitations could get stuck on the hook for expensive supplies.

"So that means you're going to be looking into this to make sure it gets solved," Autumn says. "Girl, you just can't stay away from the murder cases."

I feel my cheeks going hot. I say, "It's not like I don't think Arlo and his team are competent. But if I'm going to be up here working on the sculpture, I might as well see what I can find out. It's a whole different perspective because I'm *not* a cop."

"I was wondering how you were planning to investigate and also start the sculpture over from scratch," Autumn says. "But if you're already here, that makes sense."

I say, "It's not entirely from scratch. A lot of the frames have been built, and we still have the files for everything that already got 3-D printed. We're still going to be running behind, though. I'm probably going to be asking for extra people to help."

Carmen says, "You know my roommate is a sculptor. If you need extra hands, she could use some extra cash. She's saving money for a bicycle tour through France, to see the homes of some of her favorite artists."

"That sounds like a ton of fun," Autumn says, snagging an empanada from the box. "If Drake and I hadn't already planned our honeymoon in Turks and Caicos, I'd be interested in the details."

The turn in the conversation makes me think about what Logan had said about all of us going to Rio. I'd been blindsided by the idea, but maybe I should try diving, just to see if I like it enough to want to get certified. After all, all of my friends like the water – as do both of the guys I'm interested in. I think about why I was so resistant to the idea. It isn't just the idea of being somewhere where I'm faced with the temptations of Logan and rum. I realize now there was something else I didn't even want to admit to myself. It's sharing every level of Greetings and Felicitations with him, including letting him craft his own chocolate.

I started my craft chocolate business as a way to honor my late husband. I've been traveling solo because I wanted to keep the experiences and the chocolate that results from them as purely my creation, my response to the world and my opportunity to support and share with other people. I thought that was enough for me to feel connected to others without having to admit how much about my life had changed. But maybe that's been another way I've been isolating myself, and keeping myself from connecting to the people who are in my life long-term.

I text Logan, *Maybe we should plan a very short dive, so I can try it out. I'm not promising anything. But I'm trying to be open to trying new things.*

After about thirty seconds, Logan texts back a link. It's to PADI e-learning, a site for online scuba training. Then he sends, *Read over this tonight and we can catch a little time out on the water tomorrow. I'll let Arlo know as soon as he's done questioning the cat guy. What's up with the cat anyway?*

Wow. Logan doesn't waste any time. He must have really wanted me to say yes to the scuba, way more than I'd realized. And he's apparently very committed to the whole being cool about me spending time with Arlo thing. But at the same time – we're so completely overwhelmed with work, and he's given me homework. And he wants to take precious hours out of our day tomorrow to get in a boat, when we should be building one out of chocolate.

But I'm not going to disappoint him. I say, *Okay – as long as you can find a few volunteers to help us re-make the chocolate pieces we've lost.*

I've just hit send when Logan comes through the door from the museum into the studio. The grin on his face has wiped away all of his usual reserve. It's the happiest I've ever seen him.

He looks around the room at the artists, some of whom have gone back to work, some who seem to be waiting in broken shock for someone to tell them they can go home. Logan says, "If any of you are interested in a paid short-term project, we'll be in need of help to assemble the chocolate sculpture as soon as the police release this space from being a crime scene. And we'll be working on preparation at our shop up until then."

There's some muttered confusion – everyone seems to have assumed the gala would be cancelled – then Jonah raises his hand. I guess the EMTs decided to wait until after Arlo talks to him to get him checked out at the hospital. He says, "I'd be interested."

I put a hand on Logan's arm. Ignoring how rock-solid the muscle is under my touch, I whisper, "Can I talk to you for a second?"

He follows me over to an out-of-the-way area where there's a bunch of glass pieces laid out on a workbench, behind a vertical mosaic that divides this area it into a nook. Several of the glass pieces look like maritime salvage. And there's a discarded fishing reel, with the fishing line trailing off the table. Could this be where Amálie had been working?

But I thought she'd kept all the pieces for her project at her studio at home. Wasn't she going to show me some pictures on her phone?

Logan asks softly, "Is something wrong?"

I stage whisper back, "Do you really think it is a good idea to hire all the main suspects in a murder?"

Logan shrugs. "Can you think of a more efficient way to investigate them? There's no other way we're going to get everything done for the gala and still have time to run the chocolate shop and the puddle jump runs – and teach you how to dive."

"I can wait a week to learn how to dive," I tell him. "Especially if it means we don't have to hire potential criminals. I didn't expect you to plan a trip for tomorrow, anyway."

Logan points out, "Only one of them is potentially a criminal."

I let out an exasperated noise. "Well, if we have that many people showing up in the morning, I guess it means I still have time to go dress shopping with Autumn."

"Affirmative," Logan says. "You go do that, and I'll work out a reasonable pay scale with the suspects. I'll tell them all to be there at seven in the morning."

He sounds deadpan, but he looks amused.

Before I forget, I ask, "Do you think Arlo would be willing to release Amálie's phone? There are some pictures on there that she said she wanted to show me."

Logan says, "There wasn't a phone on the body. Do you think she might have a locker here somewhere?"

"We can ask Delores," I say.

"Who?" Logan asks.

I say, "Mrs. Cook. And if she can get the phone for us, maybe I can get a look at those photos before we turn it over to Arlo."

"I can't see how he could object to that," Logan says. He quickly sorts things out with the artists who are interested in helping with the sculpture. It doesn't sound like paying them will break the budget. Well, unless neither we nor the police manage to solve the murder. In which case, it is just more money wasted on work for a project that will likely still get cancelled. But I have to proceed with optimism.

We go looking for the phone.

Someone has unlocked the door between the studio and the museum. One of the officers is standing near it, I guess making sure none of the suspects try to leave that way. Logan and I walk right past.

Delores is just coming out of her office with a large purse in one hand and a set of keys in the other.

"Heading out?" Logan asks casually.

Delores gives him a thin-lipped smile. "I've already talked to the Detective. He said this place will be closed for a day or two, so his men can process the scene. I decided to go and visit my mother, but it's still hard to swallow getting kicked out of my own museum."

"A director's gotta do what a director's got to do," Logan quips.

Suddenly, there's a screech from one of the galleries, and Renoir says, "I love you! I love you! Love you! Love you!"

"Oh, no," Delores says, her shoulders slumping forward.

"What?" Logan asks. His hand moves like he's about to draw his gun.

Delores gestures helplessly into the gallery. "I didn't even think about making a plan for Renoir. If the building is going to be closed, I can't just leave him here. I already told my mother that I'm on my way, and she's already freaked out that her son-in-law is dead. If I tell her I can't come, she's going to assume the worst. Whatever that would be."

"I'll take him," I say impulsively. Nothing has gone right for her today, and I want to help.

"Really?" Delores looks relieved.

"If you have a cage that's small enough to transport, and instructions on what to do with him, I will. I'm currently living in an empty hotel, so there's plenty of room."

Delores nods vigorously. "Of course."

Logan says, "I can take care of moving the bird, Fee. Go do the dress shopping thing with your friends, and I'll have your aunt let me in. We'll have everything set up for you by the time you get back. Then if I can get clearance from Arlo to get back in here, I'll move the food safe 3-D printers over to the shop." He turns to Delores. "Assuming that's okay with you?"

She makes a *be my guest* gesture, with her hands in the general direction of the studio. "You break it, you bought it. That's already in the contract you signed."

I manage not to blurt out something about how she's ignoring aspects of the contract.

Instead, I ask, "Did anyone find Amálie's phone? Or is there a locker where she might have stashed it?"

Delores says, "We have lockers for staff, but the studio artists don't really use them. You can check anyway if you want. Hernan had a yellow combination lock for his stuff, and Tracie uses a padlock. The others are all probably open."

We go and check it out. Delores was right – the other lockers are all empty, and there's nothing in the break room or left behind in the bathrooms. If Amálie brought anything into the studio, she stuck it somewhere out of sight. And considering how much clutter there is in that studio, we'd have to search forever to find it.

Chapter Six

I'm still shaken from the traumatic events that had happened at the museum, but I'm trying to be there for Autumn. She told me a couple of times that I didn't have to come to the restaurant, if I didn't feel up for it. But I don't want to disappoint her again, after my reluctance to get on board with the fact that she's getting married.

This is the first time all the bridesmaids will be together. Autumn has six bridesmaids – me, as matron of honor, my friends Sandra and Sonya, who are Romanian twins, Tiff, my friend who is helping out with the flip hotel, and two other girls. I'm not sure who they are.

This whole wedding is coming together like a whirlwind. It's November now, and Autumn is getting married in February. The super-tight time frame had been the main reason I'd been reluctant to support it, given that Autumn had gotten engaged after knowing Drake for all of a month. But I've seen that he and Autumn are perfect for each other, and I get now why she didn't hesitate to accept his quick proposal.

I'm still trying to get a handle on the whole matron of honor duties. This lunch is supposed to be a chance for me to talk through some things with everyone, so I can help Autumn when it comes to dresses and shoes, figuring out who has time to help with DIY wedding favors, and planning her bachelorette party. Yesterday, I'd been excited about it. Today, I have a fake smile plastered on my face to hide the shock of witnessing a murder as I make my way into the Mexican restaurant, following Autumn and Carmen. Chalupa's is one of my favorite places on the island – especially since I'd moved back here. My friends and I have had a lot of good times here, with more chips and salsa and margaritas than I can count. This is where they'd helped me figure out how to investigate the first murder that had happened in my shop and where I first started moving forward again after my late husband's death. I picked this place for today because it is somewhere everyone can feel comfortable.

When we get a table, Autumn takes little boxes out of her purse and puts one on top of the menu at each seat.

"Aww," I say. "That's really sweet of you."

Autumn beams back at me. "I want to make sure everyone knows how much I appreciate you all dropping everything to help plan my perfect day."

The rest of the girls start showing up, first one of the bridesmaids I haven't met: a 30s-ish black woman with box braids and an easy smile, wearing a fitted gray tee-shirt that says *Coffee Before Wine*.

Autumn says, "This is Monique. She's a freelance editor. We've been friends for years, since we worked on an anthology together."

I feel a familiar pang of jealousy. Events over the past few months made me realize I wasn't always the best friend to Autumn – especially during the years when I was dealing with her long distance from Seattle and hadn't realized she'd been going through tough times. I hadn't made real friendships while I'd been away and so the idea that she'd grown and changed and made new connections without me still smarts.

But I've resolved to embrace change, and to connect with others more deeply. I need to see this as the opportunity to make a new friend, instead of the threat of having Autumn pull away.

I ask Monique, "What's your favorite color? I'm polling everyone, because Autumn said we get to choose the dress color."

"Forest green," Monique says, flashing long nails that have been polished in that exact shade, with little silver swirls decorating them. Autumn said Monique's an editor. I have no idea how she types with nails that long. I certainly couldn't do work making chocolate or filling bonbons without damaging mine

– which is why they are short and unpolished. Monique adds, "But honestly, I'm okay with whatever color everyone wants. As long as it's not a pastel. I look horrible in pastels."

"You do not," Autumn protests.

The twins show up, and both vote for teal dresses. They are both currently wearing teal – though Sandra has on a solid-color blouse and Sonya is wearing a flowy flower-print dress. It is much easier to tell them apart now what Sandra has gone back to her natural dark hair color, while Sonya still dyes hers red. They both have strong Romanian features, and look so much alike that it surprises people that they have nearly opposite personalities – but are still good friends as well as sisters. The matching elements to their outfits may well be intentional.

Tiff comes in, wearing a slim black pants suit. Her straightened black hair is cut in a bob and curled under, completing her professional put-together look. She suggests black dresses, but quickly changes her vote to hunter green once she hears that's already on the table.

Which means my poll is a tie, ready to be broken by the last mystery bridesmaid, who seems to be running late.

"I'm sorry," a breathy voice says from behind me. "I had a hard time getting away from the bookstore, and once I got here I went straight to the ladies'."

I turn, and yes, I recognized the voice correctly. Kaylee Goff, owner of Island Breeze Books, is making her way towards us. She's in her forties, with dark curly hair cut in a short bob, and a spray tan that's a shade too orange for her natural skin tone. She has an easy smile that turns wary when she sees me. From the look she gives Autumn, I get the feeling that Kaylee knew I would be here – even though I had no idea she would.

Kaylee and I had problems when we first met. She resented the fact that I was opening a store that was part bookstore – but that was mainly because she thought I had poached one of her employees. I hadn't – Emma had come to me asking for work – but then later I had accused Kaylee of murdering Emma. It had made sense at the time, since I'd found out Emma had posted on her blog that Kaylee is secretly Kay Sinclair, a popular romance author. But I'd been wrong, and things had been so awkward after that that I've been avoiding her ever since. Even though Kaylee grudgingly admitted that I make good chocolate, which she has bought from the shop a couple of times, and even though I haven't replaced Emma with another employee who's capable of curating our book section, I've had no idea what to do to fix the problems between us.

"Kaylee!" Carmen jumps up from her chair and goes over to wrap Kaylee in a hug. "How's your mother?"

"She's making it," Kaylee says, hugging Carmen back. "One day at a time, you know? Are you a bridesmaid too?"

Carmen releases her. "No, I'm just tagging along today. It's a long story." She cuts a look over at me. "There was another murder."

"Let's not talk about that," I protest. "I don't want to take away from planning Autumn's big day."

"But I want to discuss it," Autumn says. "I got there just as they were putting the bodies in the ambulance. It would be unnatural if I didn't want to talk about it."

"And we wouldn't be her bridesmaids if we didn't expect just that," Sandra says.

"You said a murder," Kaylee points out. "How were there multiple bodies?"

"One was a murder, and the other was collateral damage." Autumn leans forward. "I heard that the guy who got shot was in a big competition with several of the other sculptors who worked out of that studio for an award that came with a huge grant. I say look for the one who has money troubles, and there's your killer."

I shake my head. "The only one I know who has money troubles is Tracie. I was talking to her shortly before it happened. If Arlo is right, and there was a muzzle flash from upstairs, it couldn't have been her." Then I blink and really consider the timeline. I give an overview of what happened, then I say, "I was working. And I lost track of where everyone was. At least I don't *think* Tracie would have had time to get upstairs, shoot somebody, knock somebody else out, put a gun in their hand and get back in time to look all shocked. And she was standing right there when the door slammed. I think whoever did it either ran out of the building, or slammed that door to draw suspicion away from themselves."

"Well, who didn't you see when the door slammed?" Autumn asks.

"Everybody else." I make a helpless gesture with raised hands.

Kaylee's eyes are wide. She studies me. "You've certainly gotten a lot more careful about your investigating."

I feel my cheeks go hot, and I'm sure I'm blushing visibly. I say, "I've gotten a lot more experience at it since then. Unfortunately. I should apologize for the way I handled everything surrounding Emma's death. I just wanted to help – and to clear my own name. I was a bit clumsy and a bit hasty with my accusations."

Kaylee just stares at me. Finally, she says, "Good to know."

I have no idea what she means by that. Is she saying that my apology is accepted, and we're all good now? Or is she saying that she's glad I feel bad, and she hopes I've learned my lesson?

Either way, we're going to be spending time together, and we're going to have to make this work for Autumn's sake. In a way, I'm glad. I'm a grown woman who has been literally tiptoeing past the bookstore because I don't want to deal with potential confrontation. And now – I'm going to have to deal with the personality clash, whether I'm ready for it or not.

Autumn says, "Okay, everybody, open your boxes."

We all do, and it's vintage jewelry – which makes sense since Autumn's main gig is selling similar items on Etsy. But she's taken the time to really think about each of her bridesmaids' sense of style. She knows how much I like opals, and that the jewelry I wear is relatively simple. She's given me a necklace with thirteen teardrop-shaped opals dangling from a linked chain studded with smaller round opals. If I hadn't recently learned that Autumn is now independently wealthy and fully able to afford this extravagance, I would have felt it too much to accept.

I realize there's a box at Carmen's place too, though it doesn't match the others, which are white while hers is a soft gray. I'm guessing Autumn grabbed it hastily from the museum gift shop, so Carmen wouldn't feel left out. When she opens it, there's a square-cut sapphire in a modern silver setting, with silver waves surrounding it. Which totally suites Carmen's surfer side. Even with last minute gift shopping, Autumn gets it perfect.

I get Kaylee's tiebreaking opinion on the dress color – green – and then we spend some time chatting and eating fajitas and laughing. The mood is a lot more relaxed by the time we're ready to leave the restaurant and move on to trying on taffeta.

The inside of Dress Me Up is neon pink, and the vibe feels like we should be little kids getting ready to play dress-up. But the dress prices in here – and the expression on Autumn's face – are deathly serious. I take a deep breath and try to focus on the bridesmaids, and making sure they're happy. Still, pain settles into my chest.

I knew this was going to be hard, because shopping for wedding dresses cannot help but remind me of my own wedding, one of the happiest days of my life. Kevin had looked sexy in his tux, and he'd been adorably nervous. And still, when we'd kissed in front of everyone, he'd made it embarrassingly hot. He had been a complex man. And we had been happy together. I remind myself that even though I'm trying to move on with my life, it's still okay to acknowledge what I've lost. And to be sad if I need to.

Yet, I need to be strong, for Autumn. Because she deserves her happy memories too.

Autumn comes behind me, and wraps me in a hug. She whispers, "I know this has to be hard for you. Let me know if there's anything I can do to make it easier."

I blink back a sudden misting of tears. "Just acknowledging that makes it easier."

But then Tiff comes out of a fitting room wearing a tutu dress that makes her look like a green and teal peacock with double-fist-sized hunter green flowers at the bust – and both Autumn and I bust out laughing. And a lot of the sadness dissipates.

"Too much?" Tiff asks.

"I never knew you had such a dramatic side," Autumn says, sounding like she's trying to not still laugh.

It's true – Tiff's look is usually polished and color-coordinated – possibly bordering on bland.

Tiff puts a hand on her hip. "Oh, I can be dramatic. Just ask Ken."

Ken is Tiff's husband, so he would know. We all laugh. And this is going to be okay.

Kaylee studies Tiff's dress. "You know, if you lose the flowers, that dress could tie together the hunter green and the teal, and then everyone could wear the dress they want."

Autumn grins. "I knew there was a reason I made you a bridesmaid."

Kaylee looks at me, like maybe she's worried I think she overstepped, since coordinating the dresses is my job. But I give her a thumbs up and her expression relaxes. After all, she really does have a great idea.

Everyone goes back out into the shop to look for new selections, half of us still dressed in whatever we've already tried on. There aren't any other customers in the shop at the moment, so it's not like we are bothering anyone. I take a dress that is somewhere between teal and green into one of the fitting rooms. The hook in this room is broken, so I put my purse on the floor. I had already put my clothes in the chair when we had started changing. I drape the teal-green dress over the door and unzip the darker green one I'm wearing.

I have it half way off when suddenly, a hand snakes under the fitting room door and grabs my purse.

"Hey!" I shout, and I open the door far enough to peek out, but the purse snatcher is already running away and I'm not dressed enough to run after them.

"Stop!" Kaylee shouts, and she takes off, giving chase, despite the fact that she's wearing a floor-length green mermaid-style dress. At least she's stepped back into her sneakers.

I get my dress pulled up and zipped, then I run out of the store. There's hardly anybody on this street, so it's easy to see where Kaylee and the thief are going. The thief ducks around the corner from the shop and into an alley. I still can't run fast – lest I risk setting off an asthma attack – but the purse snatcher slows down enough to pull my phone out of my purse and then to throw the purse at Kaylee. In doing so, the thief runs headlong into a trash can and goes sprawling. My phone hits the ground hard enough to bounce.

Kaylee fumbles the purse like it was a football, but she keeps going. So does the thief, after scooping up my phone. The thief draws a gun and fires wildly.

Gasping in a terrified breath, I duck behind an air conditioning unit.

Kaylee cries out.

My heart beating fast at what I might find, I peek up over the air conditioner. Kaylee is holding her arm. She doesn't look badly hurt, thank goodness. I sigh out a calming breath.

The thief, still running, disappears around a corner. I rush over to Kaylee and pull her hand away from the injury. It might not be life threatening, but there could be significant damage to the muscle, or the bone. Luckily, there's not.

"It's okay," I tell her. "It's just a graze. A stitch or two, and you'll be fine."

She nods, but she doesn't look convinced. "It really hurts."

"That's to be expected," I say. I gesture in the direction the thief just went. "Why did you do that?"

"I don't know," Kaylee says. "I just wrote a book where my heroine had to keep up with a Navy seal. And bam. There was a real-world bad guy, so I just channeled my inner Bridgett and tried to do something about it." She looks down at her injured arm. "Not very successfully, obviously."

"It was a guy, then?" I ask as I move over to my purse. I finish unzipping it and take out a pack of Kleenex. I pull off the packaging and hand the stack of tissues to Kaylee to press against the graze. "I couldn't tell from behind."

Kaylee shrugs. "That was my first impression, but the person was wearing a filter mask and a loose sweatshirt, so I couldn't say for sure. But he just power-walked into the shop and went straight to the fitting rooms, then ran back out with your purse."

I look down at the purse. "It's weird, right? I usually keep my phone in my pocket, not my purse. I think most people do. So why would the thief take my purse if they wanted my phone? Is it possible this person was watching us at Chalupa's?"

I shudder at the thought.

Kaylee says, "Maybe? Or they just assumed that you would put your phone in your purse when you changed out of your clothes?" Kaylee seems to have gotten the bleeding under control with the compression, but she looks with dismay down at the dress. "How much you want to bet I have to pay for this?"

But instead of going back towards the shop, she moves farther down the alley.

"What are you doing?" I ask.

"Look," she says. "Our bad guy dropped something."

There's a torn strip of paper on the ground, near where the thief had drawn the gun. It must have fallen out of a pocket. I pick the strip up. It feels fragile, old. There's writing on it, in French, but most of the words seem cut in half, like this is just the edge of something. At the bottom, there's a drawing, like the edge of a coastline.

"It's a treasure map," I quip.

Kaylee looks confused. She doesn't know that I've been studying ships with sails for structure ideas for my chocolate sculpture.

"Sorry," I say. "Somebody just gave me a copy of *Treasure Island*."

"Okay." Kaylee draws out the word skeptically.

I go a bit farther down the alley, to where the thief turned, trying to see if there's anything else this person may have dropped.

And there is – my phone, which looks like somebody spiked it straight into a wall. I pick it up by one edge, looking in dismay at the shattered screen. I can't imagine that the thief would have been so careless as to drop this without wiping off prints. But I should be careful just in case we're looking for a clueless thief.

My first thought is to call Arlo, to report what just happened, in case it has some connection to the break-in at the museum, or to the murders. But I can't – because, obviously I'm holding the corpse of my dead phone. And I feel a pang of physical distress at suddenly being out of contact with everyone. Which I know is an overreaction, but knowing doesn't help lessen the anxiety.

I also find myself mad at the thief. Why would someone go through that much trouble to steal my phone only to ditch it? It must have broken when it hit the ground earlier, which I guess made it worthless to the thief, who then dropped it when they realized it wasn't going to be usable. Which means this wasn't a random crime. I think about Kaylee's blood on her bridesmaid's dress. The person who hadn't hesitated to shoot her wants something to do with me. A wave of cold fills my core and I can feel stress put an ache in my teeth.

"We should go back to the store," I tell Kaylee. "I want to get off the street."

"That's probably a good idea," she says.

I tell her, "I need to borrow a phone and call the police."

She says, "You must have them on speed-dial."

She's referring to all the murder cases I've gotten involved in. And now a snatch-and-grab. Which, I have to remind myself, isn't necessarily connected to this most recent murder.

I say, "I don't do this on purpose."

We both make our way back towards the shop. The rest of the bridesmaids are still inside, staring through the plate glass window out at us. The shop's owner is holding open the door, on her phone, talking excitedly.

"That blogger called you a murder magnet," Kaylee says, referring to the article about me that had appeared on Ash Diaz's *Gulf Coast Happenings* blog. "But maybe you're just a crime magnet."

"That's not a real thing," I say.

"Okay. How about a someone with the Nancy Drew gene?"

"Also not a thing," I say.

"How about the model for my next protagonist?"

"Absolutely not."

Chapter Seven

Autumn swings back by the shop, where Carmen's car is still parked, and we all go inside. Tam Binh waves from behind the counter. As we predicted, business has picked up in the shop, but she seems to be handling it just fine. Carmen takes over behind the counter.

"Thanks for helping me out," I tell Tam Binh. "I didn't intend to put you to work."

Tam Binh waves a dismissive hand. "I used it as an opportunity to teach Stewart Jr. about money. I told him he could keep the cash for selling the cookies he made. I hope that's okay."

"It's only fair," I say. Impulsively I ask, "Hey, where are you staying?"

"Stewart booked a hotel," she says. "But we haven't checked in yet. The fishing charter he found had them heading out immediately, and I was here. They're not going out far, so the whole tour is supposed to be maybe three hours. He wanted a longer one, but the company he called is booked through the rest of the weekend, so they just went." She makes a flitting gesture towards the door. "We're impulsive like that."

I say, "If you haven't checked in, then y'all have to stay at the hotel my aunt is flipping. I'm keeping the bird from the museum, so I know Charlotte will be ecstatic."

Tam Binh smiles. "She really will – since there's a bird and a rabbit. That would be fantastic. If you're sure it would be okay."

"The rooms on the fourth floor are finished being remodeled. Tiff is handling a lot of the decorating, and she has gotten them furnished as examples of what the hotel can look like. As long as you stay on that floor or in the lobby, you shouldn't run into construction. Naomi won't mind. She's told me a dozen times if my friends want to stay, they're welcome."

Autumn gestures to me that she needs to go. I walk her out. I tell her, "I'm sorry I ruined your dress shopping."

She puts a hand on my arm. "You didn't ruin anything. It's going to make for a great story years from now when I think back on my wedding."

I manage a stilted laugh. Then I shake my head. "Yeah. It's a bit too soon to laugh about it now. I'm still too freaked out about being targeted."

"True," Autumn says. "But we'll figure this out. We always have so far."

"Can I ask you something?" I ask.

Autumn squeezes my arm before she lets me go. "Anything."

"How do you know Kaylee well enough to make her a bridesmaid? I don't remember you ever once mentioning her."

Autumn says, "I think you and Kaylee just got off on the wrong foot. I heard about the fight you had with her at your grand opening party. It's just – you know what it's like to feel like your life has spiraled out of your control. Kaylee got diagnosed with lupus a few months ago. She's always been a super prolific writer, which means she has heavy deadlines – and suddenly some days she's too tired to sit at her computer. And she used to go walking on the seawall every day – but now she has to stay out of the sun. And I don't know how to tell her that fake tan is not working for her."

It takes a minute for the implications of all of that to sink in. I say, "So then it must have seemed that me opening a shop with a book section was another thing that was completely out of her control. And then having one of her employees show up at my place. It felt like she was over-reacting at the time – but I had no idea what was going on with her behind the scenes."

Autumn says, "You had a lot going on behind the scenes too. I doubt Kaylee had any idea that you'd lost your husband a year before opening your shop."

I feel punched in the gut. I'd been so lost in my own problems. I hadn't found any empathy for Kaylee – even after she had sucked it up and come back to my shop, admitting that she liked the truffles I had sent her and asking me for more. I could have done something after that to put things on the right track, but instead I'd avoided the possibility of more confrontation. Heat flames into my cheeks as I remember literally hiding from her when I had a coffee date at a shop near hers. I like to think of myself as a good person, as a balanced person. But I have to consider the possibility that I've been behaving childishly.

I ask Autumn, "Why didn't you tell me any of this at the time?"

Autumn purses her lips, obviously thinking about how to word what she wants to say. "I thought it was a one-time outburst, and that after the murder, there'd been so many more important things going on than that. I had no idea there was still a problem between the two of you. You didn't say anything to me about there being an issue."

My first instinct is to send Kaylee a giant basket of apology chocolates, but that's probably swinging things back too far in the other direction. I don't want her to think I feel sorry for her, or that I think she's to be treated differently just because I know about her disease.

But it makes more sense why she had impulsively run after that thief, why she had written a character like Bridgette, with action-hero skill and control in life. So how can I avoid treating her in a way she will find patronizing, but still treat her with more empathy and care? When I think about the books of hers that I've read, she shows empathy for her characters and writes strong character relationships. Some of her work is historical in nature – and her research is impeccable. She knows a great deal, and has built an impressive body of work. And from what Autumn says, Kaylee is selling herself short by feeling like her accomplishments don't matter anymore.

"Don't beat yourself up too much over it," Autumn tells me. "You've come a long way in the past couple of months – getting over being stuck in the past with Kevin, learning how to be a better friend." She waggles her eyebrows. "Finding not one but two McHotties."

I groan. "Don't remind me. I'm still not sure I'm ready to date again, but both of them sure are."

Autumn waves a dismissive hand. "They'll wait. But my point is – if you feel like your relationship with Kaylee isn't right, I'm sure you'll be able to fix it."

I take a deep breath, let it out slowly. "I hope I can. I don't like the idea of anyone thinking I'm a bad person."

Autumn leaves, and on her way out she passes Ash Diaz, who is just coming in the door.

From across the room, Tam Binh says, "Ash, what an unexpected pleasure," in a tone of voice that means this visit is anything but.

"It's okay," I tell Tam Binh. "Ash and I are friends now."

"Are we?" Ash looks pleased. He has light skin and square glasses and is wearing a button up shirt with a fitted denim blazer. Which gives him a hipster vibe. "I know I've thought of you as a friend, but I was never quite sure how you viewed me."

"I did save your life," I quip. "I wouldn't do that for just anybody."

Ash grins. After all, it hadn't been that long since I'd kept him from getting poisoned and-or shot.

"Wouldn't you?" Tam Binh asks. She gestures at Ash. "What about his irresponsible journalism? This guy gives bloggers a bad name."

I say, "I think he's paid enough for those mistakes."

Tam Binh looks skeptical. Later, I'm going to have to give her the details about how one of Ash's articles had gotten him accused of murder.

Ash says, "I've taken a few things down off the blog. But that doesn't mean I'm not going to keep working. My blog connects me to the world."

"I don't think you'd still be the same person if you gave up blogging," I tell him. I move over to the counter and give Ash the last of Carmen's piggy cookies. She's in the kitchen, making something else. Her energy today seems boundless.

Tam Binh asks Ash, "Are you here because I'm in town? I told you a long time ago that I'm not interested in an interview about my friend's murder."

"No, I didn't even know you were on the island," Ash says. He points at me. "I came by because this one isn't answering her phone. How is she going to be present at another murder scene, and not call me? She knows I have to do another article – she's still my biggest audience draw – and if she wants any input on what goes into it, there's only a limited amount of time before I have to go to press – or else the standard news outlets will beat me to it."

"About that," I say, not mentioning that it hadn't even occurred to me to call Ash and give him a news tip. "There was an attempted purse snatching while we were trying on bridesmaids' dresses, and my phone got smashed."

"What happened?" Tam Binh asks, alarmed.

I realize I didn't tell her about the incident, so I give details. Then I say, "Don't worry. I doubt the thief would be determined enough to try again. But I clearly was specifically targeted. If you don't feel comfortable staying at the hotel with your kids present, I understand."

Ash is taking notes. I give him a sharp look and he shrugs like, *What? What do you expect me to do with juicy details? Like a sprint in a bridesmaid's dress?*

Tam Binh says, "I'm sure the hotel will be fine."

I tell Ash, "I'm hoping you can keep the details about the purse snatching out of your article. If the purse snatching has anything to do with the killer, that feels like it might be giving away too much."

Ash scowls, but he nods. "Fine. But I'm keeping the notes, in case I can use them later. And in this article, I get to call you a *mega* murder magnet."

I roll my eyes, but I can't help but laugh. "Deal."

I'd been upset when his first article had come out, and he'd practically accused me of being a murderer, and when the second one had shown up, saying I was attracting murders to my hometown. But Ash seems mostly harmless now that I know him, and if he's willing to be more responsible with what he puts in this article, I'm willing to tell him what I know.

I start giving him details, and see him type *A Shot in the Dark* into his notes program.

Maybe I can get information here as well as give it. I ask him, "You try to keep up with everything going on in town. Do you know anything about the local art scene?"

Ash nods. "The arts are a big part of Galveston. Our Downtown Arts District has been named as an official Cultural Arts District by the Texas Commission on the Arts, so you've got multiple galleries and museums, and the organizations that support those. The Arts Center even organizes an art walk every couple of months. And Galveston College offers an associate's degree in art."

It doesn't surprise me that Ash can just rattle off those kinds of facts. I ask, "What about the artists working out of the studio at the Lily?"

"I only know a couple of them." Ash taps his chin with his thumb, thinking. "Destiny Dawson teaches art classes over at Pottery and Paint. It's the kind of thing where you bring your own bottle of wine. And Audrey Scruggs and Gently Drifting worked on a huge mural project last year. I did an article about it."

"Gently Drifting?" Tam Binh asks. "Is that another art organization?"

Ash laughs. "That's actually the guy's name. He had it legally changed. You'd know him if you met him – he always has this huge black and white cat with him, even when he's working. He puts it on a leash and takes it for walks."

"He was at the studio," I say. "Painting a picture of the cat."

"Sounds about right. Apparently, his girlfriend is an artist too, and she recommended him for the mural project. They won an award for it, so they've all got talent."

It doesn't sound on the surface like any of these people have a motive for murdering Hernan or Amálie.

"What about Tracie Boudreaux?" I ask. "She seems to be having money troubles. Can she not get a decent job?"

I expect Ash to say that Tracie has a criminal record, or that she has a ton of debt, but instead he says, "I know Tracie from the beach cleanup events we both do sometimes. She just adopted her twin nieces, after her sister died. The girls are thirteen. I can't imagine that's an inexpensive age."

"Probably not," I say. I remember Tracie talking about going from her museum job to another one. If she's also raising two kids, and trying to keep up with volunteering – that's a full plate. I can see why she might have been looking for some extra cash. Just like with Kaylee, I find myself feeling selfish for not showing Tracie more empathy until someone had flat out told me what was going on in her life. I ask Ash, "Can you think of a reason why any of these artists would want to hurt Hernan? Or Amálie?"

Carmen comes out of the kitchen and says, "Gently Drifting is dating my roommate, Violet. He could have been mad at Hernan, because Violet and Hernan used to date – before Hernan broke it off to marry someone else. So it's possible that Gently was mad jealous about it. But Violet has completely moved on, so that's a stretch, no?"

I try to process that information. "Violet who's going to come help with the sculpture tomorrow?"

Carmen nods. "Gently doesn't come over to our place, though. Not after Bruno chased his emotional support cat. Bruno wasn't trying to hurt Ruffles, but I thought Gently was going to have a seizure, right there in the driveway."

Bruno is Carmen's German Shephard. He's a beautiful, friendly dog. But I can see how he could be intimidating.

"So you don't picture Gently as the murdering type, then?" I ask.

Carmen laughs. "He got mad at Violet because she was playing a VR game that had shooting in it. Even if he wanted to murder someone, I doubt he would have picked a gun as the weapon."

I don't laugh. I'm not a fan of guns myself, so I know how Gently feels.

Tam Binh says, "Interesting that he chose a cat as an emotional support animal. Says something about his personality."

I picture Gently holding the cat in the dark, right after the murders. And again, knowing the context makes me feel more empathy towards him.

"I've met Audrey too, when Violet was organizing the mural project," Carmen says. "Violet mentioned Amálie at one point, as a possible part of the mural team, and Audrey flipped out. She said it was because Amálie is a sculptor, and not a very good painter, but I get the idea that there was something more to it than that. No idea what, though."

That at least gives me something to go on, and I spend the rest of my workday trying to figure out the puzzle – while barreling ahead with the museum's order for bonbon gift boxes, trusting that we – or the police – will solve the murder in time, and there will still be an event for me to sell these at. There isn't an obvious person who seems like a murderer. We've pretty much eliminated Gently and Tracie as possible suspects. But I need to look into whatever connection Audrey had with the dead artists, and how the others might fit in. And it dawns on me that I still don't know who was operating the spotlight.

The fact that two people were killed simultaneously makes this all doubly hard, since there's no way to know which was the intended target. That means two sets of possible motives. And that open studio door means that if the killer came in without a key,figuring out the connection the killer had to the target might be impossible.

I take pics of the steps I'm going through to make the bonbons for the museum, and I go to upload the images to my social media accounts. Might as well show off all the hard work. I notice that I have friend and follow requests from Ash, on all of my social media platforms. Now that he's more confident that we're friends, he didn't waste any time solidifying that. I follow and friend him back. Suddenly, he comes up first in my Instagram feed. He's gotten a kitten. Maybe he was influenced by the stowaway kitten we'd discovered on the cruise ship not so long ago. But this kitten is solid black with extra toes, and he's named it Sasha. She's adorable.

Chapter Eight

Arlo is sitting on the wooden swing on the front porch of the hotel when I get there with Tam Binh and Stewart Jr. My only vehicle is still the catering truck – and Stewart Junior got the biggest kick out of riding in it, since he got to sit in the seat that pulls down out of the wall in the back. You never can tell what will impress a little kid.

"Give me a second, would you?" I say as we all get out. "Make yourselves at home downstairs, and I'll be there in a second to sort out rooms."

Tam Binh gestures subtly towards Arlo and says, "I wonder if he's here about the case."

"I don't know," I say. "But I'm about to find out."

The two Saveurs go into the lobby, while I sit down next to Arlo on the swing.

I show him the cell phone in the shiny new pink phone case I just picked up. I say, "I wound up getting an upgrade. Better cameras could revolutionize my Instagram game."

He laughs, but his eyes look worried. He takes my hand in his and says, "Look, Lis. I know your friend Kaylee wasn't seriously hurt today, but you two shouldn't have tried to chase down a guy with a gun."

"To be fair, we didn't know he had a gun," I say.

"Still." Arlo interlaces his fingers with mine. "This case is dangerous. If you're going to keep doing things like this, you need to have some training. I told you I can give you recommendations for getting your PI license. Or at the very least some self-defense classes."

I say, "I carry pepper spray. But it was in my purse – which the thief took off with."

Arlo asks, "Have you considered a stun gun?"

I shake my head. "I'm more likely to zap myself."

He laughs. "Do you remember-"

I put my other hand on his, stopping him before he launches into another story about our shared past. Reminiscing is fun, but I'm starting to feel like we're emotionally manipulating ourselves. I say, "Arlo, I do remember. But it feels like all we do is talk about the past. Or about a murder. I'm trying to stop looking backwards. You said you wanted to see if we still have a spark, and while there's definitely something there, I find myself trying to figure out what we have in common in the present."

"Oh," he says. He starts rocking the swing, and I can practically see him trying to re-position his mind. Finally, he says, "It's hard not to focus on the murders. I don't like seeing you in danger. I want to keep everybody safe. That's why I became a cop." We swing for a while in silence. Finally, he says, "Want to go bowling sometime? I'm surprisingly good at it."

I laugh. "You're coming on the dive trip tomorrow, right?"

Arlo gives me a wry grin. "That doesn't feel like it counts, since Logan planned it and only invited me as an afterthought."

"But you're hoping I enjoy diving too, right? Since it would prove how much we both love the ocean?"

"Well, yeah, obviously. But if you don't like it, I'm not going to be disappointed the way Logan obviously will. I'm not sure why it's that important to him. I don't believe that couples need to have the same hobbies to fit together." He hesitates. "Maybe he's trying to make sure that if things do work out between me and you, that you two can still be friends. After all, you are business partners. So it would be awkward otherwise."

"And I am taking him as my plus one to Autumn's wedding," I remind him.

Arlo looks a little hurt by that. But he says, "I told you I'm okay with that."

Why is it so difficult, having Arlo be understanding? I never anticipated being in a romantic triangle – let alone one where the guys are being totally mature about it and leaving it up to me to decide where things are going. I can picture whichever one I don't choose actually coming to my wedding to the other one. And somehow, I feel like that is going to make me the bad guy in this whole situation, no matter what I do.

Arlo says, "Tell me something I don't already know about you. Something that happened in Seattle. That way you can feel like we're getting to know each other."

"Okay," I say, and then I fall silent as I try to think of something interesting enough to share. "Okay. So there was this one time. We lived pretty close to Kevin's family, and his mother liked to cook Sunday dinner for everyone. With his brothers and everything, that was about a dozen people. But one day their oven broke, so Kevin's mom did all the sides, setting them on the table outside while Kevin's dad fried the turkey. He even bought a kit for it. And he thought he had thawed that turkey, but the inside was still frozen, so when it went into the hot oil, it exploded up out of the frier, splattering oil. Kevin's dad backed away to avoid getting burned and knocked the table holding the sides over, and the mashed potatoes wound up upside down in the grass. So we went back to mine and Kevin's house – where I got to do Sunday dinner, for the first time. All I had in the pantry was sweet potatoes, but I did a vegetarian gnocchi, and pulled a salad together out of odds and ends. And Kevin's mom said it was better than a restaurant meal, so after that, we took turns doing Sunday dinner."

Arlo says, "See? We do have something in common. We both like to play the hero. There's no better feeling than getting to save the day, am I right?"

"I guess so." I can't help but smile at that thought. "I should get Tam Binh settled in. We've been out here a while, ignoring her."

"There's one more thing I remember," Arlo says.

"What?" I ask, hoping it's not going to be something embarrassing.

"This." He leans close and kisses me.

A few minutes later, I walk into the hotel feeling a little giddy.

Tam Binh arches both her eyebrows at me. "You're practically glowing. I thought you had something going with Logan? I take it you've changed your mind."

I shake my head, though the heat of Arlo's kiss is still warming my lips. I can practically still feel his hand tangled in my hair. I tell her, "When I first met Logan, Arlo had a girlfriend. But Arlo was my first love, and he wants another chance. Now, I've kissed them both. And I still have no idea what I want. That makes me a horrible person, doesn't it?"

"Not necessarily," Tam Binh says. "But if you drag things out, you're going to wind up hurting both of them. And yourself."

Stewart Jr. is watching us with wide eyes. "What did I miss?" he asks.

Tam Binh draws her son into a hug. "Nothing you should worry about sweetie."

Stewart Junior asks, "Was Daddy your first love?"

Tam Binh looks startled. Then she says, "No. No, he wasn't. But he's my best love."

That makes me smile. I'm glad Tam Binh is happy.

But is Arlo *my* best love, with all our history and his sense of honor? Or is it Logan, with his curiosity, sense of humor and generous spirit? Autumn seems to think that one day I'll wake up and know which one I'm meant to be with, just by which one I'd want to have morning coffee with. But it's not that simple, is it?

The SUV pulls up outside with the rest of the Saveur family. There's Stewart himself – unassuming, easygoing Stewart who knows how to keep things organized while never losing his cool at airports or restaurants around the world. He's very different from the guys I've found myself attracted to. But he's the right guy for the life Tam Binh wants.

Charlotte rushes over to me and asks, "Where's the rabbit? We brought him some carrot tops."

"He's up in my suite. Let me get him and bring him down." I head for the elevator. Logan had texted me that he set up the bird cage in the room that should someday serve as the hotel's office, and that he'd had to let himself in since my aunt wasn't here. Logan carries lock picks – which he's quite adept with – so I assume that getting in wasn't a problem. I take a look into the office, which doesn't have much but a basic desk and chair. The door is open, and sure enough, there's Renoir, in a somewhat smaller cage than he'd been enjoying at the museum. He sees me and says, "I love you!"

"I love you too, Renoir," I say, but I keep walking. I want to check in on Knightley too. I take the elevator up to my suite and find my bunny hanging out in his nylon tunnel. He is a white lop, so he stands out against the blue fabric. He's dragged his ratan ball into the tunnel with him and is chewing on it. Knightley doesn't really like to be picked up, or to travel, so I put him into his carrier to take him down on the elevator. This avoids a lot of squirming and potential scratches.

When I'm walking back past the office, Renoir calls out, "I'll kill you!"

I call back, "That's why I'm not bringing you out to share with company."

I put Knightley's carrier down on the carpet on the giant rug aunt Naomi has added to one side of the lobby. I had bought some furniture to go on the rug, and we've been using it as a shared living room. We're going to be living in this hotel for a while, since there's so much work left to be done before we can flip it, so we figured we might as well be comfortable.

The kids all come over and I get them sitting on the sofa, then I open the door to Knightley's carrier.

He makes no move to exit the space.

I tell Charlotte, "Bring the carrot tops down close to the door of the carrier – but move slowly so you don't scare him."

She does as directed, and Knightley immediately shows interest. He hops to the front of the carrier and starts nibbling on the far edge of the carrot greenery, without moving his feet out onto the carpet. I get Charlotte to carefully pet him, again without startling him.

The other three kids start oooohing and asking when it will be their turn. I hope Knightley has enough patience for them. I don't want to stress him out.

Suddenly, I sense movement out of the corner of my eye. I turn and there's Renoir, flying silently this direction, swooping through the hall like a determined cloud. Not to be denied the attention he feels belongs to him, he lets out a squawk and lands right on Knightley's carrier. Startled, Knightley jumps back, pressing himself up against the back corner.

Renoir starts dancing on the carrier's edge, bobbing his head and shaking out his feathers. I put out two curved fingers – just the way Delores Cook showed me – to give Renoir a perch to grab onto, and he climbs up onto my hand. I ask him, "How did you get out of your cage?"

Charlotte says, "Cockatoos are the Houdinis of all the parrots. The ones with the yellow crest like this are the most talkative, too." She bobs her head, imitating the way the cockatoo had been dancing, and Renoir gives her his full attention. Charlotte asks, "Who's a good bird?"

Renoir says, "Au Nord des fleurs!"

There's something familiar about that phrase, but I can't remember what.

Stewart asks, "Who taught this bird to speak French?"

And it hits me – *fleurs* had been one of the words on the piece of paper the thief had dropped. It is feeling more like the attempted purse snatching, and the break-in at the art gallery are connected. I'm trying not to assume that the murder was connected to it too – because one thing I've learned is that narrowing your pool of suspects too early can cause you to miss things – but it's certainly a possibility.

Renoir focuses in on Charlotte's long hair, or maybe her tiny diamond stud earring, and I can feel him preparing to jump from my hand over to her shoulder, so I pull him back farther away. I'm not sure what to do if he tries to fly, but thankfully he doesn't. Instead, he squawks, "Ma chère Josephine!"

Charlotte giggles.

Tam Binh says, "I think that was a compliment."

Renoir says, "I have Culliver's diary!"

"Who's Culliver?" Stewart Jr. asks.

"I don't know," I admit. "I think the bird has been watching the History Channel. There must have been a TV at the museum."

"Oh," Stewart Jr. says. He sounds disappointed. But his smile brightens. "Then can I pet the rabbit?"

I hand Renoir off to Tam Binh and check on Knightley. He isn't plastered against the back of his carrier. But he isn't exploring at the front either. I tell Stewart Jr., "If you move very slowly, and then only pet him for a second, you can. But the bird scared him."

"I know what that's like," Stewart Jr. says. "I'm scared of wombats. Hey, did you know wombats make square poop?"

"I did not know that," I say. I look over at Stewart Sr., who nods gravely, verifying that this is true.

Stewart Jr. takes a carrot top from Charlotte, and kneels down in front of the carrier. He puts the greenery part way inside the carrier and starts to put his hand inside to pet Knightley. He freezes when Renoir says, "If you do that, I'll kill you."

I giggle, but it's a nervous sound. I tell Stewart Jr., "Don't worry. He's not talking to you."

Tam Binh asks, "Are you sure Renoir has been watching TV? He's said that three or four times since we got here. Birds tend to remember things that were said around them with emotion."

Charlotte says, "That's not always true. Sometimes they remember random stuff too."

"If not TV, what else could it be?" I say. "Do you think someone at the museum threatened Renoir when he did something he wasn't supposed to?"

"Maybe," Tam Binh says. "Either that, or maybe he heard someone being threatened."

"Maybe someone speaking French," I say, thinking about my feeling that the dropped paper could be connected to the museum.

We let Stewart Jr. pet Knightley, then I take Renoir back to his cage. Somehow, the cockatoo managed to unlatch the door from the inside, and it's standing wide open. I don't know how to keep him from doing that again. And the main floor of this hotel is huge. I don't want him getting outside, or getting hurt in the kitchen, or just plain lost. How would I explain that to Delores? I still need her good graces for the exhibit opening to happen.

I carefully close the office door. I'm pretty sure there's no way a bird can turn a ball-shaped doorknob. I instruct all the kids not to open the office door, even if the bird really looks like it is hungry or wants out or under any other circumstance.

Then I take my rabbit back up to my suite.

Afterwards, Stewart gets his luggage out of the car, and I get our guests settled into three rooms, next to each other on the hall of the mostly remodeled fourth floor.

Their rooms are on the same floor as my suite, but I go back downstairs before settling in for the evening. I check that the doors and windows are locked, and I put a light on for Aunt Naomi, for when she gets back. I grab a snack from the kitchen – leftover etouffee my grandmother made when we brought her over yesterday – and take it up to my suite. Knightley is already back in his tunnel, chewing on his ball like nothing had happened. He can be easygoing like that. Sometimes.

I eat, trying to process everything that has happened today. It has been a lot. It's hard to believe that there was a murder earlier, and then I kissed Arlo and that I'd promised Logan I'd go diving, all in less than twenty-four hours.

I keep thinking about what Tam Binh said. What if the bird really *had* heard someone being threatened? Could some of the other things he had said be real, too? I take out my laptop and search for information on Culliver's Diary. After all, that had been a very specific phrase. Maybe it's a famous art piece.

Nothing comes up, though. There are a number of people named Culliver, including at least one famous sports guy – who's not local. And there are references to Gulliver's Travels, which is apparently a fictional diary. Could I have heard the bird wrong? Transposed a C in place of a G? It's possible, I guess.

But there's nothing that seems like a promising lead to finding Hernan and Amálie's murderer. So I click over to the PADI website and start reading over the material Logan wanted me to review before the dive tomorrow. What exactly have I gotten myself into?

Chapter Nine
Thursday

When I walk into the shop early the next morning, I am greeted by the smell of coffee. It's a bit surprising, since it is six in the morning. Sometimes Carmen is here earlier than that, baking, but she usually waits until close to opening time to make coffee.

I wanted to make sure to arrive before any of the artist suspects. I came in through the back door, directly into the kitchen, since it is possible people might be waiting out front. That has happened before after a murder.

Carmen and Tam Binh are already in the kitchen, both wearing aprons, and all of the ovens are going. Tam Binh hands me two cups. One of them has a phin – a Vietnamese-style coffee press – perched on top. That cup is empty, but has hot coffee dripping from the phin into it. The other cup has ice and condensed milk, and a thread of red syrup turning some of the milk pink.

"What's the flavor?" I ask.

Carmen says, "Cinnamon and cherry. That's the one that came out the best."

She is talking fast, moving fast. She's taking cupcakes out of the oven, pulling them out of the pan and onto cooling racks at record speed.

"How many of these coffees have you had?"

"Two," Tam Binh answers for her. "And she can't have any more. I'm glad you're here. We're making notes for the podcast. We can record it whenever you have time."

"I hope you can wait until tomorrow," I say. "This is going to be a busy morning, and then we're going to do a quick dive trip this afternoon."

Tam Binh looks confused. "Why would you do that, if you're so busy?"

Carmen says, "It's because she likes two guys, and doesn't want to tell either one no for fear of hurting their feelings."

"If you don't have a suggestion for fixing the situation, let's talk about something else," I say.

Carmen says, "It's simple. Ditch Arlo, and commit to Logan. He's the one who made you happy again, after you moved back here. Arlo could have come looking for you any time, but he waited until you were already into somebody else. That's just not right."

"I disagree," Tam Binh says. "I'm a sucker for a second chance romance. Arlo showed up when the timing was right for him – and for Felicity. He doesn't have Logan's mysterious past or a history of love interests dying on him. He's the more stable choice."

And . . . now they're talking about me like I'm not even there. I say, "If y'all aren't on the same page, how do you expect me to be? I haven't even decided if I'm really ready to date again. I'll make a decision when I'm sure it's the right one."

Logan walks in. "A decision about what?" he asks.

I feel heat flame into my cheeks. I lie. "A decision about the next cacao bean I want to experiment with."

He gives me a skeptical look. "That sounds a bit overdramatic."

"That's my story, and I'm sticking to it." I take the phin off the top of the cup of brewed coffee and pour the coffee in with the condensed milk and ice. I shake it gently to combine it and take a taste. It's sweeter than most of the coffee drinks I go for, but the subtle cherry note and warmth from the cinnamon actually makes for an excellent brew.

Logan says, "I've turned the book nook into a 3-D printing lab, since you seemed uncomfortable with having a bunch of temporary employees back in the chocolate finishing area. They should have more room to spread out in the front of the shop anyway. Tracie should be here soon to get the files started. She's a bit of a whiz at rendering details."

Someone knocks on one of the plate glass windows that face onto the Strand. I go up front. It's Tracie. I'm a little surprised to see her here this early, given everything she has going on in life. I unlock the door and let her in. Tracie looks like she's been crying. Her eyes and nose are red.

"Are you okay?" I ask.

Tracie says, "I'm trying to be." She has a backpack slung over her shoulder. She moves over to the area where the huge 3-D printer has been set up. Logan had to move the display case housing the rare books back behind the counter and shove the sofa up against the bookcase to make room for the other equipment. Tracie drops the backpack on the sofa – a small dove gray affair I think makes the space look elegant. She unzips the backpack, pulling out a laptop.

"Were you close to Hernan?" I ask. She seems really broken up over the death of a co-worker. Maybe there was something more to it? She gives me a bewildered look, so I add, "Or to Amálie?"

She shakes her head, then plops down on the sofa and starts setting up the laptop. "It was just the opposite. I feel so guilty. Amálie was something of a mentor, since she often worked out of the same studio. I really need to win this upcoming grant, but I found out she'd recommended against me advancing to the final round of judging – after agreeing to act as one of my references. One of my friends was helping out the grant committee with paperwork. She wasn't supposed to tell me, but she did. I was so mad at Amálie. And then she started taking over the job I was supposed to do for the chocolate sculpture, because apparently I wasn't going to do it up to her standards or whatever. I told her I wished she was dead. It was probably the last thing anyone said to her. And then – five minutes later, she was."

"Oh, Tracie, I'm so sorry." I sit down on the sofa on the opposite side of the backpack. "You shouldn't feel bad. The only person at fault here is whoever shot Hernan."

I know my words probably won't help Tracie. Because that kind of illogical guilt sticks with people. I'd had a taste of it myself, yesterday. But I can't help but think – everything Tracie just told me is the closest thing to a motive anyone's had so far. I don't think she'd have been so straightforward about telling me all that if she was the killer. But it's not going to look good to Arlo or his team.

Tracie says softly, "I was just frustrated. I had a good project. And to prove a mind for innovation, all the grant applicants had to make a Rube Goldberg machine. Mine was really cool." She pulls out her phone and flips through to a picture of a series of levers and cups and pipes, all painted purple and green and red. "It's supposed to be a visual S.O.S., and in the end the machine sets off a road flare. You should come see it in person. It's in a duffle in my garage, but I can put it back together in like ten minutes."

"Very cool," I say, though I don't really understand it.

Partly to distract Tracie from her complicated feelings, and partly because of genuine curiosity, I say, "I haven't seen the 3-D printer in action yet. Any chance you could show me how it works?"

"Only if there's coffee," Tracie says, eying the cup in my hand. "That smells amazing."

"It's Cà Phê Sữa Da," I say. "Vietnamese iced coffee, which is a bit on the sweet side."

Tracie frowns. "Can you do an unsweetened version?"

"I'm sure that can be arranged." I go back into the kitchen, and Tam Binh gives me a fresh phin and cups. By the time I get back, Tracie has a file open on her computer. It's a line drawing that looks like a porthole, with detailed filigree on the edging. Tracie says, "The thing about 3-D printing is that you can't have pieces that are cantilevered. The printer lays down the substance – in this case the chocolate – in thin layers, with each layer building onto the thickness. I like to think of it like building with ultra-thin Legos. But it's also like building up a design with a glue gun – you can hang over a tiny edge, but it can't be dramatic. That means that with something like this porthole, it would be impossible to print it standing up. But if you rotate the drawing, you can build an initial disc, and build the layers up from there."

"That's so cool," I say, impressed by the possibilities. "People are always asking for things like chocolate Eiffel towers and elephants, or whatever. You can only get so much detail on something like that using a mold, so a lot of times people decide not to place the order. But something like this could change that."

"I bet it could." Tracie hands me the laptop. She gets up and steps over to the printer, where she opens the side of it and pulls out a cylinder with a tip on the end that looks like an overgrown cake decorating tool. She says, "This is the cartridge. We need to fill it with tempered chocolate, and then you can hit print to start the design." She gestures over at the chocolate tempering machine Logan has set up next to the printer. The printer looks like a magician's cabinet with translucent sides. The tempering machine is far bigger, with more features than anything I'd had in the shop before. The whole setup is exciting to a chocolate geek like me. Tracie moves closer to the tempering machine. She says, "It looks like it's on and ready."

"Logan must have prepped it," I tell her. "He's a morning person, so who knows what time he got started."

Tracie nods in acknowledgement, then says. "It's simple to cleanly fill the cartridge." This tempering machine has three spouts. Tracie takes the cartridge over to one of the spouts and allows chocolate to flow into it to fill it. She puts it in the machine, and I hit start. Then I move over to the printer to watch it in action. The machine starts by laying down a thick line of chocolate, which looks a bit like the strokes used in cake decorating, to make the outline of the widest bottom edge of the porthole. Once it has outlined the entire disc, then it goes back and makes a line inside that, building that layer's structure in a shrinking spiral. Tracie says, "The piece on the actual sculpture has a layer of glass in it. I didn't try to replicate that, because you'd lose a lot of the details, and it might not make sense what the object is supposed to be. When Audrey gets here, you might talk to her about filling in that kind of thing. She's a glass artist, but she's done some pieces out of sugar too."

"I've seen sugar sculpture before," I say. I'd seen a sea collage, where translucent sugar had been blown into bulb-like shapes to make the bodies of jellyfish, and then opaque molten sugar had been pulled out to make the tentacles. It really had looked like glass. Instantly, I can see how a few pieces of pulled and blown sugar might really bring this ship sculpture to life.

I watch for a while as the chocolate porthole takes shape, and I begin to think of all the possibilities the shop would have if we had technology like this on hand on a regular basis. Printing custom chocolate sculpture on the fly. Creating shaped single-origin solid chocolates with elaborate designs to go in gift boxes. Chocolate art parties where people pay to have their name on a chocolate bar.

We're keeping the tempering machine – Logan and I had bought it after accepting the commission for the giant chocolate sculpture. But 3-D printers in general are very expensive and my personal funds are tied up in the flip hotel. Maybe after my aunt sells the hotel, and I get my share of the profits, I could consider buying a printer like this for the shop. Or at least a smaller one.

Audrey comes in, carrying a case of sculpting tools. I don't recognize her, but Tracie makes quick introductions.

I say, "I didn't see you at the studio the other day when we invited people here to work."

Audrey, who has her red hair in pigtail braids and is wearing combat boots and a red and black flannel shirt, says, "I refuse to work anywhere Amálie Timbers is going to be." She stops and looks remorseful at her choice of words. "Was going to be. Violet told me to be here. I hope that's okay."

I say, "Absolutely. I was just discussing with Tracie how having a sugar artist could take the sculpture to a whole other level."

"That would be so cool!" Audrey immediately starts sharing her ideas. She gets very animated, talking with her hands and fidgeting. She has a similar face shape to mine, and a smile that's infectious. I instantly like her.

A few minutes later, Gently Drifting shows up, carrying his cat, which is trailing a leash. Violet is with him. Violet has short fluorescent pink hair and delicate Asian features, and there's a tattoo of a tree taking up much of her left forearm. Even though we're obviously working out here, she gives me a curt nod and walks straight to the back, where I hear the squeak of plastic as she moves some of the cheap chocolate around. Gently looks nervous, now that she's left him alone.

But then Jonah – the guy who got knocked out by the killer at the museum – walks in, and Gently visibly relaxes. Interesting. He seems to need a friend present to feel at home – but neither Tracie nor Audrey fit that description.

Jonah says, "Hey."

Tracie asks, "How's your head?"

Jonah grimaces. "You know that feeling when you have a hangover so bad your headache has a headache?"

"Yeah," Tracie says sympathetically.

"It's like that." Jonah sits down at one of the tables. He runs his hands across his face, stopping short when he gets near the bruised part of his temple.

While Jonah and Tracie are distracted, I ask Audrey, "Can I ask you something?"

"Depends on what it is," Audrey says.

I ask, "Why didn't you want to work near Amálie? Did she do something to make you mad?"

Audrey pulls at the end of one of her pigtails, lifting it up to study the hair at the end. She says, "It wasn't Amálie herself that I disliked. I used to work with her husband at a local insurance firm. He got me fired."

"I didn't realize Amálie was married," I say. After all, the way she had been talking to Logan had seemed like flirting. But maybe I was wrong, and that been just more of her eccentric honesty.

"Oh, yes, she was married to a crazy liar. There had been – irregularities – and I think he was afraid of me." She wrinkles her nose. "Amálie was the one who had recommended me for the job. It's really hard to make a living making art, and she knew I was struggling. But when I got let go, she believed every word her husband said, and I just couldn't handle being around someone who could think so little of me."

"I get that," I say. It also sounds like motive – sort of – except for the fact that Audrey wasn't at the museum last night. I ask her, "So where *were* you working yesterday?"

"My room," she says. I must look confused, because she says, "I wasn't building a sculpture. That's far too messy to do at home. I was working on my website for most of the day yesterday."

"So you were by yourself?"

She shrugs. "At some point I ordered a pizza. But other than that, yeah. If you're asking if I have an alibi for the murders, I don't. But I really don't have a motive either. I have another job now, which I enjoy a lot more. I've been cataloging oral history interviews at the library for the past six months. I'm a bit of a history buff, so it's been fascinating."

"That does sound more interesting," I say.

She drops her pigtail. "I can only stay for a few hours this morning, because I have to get over to the library when they open."

I nod. "I'm happy for whatever work you can get done. Just give me a list of supplies for the sugar work, and I'll find a way to get whatever you need before the next time you come in."

"I have the tools," Audrey says. "I just need a couple of bags of isomalt. It's so much easier to work with, I prefer it over sugar for anything people aren't going to be eating. Because obviously, sugar has it hands down when it comes to taste."

I'm familiar with isomalt. It's a beet-based sweetener that doesn't caramelize the way sugar does, so it makes for clearer sculpture pieces. I've never really tried working with it, but I have seen demos. I say, "We can get that by the next time you come in."

I go and ask Carmen to get us a bulk quantity of isomalt from one of her baking suppliers.

Violet is in the kitchen, talking to Carmen. They are bantering comfortably, which is logical, since they are roommates.

I say, "Thank you for coming to help out today. I feel like we're making up some of the time we lost with yesterday's incident."

Violet says, "Anything for a friend of Carmen's. Plus, you're paying me."

"Of course," I say.

Carmen nudges Violet. "Ask her."

Violet shakes her head. Carmen gestures towards me, and Violet rolls her eyes.

I can't help asking, "Ask me what?"

Violet heaves out a sigh. "Carmen thinks that I should tell the police that I used to go out with Hernan, before he dumped me for Rosa. She thinks that gives Gently a motive. Though everybody knows he wouldn't hurt a flea. Like literally. If there's a bug, I'm the one who has to deal with it. So can I get in trouble for *not* talking to the police?"

"I don't think so," I say. "But the cops are bound to look into Hernan's ex-es anyway. I'd be surprised if they don't already know. What if they ask where you were yesterday?"

Violet says, "I was at home, binge watching *Business Proposal.*"

"I love that one," Tam Binh says. "I hate starting a new Korean drama, because I know I'm going to want to binge watch all the way through it, and that's like fourteen or sixteen episodes at an hour or an hour and a half a pop."

"Exactly. And since somebody works all the time these days-" Violet casts a significant look at Carmen. "The only one who can vouch for me was Bruno."

And it's not like a German Shephard is going to prove a communicative witness.

I say, "Maybe there's a way you can at least prove the program was playing all day. I'm not sure how much that helps, though."

"Not much," Logan says, coming in from the chocolate processing room. "Really, the best thing is for us to figure out who the killer actually is."

Like I haven't already been trying to do that. I haven't gotten very far, but I've at least been collecting information. So I ask the obvious. "Violet, you're also a sculptor. Are you up for the same grant Hernan was competing for? I heard that several artists here had entered."

Violet says, "Well, yeah. It was a lot of money, and a space to work. Who can't use that?"

I wonder if she realizes that that gives her even more motive. Still, she doesn't seem desperate for cash or space. I have a hard time imagining her killing Hernan just because he was in the lead in the competition. There has to be something else that I'm missing. I head back out into the main part of the shop with the intention to talk to Gently and Jonah, and find some other perspectives on all of this.

The two guys are sitting at the same table, which now has several giant blocks of chocolate on it. They both have carving tools, but they're still discussing what to do with the block. Eavesdropping, I get the idea that they're trying to figure out how to create a mast without making it weigh too much. Gently wants to solve the problem by getting a PVC pipe and dipping it in melted chocolate."

Jonah sees me and says, "You must have seen something yesterday, Mrs. Koerber. You were working near the sculpture."

I say, "I didn't see much. The lights were out by the time I realized anything was wrong. And then when I ran over to Hernan, it was too late to do anything."

Jonah says, "You were at the museum right before the break in, and right there when the artist who made the sculpture that got defaced got killed. Did you have any reason not to like Amálie Timbers?"

"Why would you even ask that?" I ask, mortified. I'm being unjustly suspected of murder – again. And this time, it's by a skinny artist kid.

Jonah takes my question more philosophically. He says, "I need to know who attacked me yesterday. I didn't sleep all night last night, because I kept jumping at every little noise, convinced whoever hit me was coming after me again."

Gently grabs on tighter to the cat and says, "You really think you can solve a murder?"

"Why not?" Jonah gestures at me. "She's solved three of them. And I've got the advantage that I'm addicted to mystery novels, and a couple of crime-solution animes. I've already uncovered a couple of clues."

"Like what?" Audrey asks skeptically.

"For one, that inch of fishing line that was taped to the door. In one of the animes I watch, the bad guys are always setting up misleading effects with fishing line. I think somebody actually did that, to create a specific timing with that slamming door everyone's talking about."

Startled, I choke for a second on the spit in my own mouth. I think Jonah might be right. There was that reel I had seen, with the fishing line trailing away off the table. I ask, "You're sure that piece of fishing line wasn't there earlier than yesterday?"

"It wasn't," Tracie says. "I remember wondering when somebody had had a party." Then she asks Jonah. "When you got hit, was it before or after the door slammed?"

"Before, definitely."

I ask, "Was it before or after the gunshot?"

Jonah looks down at the table, presumably playing back through events in his mind. Eventually, he looks up at us and says, "After. I don't actually remember it as a gunshot. I thought I heard a noise on the stairs after the lights went out, so I turned towards it, and then there was a bang that seemed to echo through the entire space. I couldn't tell where the shot came from, but that's the last thing I remember."

"Didn't you tell the police this?" I ask.

"Not yet," he admits. "I was pretty out of it last night. I think they were more concerned about me passing out again with a concussion."

I really need to talk to Arlo. All of this information could save time in his investigation.

"I have a question," I say. "Who had the spotlight? I don't think I ever saw that person last night."

Tracie says, "That was Syed. He's an industrial artist, and he's not here today because he's independently wealthy and couldn't be bothered."

"What he said is that pirates are stupid," Gently says. "And he doesn't want to build the ship of a criminal."

"It's not actually supposed to be a pirate ship," I point out. "Amálie said the sculpture was supposed to represent the maritime history of Galveston, and the resiliency of hope by using re-claimed metal from cars and structures damaged by hurricanes."

"But it looks like a pirate ship," Gently points out. "A pirate ship out of someone's dream."

"That's right," Tracie says. "That's how Syed put it. I think he was in talking to the cops when you came through looking for Amálie's phone."

"What did you want with her phone?" Jonah asks. He still looks suspicious.

I ignore the heat coming into my chest and neck in a mix of embarrassment and disbelief. I should not be a suspect. I say, "She said she wanted to show me something. I figured it might be important."

And that makes me think – Amálie's phone going missing – my phone being stolen and then destroyed. That doesn't feel random. Could the killer think one of us had received a text or something that could be incriminating? Or have some kind of information that the killer would find beneficial? But there wasn't anything unusual on my phone. So potentially, the purse snatching could have been a mistake, and the information had been sent to someone else.

"Excuse me," I say, taking my new phone out of my pocket. "I need to make a call."

I go outside and walk over to the turtle sculpture that is on the sidewalk, not far from my front door. I call Arlo.

He picks up, saying hesitantly, "Please, Lis, tell me you didn't find another body."

"For once, the answer to that is no," I say.

Chapter Ten

Logan is driving when we pull into the museum parking lot. Arlo is standing outside, waiting for us. He gives Logan a skeptical look. Logan just gets out of the car and heads for the studio. I follow.

Arlo asks, "What did you want to show me? Or is this just a ploy to get a look at the crime scene?"

"I definitely have something to show you," I say. "But I'll be honest, I also wanted to look around and see if I remember things right. I'm sorry. I know I said I would stay out of this case, but people just keep volunteering information. Plus, you have another amateur sleuth on your hands. Jonah thinks he's going to solve this thing."

Arlo groans. "Just exactly what I don't need." He unlocks the door, and we go through into the building. Logan switches on the lights.

I turn back to the door. Sure enough, there's a piece of Scotch tape securing a fragment of fishing line to the door's surface. There's a couple of bits of crepe paper also attached. If I didn't know what I was looking for, I would have assumed that I was seeing the leftovers from party decorations that had been pulled down. I can only assume that's the calculated effect the killer was going for, so that anyone seeing it would discount it. Only an artist would think in that kind of detail. Too bad that describes every one of our current suspects.

I explain what Jonah had said about the fishing line appearing after he arrived yesterday. Arlo takes a picture of it, but from the look on his face, he's just humoring me.

I wind my way through the maze of workstations, to where I had seen the rods and the reel. I call Arlo and Logan over.

With a gloved hand, Arlo starts to pick up the reel – only to find that it is attached to the table.

"What the heck?" Arlo says. Suddenly, he seems a lot more convinced that maybe I'm onto something. We all take a closer look. There's a drawer in the table, and inside the drawer there is some kind of mechanism involving a kitten-shaped kitchen timer. It really does look like someone had timed the lights going out and the door slamming. Maybe the earlier break-in was just to set up the problem with the breaker box, and the vandalism with Amálie's sculpture was just to cover the intruder's true intentions.

I discuss this with Arlo and Logan, but at this point, I'm just making guesses.

I say, "Jonah said he heard a noise on the stairs leading up to the loft, right before the gunshot."

I walk over to the stairs before Arlo thinks to stop me. I may have shown him what I came here to show, but that doesn't mean I can't look at anything else while I'm here. I spot another piece of Scotch tape, but this one doesn't seem to be attached to anything. I go up the stairs, and near the top, there's another piece of tape. This one has part of a popped balloon attached to it. There's so much junk up here in the loft – who would have even noticed a deflated balloon in the midst of all the half-completed sculptures and canvases with riotous colors and haphazardly stored equipment?

Arlo had come up here looking for a suspect, and come back to look for a weapon. But this killer seems to be all about misdirection. Maybe Arlo had seen something – without recognizing it as a weapon or a clue.

I feel a tickle at the back of my throat from all the dust, and I cough.

Both guys come up the stairs. Logan asks, "Do you have your inhaler?"

I pull the inhaler out of my purse. "Y'all are overreacting. Anyone would cough with this much dust." But I take a puff on the inhaler, preemptively, just in case.

Logan asks, "What are we looking for?"

"I'm not sure," I say. "I'm just trying to think like whoever stuck a kitchen timer on a fishing reel."

Arlo says, "Yeah. I get what you mean."

Logan sighs heavily. Maybe he's not as cool about me and Arlo vibing on the detecting front as he would like to be. But I try not to focus on the awkwardness.

Instead, while Arlo is in a good mood, I ask, "Did you learn anything interesting about Syed? He's the only artist who was here yesterday that I didn't really get to meet."

Now it's Arlo's turn to sigh. "Lis, you know I can't talk about an active investigation with a civilian – especially not one who was present at the scene of the crime. I shouldn't even be letting you look around this place. If you touch anything and it is hypothetically something you could have placed at the scene, it could break the chain of evidence and eventually get the case thrown out of court. Do you want a murderer to go free on a technicality?"

I freeze, only listening to the last part of Arlo's statement. But he seems to take it as me agreeing with him.

"Good," he says. "Let's go back downstairs."

"No," I say, pointing at a familiar-looking purple and red and green tube. The end of it is blackened, and there are faint black streaks on a piece of plywood propped nearby. "Look. That's Tracie's project for the grant she's trying to get. What is it doing up here?"

Logan moves over to the project machine, examining the black smudges. Then he turns around, sighting from the end of the pipe out into the room. He says, "I think we're looking at the murder weapon."

I turn around too, following the trajectory from the pipe to the scaffolding where Hernan had been standing. It's a straight line to the approximate height of where he'd been shot. There doesn't seem to be a way to aim or adjust the tubing, so if it is the weapon, the killer would somehow have to have been sure Hernan was standing in the right spot. "But it doesn't make sense," I say. "Tracie said the device was supposed to set off a road flare, not shoot anything – let alone a bullet."

Logan says, "It's been modified. The inside of this has been damaged from being used as a gun. You said Tracie was mad about Amálie tanking her chances for that grant. What could be more poetic justice than killing her with the device she didn't think was creative enough? And even more – by using Hernan as one more step in her Rube Goldberg machine?"

"Tracie didn't do this," I say.

"Do you know that for a fact?" Arlo asks.

"Let's just call it intuition," I say. "She's not this kind of person."

Arlo says, "I think I should probably still have a long chat with her anyway."

I say, "Tracie wasn't the only one involved in the grant competition. Apparently, Violet was up for it too. And likely some of the other sculptors here at the studio."

"And I'll talk to them too, Lis," Arlo says. "Somebody has to know who was last in possession of Tracie's project."

I tell him, "We got to talking about the grant competition. Tracie told me her project was dismantled and in a duffle in her garage. She offered to show it to me. Which means she doesn't even realize it had gone missing."

"That's one possibility," Arlo says. "But she could be building a false alibi. She's definitely a suspect."

The guys already have their dive gear, but I'm renting equipment. We wind up going straight to the dive shop from the museum. It makes more sense than going back to the chocolate shop just to come back out later. It's a quiet drive, because we're all thinking about what we found in the loft.

I try to switch gears, to get excited about the adventure I'm about to have underwater. Logan has planned a rig dive. At first, I thought that meant we'd be diving near the rigs in the bay – which in a way is confined water, right? But apparently the visibility in the bay is nonexistent, making diving there not only unsatisfying, but also dangerous. We're going out farther.

There are a few other customers in the shop. A woman comes over to help me.

"Are you just getting into diving?" she asks.

"Yes," I say. "It's actually my first time doing SCUBA. I need the basics."

Her face lights up, and at first I think she must be on commission. But she says, "Oh, wow, your first dive. My first dive, I was so nervous, but once I got into the water, it was magic. Your life is never going to be the same."

What is it with all these divers? It's like a cult. I stammer, "Uh-I guess so."

"Let's look at wet suits for you."

She takes me over to a section on the other side of the store. On a nearby aisle, I spot a woman with a vaguely familiar pixie cut. It's the artist who had been texting or posting to social media after the murder. Today, though, her gelled hair looks sleek and shiny under the store's bright lights. I ask the saleslady to give me a moment.

"Sure," the saleswoman says. "Let me pull out your size in my favorite wetsuits."

"Hey," I say to the artist. "Weren't you at the museum yesterday?"

She turns and offers me a hesitant smile. "I was. I should have introduced myself. I'm Marissa Reid. I paint watercolors – mostly of underwater subjects." She gestures around herself at the contents of the dive shop. "Obviously."

I say, "I don't know if you heard, but Logan invited everyone to help out with the chocolate sculpture. I don't suppose you'd be interested?"

Marissa looks embarrassed. She hands me a business card. "I don't need another gig. I have a day job crewing a fishing charter. I spent the entire morning today doing maintenance on the boats. I'm sorry. I know it looked like you need some help. I hope some of the others showed up."

"They did, actually." I pick up a random piece of equipment off the shelf and pretend to be looking at it. I surreptitiously look up at Marissa. "Have you ever worked with sculpture? I understand there was a big grant competition."

Marissa makes a derisive noise. "That medium is not my calling. And I don't do contests anymore. Most people don't seem to understand my art."

By which I take her to mean that she bombs out in competition. Maybe she's the one artist I've met so far who doesn't have talent. I know that watercolor can be a complex and nuanced medium. But in unskilled hands, it can also be one step away from finger painting.

"Have you ever worked with Hernan or Amálie?" I ask.

"You do know regulators tend to flood if you use them like that." Marissa takes the instrument I'm looking at out of my hands and hands it back to me. Apparently, I was holding it upside down. I feel a spike of embarrassment. She says, "I didn't know either of them very well. I once took an art history class with Hernan. But he seemed a bit too assertive for my taste, so we never hung out."

"Oh, okay," I say. She isn't giving me anything to work with here. So I say, "Enjoy the rest of your day."

Marissa says, "If you're looking for someone who had a problem with Hernan, you should talk to Destiny. There was something between them. I thought they were dating last year, between when Hernan broke up with Violet, and when he started dating Rosa. But Destiny claims they never were. Just that they were friends – and then one day about a month ago, they weren't friends anymore."

"Really?" I say, trying to keep my voice neutral. But some of my excitement still comes through. I had thought the conversation with Marissa was a bust, but she's given me a new lead to look into. "You think I can find Destiny at that paint and drink wine studio?"

Marissa nods. "She's there most evenings."

"Which means I can go by after this dive," I say.

She looks at the regulator in my hands. "Be careful. You need to make sure you know what you're doing before you even get into the water."

I gesture in the general direction of Logan and Arlo. I tell Marissa, "I have two excellent tutors."

It doesn't take long to assemble all the equipment I'm going to need. It takes a bit longer to run through all the practice stuff the guys want me to do in shallow water before we get on the boat. It feels a bit ridiculous, putting my face in the water when I practically have to sit on the bottom to do so. But it does make me feel better that they're not showing complete disregard for the safety rules of diving. And eventually, we do get on the boat, and I get to see the GPS. When I get a look at where we're going, I realize we're headed for the same offshore oil rig my uncle works on.

He's going to get the biggest kick out of that. I call him, to let him know. It's not like he can come outside and wave as we go swimming by, but it is still cool to know that we're in the same place.

When I tell him, though, Uncle Greg says, "You be careful. We had a theft out here this morning."

"How does somebody steal something off of an oil rig?" I ask.

"They took a piece of equipment, and somehow just lowered it into the water." Uncle Greg says.

"Was it expensive?" I ask.

"I'll say. It was a remote operated vehicle, what we call a ROV. It's basically an underwater drone. At first we were afraid the thief was planning to sabotage the rig, but there's no sign of them now."

"That's crazy."

"I agree." Uncle Greg tells me to be careful on my dive.

As soon as I hang up, both Logan and Arlo are giving me rapid-fire advice on the proper technique for different aspects of diving. I'm ready to get into the water, just to get some quiet. Logan asks again, "Are you sure you understand the hand gestures for communicating underwater?"

"Yes," I say again. I make an okay gesture, bringing my thumb to my forefinger to form a circle – the way to say *yes* underwater – to illustrate my point.

Finally, we go over the side of the boat into the water. And yeah, it is magical. The scale of the rig is enormous, with the chains that anchor it to the bottom spreading out into the distance. Each one of the links is almost as big as I am. It's all a bit disconcerting at first, being able to hear my breathing so loud. And I flinch the first time the bubbles touch my face. But the bubbles tickle more than anything.

The pipes leading from the bottom of the rig down to the ocean floor have things growing on them, attracting fish. We swim down a little way to look at some of the fish, though it is about eighty feet to the bottom, and I know I'm not ready to go down that far. The area to our left has an underwater mound which makes the bottom over there much shallower, and there's a bed of seagrass growing there.

The fish surrounding the rig are colorful – red snapper, mostly, though I also recognize some speckled trout. Some of those fish are big enough to be intimidating, but they don't seem interested in me, so after a bit I relax. I listen to my own breath, feeling buoyant in the water, finding the edge of absolute peace. Logan makes the gesture for *okay*, and both Arlo and I make it back.

Arlo points at the area with the stand of sea grass. We swim away from the rig, towards the sea grass. Arlo gestures for me to turn back and look at the rig from a distance, but I notice something big floating in the grass. Fear spikes through me, as my brain says *shark*! But it isn't a shark. Because sharks don't wear red plaid. I motion to Logan to look in the direction I'm pointing. He does, then he swims strongly towards the sea grass. I follow hesitantly.

Logan reaches down and untangles a very human hand from part of the grass. I suck in a massive gulp of air, which then startles me as my regulator responds to my change in breathing. As Logan moves, the person flips over in the water. It's Audrey, the glass artist who supposedly had to leave my shop about five hours ago to go work at the library. Obviously, she had been lying. Why had she come here? Had it even been voluntary, or had she been kidnapped on her way to the library? And why had she wound up dead?

I feel a scream building in my throat, and Arlo is there next to me, supporting me in the water, and making sure I don't lose my regulator when the scream finally comes out of my mouth.

Chapter Eleven

I'm wearing a wet suit, and it's really not that cold out anyway, especially for November, but I find myself shivering, sitting on the boat. Logan hands me a cup of coffee from a Thermos. It's pretty good coffee, but I find myself just holding the metal cup, to absorb the warmth.

Arlo is driving the boat. He looks very serious. This is not at all how my first dive trip was supposed to turn out. I had made so many strides in recent months towards recovering my love of the ocean, of coming to terms with the fact that while Kevin had died on a boat, the boat itself wasn't responsible. I would have thought that something like this would be more triggering. But instead, I keep coming back to the *why*. Why would Audrey have wound up here? Is it just coincidence that she's near the same rig we'd decided to dive at? Why would she have been out this far without a life jacket or dive equipment, or anything?

The most obvious possibility is that Audrey was somehow involved with the theft that happened earlier on the rig. Maybe she'd been driving the getaway boat and hadn't intended to go in the water. After all, she'd still been wearing heavy combat boots and that open flannel. So what could have happened?

I say, "I guess it was too soon to make jokes about me *not* finding a body for once."

I had liked Audrey. It's hard to believe that she could have been wrapped up in something that would have gotten her killed. Of course, I had known her for all of a couple of hours. But first impressions are hard to overcome.

Arlo says, "This complicates things. Potentially, the person who killed Hernan and Amálie is lying at the bottom of the ocean. And that makes this partially the Coast Guard's problem."

Not the least of which was going to be retrieving Audrey from the bottom of the Gulf. We're stuck here waiting for them, as a sort of buoy for the location.

Logan crosses his arms over his chest. "I think what we have to ask ourselves here is who would have wanted to steal an ROV from that rig. And how they could get away with it in broad daylight."

I add, "And whether that person would also have an interest in a museum." I take a sip of my coffee. I see a boat approaching in the distance – likely the Coast Guard. "What could you even do with that kind of equipment?"

Logan says, "Rig divers use them to repair pipe, at depths where it wouldn't necessarily be safe to go in person, or for jobs that are going to take too long to do. So conceivably, if you wanted to pull a heist, or destroy something, you could cut a hole in the side of something and then drag something out of it. Or if you wanted to do salvage, you could cut apart something that was too big to move."

Arlo says, "Treasure divers are often financing their own operations. I can see someone illegally borrowing industrial equipment if they were broke – or if they were new and didn't really know what they were doing."

"What's a treasure diver?" I ask.

Logan says, "Legally, if something has been at the bottom of the ocean for a long time, a salvage diver can claim ownership just by recovering it. Treasure divers look for wrecks that are worth something, or have historic value. Then they sell off whatever they find."

Arlo adds, "There are a ton of documented wrecks in the Gulf Coast, both historically and more recent. When you dive to explore a wreck, that's just called a wreck dive, like what we just did was a rig dive. But if you're removing things from it, that's something else entirely. There's a lot fewer divers who are willing to put in the work to do something like that, because if a wreck has already been identified, chances are anything valuable has been taken off it. So they have to find something that's been lost. Which is obviously difficult in itself."

"Or maybe they could take a shortcut, and just take something someone else has found," I say. I can't help but think about that copy of *Treasure Island* that Delores Cook had given me. I've always thought it was such a well written story. You have a good kid who is given a treasure map – and a bunch of pirates who want to mutiny on the ship to take the treasure for themselves. The idea of pirate gold makes for a good literary conflict, but it's impossibly unrealistic for real life. Or is it? I think about that piece of paper the purse snatcher had dropped. I had joked that it was the edge of a treasure map. But . . . what if it was? I laugh out loud. Because I'm being completely fanciful.

"What's so funny?" Logan asks.

"I was just thinking about pirate treasure. But none of that stuff was real, even in that time period. It was a thing for adventure books and entertaining children." I gesture back in the general direction of the island. "It's like when Arlo and I went looking for Lafitte's treasure when we were kids. And we found out that pirates didn't actually bury treasure – except for one guy, one time, and then it became a legend."

Logan crosses his arms over his chest. "Buried treasure, yes. That's a myth. But pirates – both historical and modern – did amass fortunes. And sailing has always been a dangerous business, so sometimes those fortunes wound up at the bottom of the ocean. It's possible for a maritime chart to be a treasure map of sorts."

I'm a bit bemused by all of that. Especially because I never realized that Logan is quite that much of a romantic. I think of him as the practical one, the one ready to spring into action, the one who reads weapons manuals instead of novels – but I forget he's also the guy who, back when he'd been a bodyguard, tortured himself over the client he couldn't save.

Arlo says, "Stop looking like you're laughing, Lis, or you're going to have some awkward explaining to do to the Coast Guard."

We are still at a murder scene, and the Coast Guard boat is rapidly approaching. It manages to stop far enough away that it doesn't smack into us, and Arlo moves from our boat over onto the larger vessel. He and an officer in a white uniform talk for a bit, and then two divers in black wet suits go over the side. I don't want to think about what they're about to bring up to the surface.

I say, "If this is about salvage, or about a heist, then it's all about greed. I don't understand how three dead artists fit in."

Logan says, "I don't either. Maybe we're wrong. Maybe Audrey was out here for some reason that had nothing to do with the theft. She could have had a boyfriend aboard the rig. Or maybe she came out here to paint. And after she went overboard, whoever was with her panicked and didn't report it."

"Maybe," I say, but honestly that feels like more of a stretch, given the break-in at the museum, the purse-snatching, and the theft of equipment from the rig. For Audrey to die by accident in the same place as the theft just seems one coincidence too many. And it doesn't explain how thoroughly her body seems stuck in the sea grass.

Logan sits down next to me. It's comfortable here, with him, watching the water from this gently rocking boat. We could sit here a long time without the need to even say a word. I like that feeling. I don't want to lose that. But I will, if I keep kissing Arlo.

A dolphin jumps in the distance, and Logan points to it. "That's one thing I love about this place. When I first moved here, I rode the ferry every day for weeks, just to dolphin watch."

"It must not have been in the summer," I quip. After all, the line for the automobile-carrying ferry that goes between Galveston Island and Port Bolivar on the mainland can stack up for hours during peak tourist season.

"It was the off season," Logan says. "But I didn't drive onto the ferry anyway. I just parked my car in the lot and walked on. After all, I wasn't going anywhere on the other side. I could just walk around and get on another boat going back."

"I thought you were all about the sea turtles," I say. After all, Logan had named his flight business Ridley Puddle Jumpers, after the endangered Kemp's ridley sea turtles that sometimes nest on the island.

He gestures out at the water. "Dolphins are pretty cool too. Though they can be jerks to each other, and to marine life like fish, so sea turtles are definitely cooler."

Arlo climbs back aboard the boat. His expression is grim, and his lips look pale. He says, "The divers found what was holding Audrey underwater. Her ankle had been chained to one of her own sculptures. It was a mermaid made out of junk she'd found during a beach clean-up. Somebody involved in this case has one sick sense of irony."

I keep thinking about that the whole ride back to shore. Which of these suspects has an art style that implies a love of irony? Destiny, perhaps? With her whimsical and irreverent takes on wooden sculpture, done to look traditional at a distance. She didn't come to the shop this morning. Either she doesn't need the extra money, or she doesn't like working as part of a team – or maybe it's possible that she didn't want to give anything away that could tie her to the murders. I really do need to go to her class later and see what I can find out.

Logan asks Arlo, "Whose jurisdiction is it?"

Arlo closes his eyes for a long moment, like for some reason he's wishing this particular murder was someone else's problem. "The two murders that happened at the museum are clearly mine. The one here belongs to Chief Warrant Officer Walls. We've decided to share information. Keep it genial instead of competitive."

Logan grins. "Because you've always been so good at that."

"Not everyone brings out the worst in me like you do," Arlo says. But I can tell Arlo's shaken.

I ask him, "Why is this case getting to you? Did you know Audrey somehow?"

"No, nothing like that." Arlo looks hesitant to share what's bothering him. Maybe he doesn't want to show weakness in front of Logan. Finally, he says, "It's just that I never saw Audrey up close before they pulled her out of the water. She looked a lot like you, when you were her age."

"I never had red hair," I point out. And while there were some similarities between mine and Audrey's appearances, we didn't look alike enough to really justify this response. Unless Arlo is even more stuck in the past than I'd realized.

"She did look a bit like you, though," Logan says. "Not like twins or anything. But I understand why he's shaken."

Or maybe Arlo's not so stuck, and I just don't really see what they do. After all, when you like someone, you tend to see their face everywhere, just like when you miss someone. After Kevin's death, I can't count the number of times I imagined I saw him, only to realize it wasn't him after all.

We head for shore, and Logan goes below deck to stow some of the gear.

From his spot driving the boat, Arlo says, "I lied to you earlier. I'm not okay with you taking Logan as your plus one to Autumn's wedding. We missed our timing before, when we were young, and I don't want to miss it again." He gestures back at the water where we had been diving – where someone equally young had just lost her life. "Today has reminded me that you never know how much time you have, and I don't want to waste any of it. Forget dancing around, trying to logically weigh who's going to make you happiest. Marry me, and let's just move on with living it."

I just stare at him, unable to form a response. Was that just a proposal? I hear the creak of Logan's footstep on the stairs, coming back up to join us. It suddenly feels like this boat is very small, and I have to fight an irrational urge to jump overboard, just to get away from the pressure of a decision.

Did Logan hear what Arlo said? I can't tell, from the inscrutable look on Logan's face. And nobody says a word until we reach shore, at which point, I quickly escape into my car and drive back to my chocolate shop. Mine and Logan's chocolate shop.

Arlo was right about one thing, though. Life is too short to walk around waiting for relationships to solidify themselves. That counts for friendships, too.

At the shop, production on the sculpture is in full swing. Marissa decided to come help after all. I guess I made her feel guilty when I ran into her at the scuba shop. Or she felt really sorry for me. Gently has his cat draped around his shoulders as he programs images into his laptop, and Tracie has her head down on the table, taking a nap. The others are all hand sculpting blocks of chocolate.

Autumn has stopped by, and she's sitting with Carmen and Tam Binh, sampling pieces of something that looks suspiciously like wedding cake. I wonder why Autumn's fiancé Drake isn't here – until I see him walk out of the bathroom. He's a clean-shaven black guy with a tight fade haircut. Today, he's dressed in a white button up shirt with an orange-and-gold swirl-design tie.

"Hey," he says. "You're just in time. Carmen knows how much my Autumn likes lavender, so she's about to bring out a chocolate cake with lavender buttercream."

"I wasn't planning on staying," I say. "I need to go sort something out with one of the bridesmaids."

"Before you go," Drake says, "I was wondering if I could have a look at that copy of *Treasure Island*. Autumn told me about it, and I love those old illustrated editions. Occupational hazard."

Which makes sense. Drake is a restoration librarian at one of the local universities.

"Sure," I say. I go and get the book from my office. Looking at the cover, I keep thinking about what Hernan had said about loving this book too. I'm no closer to figuring out what motive anyone might have had to have killed him. I flip through the pages, but there aren't any answers here either, just a note that the book was a donation from the personal library of J. Mills.

I hand the book to Drake, who starts examining the binding with interest.

Autumn scolds him, "Focus, Honey. Cake now, books later."

Logan comes out from the back of the shop. I didn't realize he'd already gotten back from the police station, where he'd gone with Arlo to record a statement. He says, "Maybe I should get in on this tasting. Since I'm here . . . and since I'll be at the wedding."

"About that," Drake says. He puts the book down on the table, careful to keep it out of range of the frosting. "I was wanting to talk to you."

My heart lurches – is Logan for some reason being disinvited to the wedding? Did Arlo talk to Autumn and Drake about him not wanting me to take a plus one? Logan looks a little concerned too.

Drake says, "My cousin Andrew won't be able to come to the wedding after all, which leaves me short a groomsman. I know we haven't known each other that long, but I'd be honored if you step in."

"I'd be the one who's honored," Logan says.

I let out a tight breath. So now Logan is not only going to the wedding, he's going to be in it. Arlo really isn't going to like that. And I'm trying to decide why I care so much about that. Do I love Arlo? Or am I desperate not to hurt him, because of everything I did wrong in the past?

I decide not to focus on that. Instead, I grab a couple of bars of my Ecuador chocolate and box up an assortment of truffles. I put them all in a bag so they'll be easy to carry as I walk over to Kaylee's bookshop. It feels good to have the sun on my face, to shake off the horror of earlier today, to know that my lungs feel stronger than ever – that I am, in short, alive.

Chapter Twelve

When I get to the bookshop, Kaylee is at the register, helping a customer, so I browse for a bit, until Kaylee comes to find me in the stacks. She's wearing a tee-shirt today that says, *No Talkie 'til Coffee.*

I gesture at the shirt and say, "I totally agree. Cutting back coffee when I was doing the treatments for my asthma was one of the hardest things I've ever done in my life."

Kaylee laughs, but she looks a little sad at the same time. She says, "At least you found a treatment."

I say, "Yeah, it was a bit of a miracle, the silver lining to the darkest cloud I've ever walked under. I found out about the experimental program at the hospital where they took Kevin, after his accident."

Kaylee leans against a corner of one of the bookcases. "I'm sure that makes you feel bad, because obviously you'd rather still have the asthma symptoms, and still have him."

I nod. "He was a good guy." I'm a lot more okay talking about this than I would have been a few months ago. I'm still sad, and a bit nostalgic – but not overwhelmed.

Kaylee says, "For what it's worth, I didn't know why you'd come back to Galveston, back at your grand opening party. Everyone was talking about how excited they were for your return. You had been so popular in high school, a lot of people were excited to see you again. I was the geek reading quietly in the library back in high school, so that made me a little jealous. And all this Local Girl Follows Dream stuff was annoying – especially since I've decided to hide my own success as a romance novelist."

I blink. It's hard to imagine someone as successful as novelist Kay Sinclair being jealous of me. I hadn't really even been super popular. People just liked me because I avoided drama.

Then something she said hits me. I say, "Wait. We went to high school together?" I had assumed that Kaylee was a good decade older than me.

"Not exactly. You were in school with my baby sister, Sarah. You came to my house once, working on a history project."

"I remember Sarah," I say. "But I don't remember the history project."

"I've always liked history," Kaylee says. "Sarah kept bugging me to answer questions so she wouldn't have to look things up. You really don't remember?"

I shake my head. "I'm sorry. That was a long time ago." I haven't thought about most of the people I went to high school with in years. I ask, "Where's Sarah now?"

Kaylee says, "She's living in Dallas. She's an advertising executive."

"Sarah?" I say, incredulous. "I thought she wanted to be an anesthesiologist."

Kaylee shrugs. "Very little about life goes the way you expect when you're that age."

I sigh. "That's true enough. And for what it's worth-" I mirror the language she'd used, trusting her to get the irony. "I didn't know about your diagnosis. It's hard having medical issues that other people don't automatically see."

Kaylee scowls. "I don't want pity for my medical condition. I'm the same person I was before."

"I get that," I say, holding out the bag full of chocolate I brought. "So don't think these are pity chocolates. They're a thank you for saving my purse, and almost saving my phone."

She takes the bag. "Did the cops ever catch the thief?"

"Not yet." I take my new phone out of my pocket. "Though I'm pretty happy with the upgrade."

"I like the camera on that model," Kaylee says.

"Me too. Don't be surprised if this winds up on Instagram." I snap a picture of the bag in Kaylee's hands. But then I focus in on the phone itself. "It is odd, though. Obviously, whoever snatched my purse mainly wanted the phone. So maybe they thought I had something on it about Hernan or Amálie. So I can't figure out why the thief would have dropped the phone, even though it broke, if they could have used the SIM card in another phone to access the information."

Kaylee says, "But that's not how it works. SIM cards only give you basic information. You have to reconnect everything else. The thief could have accessed your phone's native messages, or your billing information, but that's about it."

I stare down at the phone in my hand. I had spent a while at the phone store, while they pulled all my phone's backed-up data from the cloud and put it on the new one. "So if the thief knew that, it makes sense why they dropped it. And if there was something on my old phone that the thief wanted – it's still here."

"Well, yeah. But wouldn't you know if you had something on your phone that someone would want to steal?"

"I should – unless I didn't realize it was important." I flip through the screens, thinking about what information I have stored in the different apps. I say, "I didn't have any communications from Hernan or Amálie, either by text or by e-mail, and the only stuff I have from Delores Cook is about deadlines and budgets. But I did take some pictures at the museum. I don't think they were anything special, but what if I caught the killer in the background of one of the images or something?"

I go back to the first screen and pull up my photo roll, scrolling back through to where I had taken pictures of the exhibit and Amálie's sculpture. Renoir is in the background of several of the images I'd taken, and preening his feathers for the camera smack center in several others.

"Cute bird," Kaylee says.

"With a bit of excess personality," I say. I show her a photo of the ship sculpture, with its hodgepodge of found pieces. "This is the sculpture Amálie was exhibiting. A lot of it is made of marine salvage. It was damaged during the break-in, where I assume someone was trying to give a reason for messing with the fuse box. Keep the police guessing, you know." I hesitate. I just had an idea, and I let it gel for a second before putting it into words. "Wait. What if it wasn't just a misdirection? What if something about the sculpture itself was important? I texted Delores several times asking if there were other photographs of the sculpture, with better details than the pics I have. She doesn't seem to think there are any – though she doesn't seem that interested in tracking anything down. And Amálie's phone disappeared off her body. She probably took photos of her own work. What if the killer is looking for those pics?"

"It's possible," Kaylee says. "But if the killer and the thief are the same person, and they took Amálie's phone – then why would they need yours? They could have taken pictures of the sculpture before it was damaged, or gotten whatever they needed off of her phone."

"I don't know." Stumped I look at the picture of the sculpture. "Unless . . . what if they weren't trying to collect the images, but destroy them?"

Kaylee's eyes go wide. "Who knows you took photos before the sculpture got damaged?"

"Hernan, possibly. And maybe Tracie. One of them is dead, and I'm pretty sure the other one doesn't have a motive." Though I'm going to have to re-think that, because so much of this keeps leading back to Tracie. Though I'm sure she wouldn't be stupid enough to use her own Rube Goldberg machine as a murder weapon.

"What if Hernan told the person who killed him about the photos?" Kaylee asks. She reaches into the bag and gets out one of the boxes of truffles. She takes a bite out of a bourbon pecan truffle before adding, "Maybe that's why he got killed."

I consider this, but it doesn't completely make sense. "It was Amálie's sculpture. If someone died over it, wouldn't it make sense that she was the intended target?"

"Maybe?" Kaylee finishes the truffle, not looking convinced. "There's no way to know which one the killer was after until you unravel the rest of this. Not for sure, anyway."

"So, assuming that I have some of the only existing pictures of Amálie's sculpture, and the purse snatcher wanted to destroy them – I need to figure out why. Here's my best close-up of the side of the ship that got damaged." I swipe over to the photo I want to show her, and use my finger to outline the irregular oval that was cut and damaged. "This part was cut into pieces. It seemed savage and personal at the time. But what if there was one piece of it that was valuable? Or incriminating? Or – something? Look at this telegraph thing. It looks fairly unique. Maybe it's made out of gold?"

Kaylee laughs. "I seriously doubt that is worth anything. Engine order telegraphs are used to transmit information from the bridge to the engine room, so there's no reason it would have been made out of anything valuable. Besides, gold doesn't rust."

"True." I look closer at the image, and she's right—there are a few flecks of rust at the edge of the dial. I ask, "How do you know so much about boats?"

She takes me over to a shelf farther down the same aisle and pulls out a book with a buxom blonde on the cover, leaning against a ship's mast, looking longingly down at the sea. *The Pirate's Secret Love* by Kay Sinclair. Kaylee says, "This is the first in my *Pirate's* series. They're all guys with hearts of gold, misunderstood by their times and forced by circumstance into lives of crime – until they get redeemed by love. They're nothing like real historical pirates, but I did get to put in a lot of stuff about boats and marine life and history. It was some of the most fascinating book research I've gotten to do. I even spent a week sailing on the *Tall Ship Elissa*, as sort of a ride-along, so I could get the feeling of living on a boat right. The ship is from the

1870s, which wasn't exactly the decade I was going for, but it was probably as close as I was going to get."

"People actually sail the *Elissa*?" I say, surprised. I thought the *Elissa* was just a museum. I'd toured it back in high school, before it had been damaged by Hurricane Ike. It's been restored now. But once I'd seen it, I hadn't really felt a need to go back. And once I became an adult, I turned to more modern boats. After all, my late husband designed boats and other marine equipment for a living, so I learned a little bit about the technology involved from his point of view.

"Most of the times, it does stay in port," Kaylee admits. "But it is used for day sails in the spring, and sometimes for sail training. On the trip I took, I got to climb up into the rigging and furl sails. It was a full working experience."

"That sounds fascinating," I say, meaning it.

Kaylee says, "If I had the opportunity, I'd find a way to do it again – despite the lupus. I refuse to let it sideline me from life."

I imagine she would manage it, too. She seems a very determined person, and I can picture her with long sleeves and a giant hat, tied on to keep the wind from blowing it off. Protecting herself from the sun sensitivity.

I return my focus to my phone, zooming in on different parts of the picture, trying to find anything that looks valuable.

"Wait," Kaylee says. "Go back."

I move back towards the left side of the image, and Kaylee points to an unassuming iron bell, which appears to have been cut in half vertically to fit flat into the collage just below and to the right of the telegraph. It's about ten inches tall, and there's something inscribed on the side.

Kaylee points at it. "That's the piece that's valuable. Or at least it was, until somebody hacked it in half. If it's what I think it is."

I look closer. The inscription seems to say RIDE, but the writing is faded so it is hard to be sure. I say, "I don't understand."

Kaylee says, "A ship's bell is usually the only thing that can be used to identify it in the case of a shipwreck. Especially in the case of a wooden ship. Wood disintegrates after about fifty years, so the main things that are left are bells and cannons, or anything else made out of metal."

And here we are, back to the idea of treasure diving ROV thieves and pirate maps and a bird that randomly shouts, *pieces of eight*. "But what would make a bell worth that much? And if it was valuable, why didn't it wind up in a museum?"

"Did you know that Lafitte's flagship ran aground and sank somewhere in the Gulf? It was called the *Pride*." She pauses to let me figure out that it could potentially be what the partial inscription on the bell is referring to. "There's the historical value involved in that discovery, since Lafitte was not only a dangerous and notorious pirate, but also participated in significant events in the history of this country. But rumor has it that when Lafitte was run out of Galveston after causing trouble here, he burned his house and fort and loaded all his money onto the ship. Which then sank. Over the years since, people have gone broke looking for it."

I look at Kaylee, trying to decide if she's joking, or trying to see how gullible I am. But she looks serious. I say, "Then why didn't this find make the news? Amálie said she shopped ship breaking yards and marine salvage suppliers, and places like Craigslist. It just seems odd that something would move through the hands of all those professionals, and nobody would recognize it."

Kaylee considers this. Finally, she says, "Unless there was an individual treasure diver who found the bell and decided to keep it. Which would be perfectly legal. It would have to be someone who was really into history, and cared more about owning a piece of it than about fame or money. Then if something happened to that person, and someone who didn't know ships inherited the estate, the bell could well have wound up on Craigslist or whatever, without either the buyer of the seller realizing the value."

"But would that be worth killing for?" I ask. Though I have learned through experience that people have strange reasons for killing. It doesn't have to make logical sense.

"The bell itself would be worth a bit of money, even damaged, if it could be authenticated as belonging to a famous pirate ship. But the location of the ship – that would be worth significantly more. But if the diver who found it died or skipped town or whatever, I don't see how that location would be able to be uncovered. Therefore the import of the find becomes much less significant."

As she's talking, I'm piecing things together. When I'd done that search for the name Culliver, there had been a hit for a dive instructor headquartered out of Florida. The website was years out of date. I'd attributed that to lack of technological expertise – but it's possible that the owner had been dead for some time, and no one had taken down the site. It hadn't said anything about treasure diving – but potentially this Culliver could have done some diving in Texas.

How Renoir the cockatoo would have known about that is anybody's guess.

Chapter Thirteen

I forward the photos to Arlo, along with a brief description of what that bell just might be. I text because I don't want to call him, because I'm not ready to deal with his proposal – if that's really what it was.

I'm about to send the same message about the bell to Logan when Logan calls me, asking me to come back to the shop. Apparently, Drake is upset because the copy of *Treasure Island* has gone missing. Drake has to leave, because he has another appointment and he only discovered the book was gone because he was about to hand it to Logan on his way out the door. He's afraid someone stole it. I'm not sure exactly what Logan expects me to be able to do about that. I hang up the phone.

Kaylee gives me an odd look, and I realize I'm rubbing at my temples. I'm getting a headache from all the back-to-back problems.

When I get to Felicitations, the artists who had been working on the sculpture are all sitting glumly together at one table, staring at each other with suspicion. Gently is hugging his cat, but the cat does not seem to be enjoying it. Violet has a comforting hand on Gently's arm. Tracie is still half-heartedly working on her programming, while at the same time trying to get a look into the backpack at the base of Marissa's seat. Marissa is typing on her phone.

Jonah has a sketch pad open to a page where he's written the names of all the artists who were in the studio when the murders took place. My name's also on his list, along with Delores and Logan. Audrey's name has a huge *x* over it. I guess the news has broken that there's been another murder. In much smaller print, he's written other text under each name. I sidle closer to get a better look.

Under my name, he's written something that starts with, *Present at an alarming number of murders, easily flustered, probably has something to hide*. Before I can catch anything more, he realizes I'm standing there and covers the page.

Jonah says, "Is there something you want?"

I say, "I'm just curious how you're getting along with your investigation."

Jonah points at Tracie and says, "She's the one that suggested we all take a break after Audrey left this morning. Gently and I were the only ones who stayed here the whole time."

Gently says, "Violet had to go get my anti-anxiety medication. I made a mistake on my carving. I – wasn't doing well. Especially when I realized I'd forgotten to take my meds this morning. And Jonah said he'd stay right here with me, because he's good at keeping me from spiraling."

Tracie looks embarrassed. "I suggested the break because the school called. One of my girls got in a fight, and I had to go down there and sort it out. I was so upset that afterwards, I took a long walk along the beach."

Which means that neither Violet nor Tracie has a solid alibi for Audrey's murder. The only ones who are in the clear are Jonah and Gently, and they weren't strong suspects anyway.

Gently says, "I had a line of sight to the table. None of us went anywhere near that book. And I don't think anyone at this table is a murderer, either."

Tracie asks, "Does that mean you suspect Destiny? Or Syed?"

Gently says, "That's not what I was saying."

Violet says, "Syed does own several of Hernan's sculptures. They're bound to be worth significantly more now that Hernan is dead. That could have been a motive."

Tracie says, "Destiny was also taking part in the competition for the grant. And she had moved on to the final round. Unlike me – she had a real motive for getting Hernan out of the way."

Well, they're not hesitating to throw each other under the bus.

Gently says, "I don't like to think about people I know as capable of violence."

Jonah says, "Especially not your girlfriend."

"Hey!" Violet says.

"What does that mean?" I ask.

Jonah says, "I did a basic search on each of my suspects. I found out Violet assaulted Ryker Brody a couple of months before he was killed."

I suck in a startled breath. Not terribly long ago, Carmen and Violet had had another roommate. Another roommate who had gone to jail for hiring someone to murder her ex-husband, Ryker, who was trying to get custody of their child.

Violet says, "Ryker showed up drunk and tried to make Tasha go with him so they could talk. He wanted to get back together or something. She wasn't interested. I kicked him in the face to convince him to leave." Violet shrugs. "It's the only time I ever did anything like that. Mostly, kicks at the gym are just for getting sculpted abs"

That does show that she has a history of violence – but it's a long distance from kicking someone in sort-of self-defense to coldly murdering someone because they dumped you a year or two previously.

The door to the shop opens, and Ash walks in. He's holding his phone, still looking at it as he walks. He looks up and sees the artists sitting all grumpily together. He zeroes in on Marissa, saying, "I saw your comments on my article."

She shrugs. "I can't help it if you don't have the guts to tell things like they are anymore. Your blog, at least, used to be fun."

I look from one to the other. I say, "I take it you two know each other."

Marissa says, "I used to be friends with Imogen – before she became Ash's fiancé. Ash and I have never gotten along."

Ash says, "It's not my fault you left the LARP group."

I'd met members of Ash's Live Action Role Playing group not long ago, when they'd been part of the entertainment aboard the cruise ship I'd gone on. They were a group of folks with strong personalities.

Marissa says, "You couldn't be bothered with historical accuracy. And everyone took your side. What was I supposed to do?"

Ash says, "I did offer to do the doublet things."

"Too little too late," Marissa says.

I can sympathize with Marissa. Ash is a bit of an acquired taste. And I don't really need to know the details of what they're arguing about to get the gist.

Ash turns to Tracie and says, "I'm glad you made it back okay."

Tracie blushes. She says, "I'm sorry you had to see that. When I cry, I really ugly cry."

I give Ash a questioning look.

He says, "I was jogging on the beach earlier, and I ran into Tracie taking a walk. She needed to talk, so we talked."

Well, I guess that gives Tracie at least part of an alibi.

"Ash is such a nice guy," Tracie says, giving Marissa a significant withering look.

Marissa makes a face back. I get the idea that the two of them aren't particularly friends.

Gently says, "He really is. Ash said such nice things in that article about the animal shelter. He loves animals – especially cats."

"Unlike Amálie Timbers," Jonah says. "She hated cats. She was trying to get Mrs. Cook to ban Ruffles from the building. She claimed she was allergic, but she never showed any symptoms, so we assumed that it was just a matter of ego. She was the most famous of any of us, and she never let anyone forget that."

Marissa half laughs. "Are you saying Gently had a motive?"

"I wouldn't hurt someone just because they didn't like my cat," Gently protests.

Violet pats his arm again. "She's just joking sweetie. Take a few deep breaths."

Jonah says, "Gently was here all day. He couldn't be the murderer."

Tracie says, "You're assuming that whoever killed Audrey is the same person who killed the other two. We don't know that. Audrey was always a bit mysterious about how she spent her time away from the studio. She might have gotten herself into completely unrelated trouble."

I ask Tracie, "What about Hernan? Could he have upset anyone enough for them to want to kill him?"

Tracie says, "You mean aside from being insufferably arrogant."

Violet rolls her eyes in agreement. "It only gets worse the better you know him. You should talk to his wife. I bet she wanted out of the relationship, and she just snapped."

I can't tell if Violet is joking or not, but I need to add visiting Hernan's wife to my list, along with Destiny and Syed. I probably should have dropped by to talk to them already – but I've been so busy with my actual job.

"What happened to the book?" I ask. Drake and Autumn had left before I'd gotten back here, but Drake has texted twice, apologizing and asking if there's any updates about the missing volume.

Gently says, "I promise you, none of us could have taken it. We were all focused on the project."

Tracie says, "How are we supposed to focus? How do we know that whoever has decided to start killing off artists won't decide to pick off one of us next?"

They all look uncomfortably at each other. It seems that they each have their suspicions. And none of them seem to have noticed that Ash is taking notes. Jonah is too – but he's being more obvious about it.

How does this all fit together? Is this about the artists and the Rube Goldberg grant thing? Or about the sculpture and the ship's bell? Nothing I've done so far has narrowed anything down.

Logan walks over and puts a hand on my arm. He asks, "Can I borrow you for a minute?"

"Sure," I say. I have a feeling I'm not going to get much more useful information from this group anyway. I assume Logan has run into some sort of snag with the sculpture.

Instead, he leads me into the bean room, and there's Stewart Jr., leaned back against a bag of cacao nibs, sound asleep with the vintage copy of *Treasure Island* open across his chest.

Logan says, "*Treasure Island* is a children's book, and you told him yesterday that he could read any of the books off the bookshelf. What did we expect?"

"Where's Tam Binh?" I ask.

"She and Carmen went to go get some more supplies for their projects. I thought Stewart Jr. went with them. When I called her a minute ago, Tam Binh said she thought he was working on the sculpture with us."

I say, "At least he didn't wander off. And there's not a thief in our midst after all."

Logan says, "That's the least of our worries, but yeah. No thief is always a good thing."

I ask Logan, "Am I easily flustered?"

"Not particularly," Logan says. "Why do you ask?"

"That's what Jonah wrote about me on his murder board. I didn't get to see much else, but I bet you could get him to share what he knows. He likes looking clever."

Logan says, "That's good to know. We need more clues on this case. Nothing is fitting together yet."

I say, "Kaylee and I figured out something important about the sculpture." I take out my phone to pull up the image to show Logan the ship's bell. Only – none of the images in the sculpture are in my camera roll. I go to where I texted the image to Arlo, but the copy of the image has disappeared from my end of the thread.

I have a little freak-out inside myself, then I show Logan what isn't there. I need him to take my word for it, and he does.

He asks, "Where's your tablet?"

"I think I left it in my catering truck," I say.

"Then don't be so sure there's not a thief in the vicinity after all."

I gasp. He's suggesting that someone used my tablet to access my photo archive on the Cloud. I forwarded the images to Arlo – and apparently the killer knows that.

But is Arlo being a cop enough to make the killer back off? Or is Arlo in danger too?

Chapter Fourteen

I call Arlo, but he isn't picking up. Which is a bit worrisome. I really don't want something I've done to put him in danger. I call the police station, but they say he went out.

Logan says, "Give me ten minutes, and I should be able to find out the location of his car."

I go over to the table where the artists are still gathered. I explain that the whole thing with the missing book was just a big misunderstanding. I ask, "Do you think you can put all this suspicion aside and continue to work together? Please?"

They look around the table at each other.

Tracie says, "I need to get home soon anyway. The girls will be done with school in a bit, and I need to figure out how to punish a thirteen-year-old who actually enjoys doing homework. But I can be back early tomorrow."

"Same," Marissa says. "I have to get the boat in order for a fishing charter going out in the morning. But I can come in the evening tomorrow, if you're still working. Or during the day the day after."

Violet says, "Gently and I can stay for pretty much the rest of the day today. I have some ideas for how we can take away a significant amount of weight from the sails of the ship by suspending hollow plastic boards in the chocolate as it sets. I want to do some experiments here before we try to do it full scale at the studio."

They all look at Jonah, who looks down at the floor and says, "I have a couple of leads to follow up on. But I'll be back in the morning too."

That settled, I go in to where I had left my bonbons to finish setting. I crack them out of the molds – flipping the mold over in one smooth motion and banging it against the counter. That is one of the most satisfying sounds in all of chocolate making, but I can't enjoy it, because I'm too worried about Arlo. There's nothing I can do until we have some idea where he is, but that doesn't make boxing up chocolates feel any less frivolous. The museum had asked for a selection of tropical flavors, and I'd splatter painted each mold with colored cocoa butter at the beginning of the process, so that the outside of each bonbon is a different vibrant color. The lime ones are green, the pineapple ones are yellow, the mango ones are orange, and so on. It's a simple technique, which can be accomplished with the flick of a paintbrush into each mold cavity before the chocolate that forms the outer shell is poured in. It's also one of the quickest ways I can think of to mark so many bonbons in such a short time.

The back door to the kitchen opens, and I can see into the kitchen through the open doorway of the chocolate processing room. Tam Binh has a panicked look on her face as she rushes in. She sees me working, then looks out into the main part of the shop – which I can't see from where I am, but probably offers her a view of Ash taking video of the two artists working on chocolate sculpture technique. I can see the tension going out of her, and she's moving more slowly as she crosses the kitchen and comes through the doorway into the chocolate processing area. She says, "I take it everything is okay now?"

"Not everything," I say, "But Stewart Jr. is still conked out in the bean room. We didn't have the heart to wake him up."

Tam Binh says, "I am so sorry. I'm so embarrassed. I've never left one of my kids behind before – and we've been on some chaotic trips."

I say, "It makes sense that you thought he was with us. And he obviously wasn't any trouble."

Carmen snorts a laugh. "Aside for having the shop turned upside down looking for the book he was reading."

"But *he* wasn't the problem," I insist.

Tam Binh goes into the bean room, presumably to verify that her son is, in fact, not causing any trouble. Then she washes her hands and starts helping me box up the bonbons. She says, "Would you believe that Rosa Núñez works at the bakery supply store Carmen likes to go to? She didn't even take the day off out of sympathy for the dead."

It takes me a second to remember that Rosa was Hernan's wife. I say, "People cope with grief in different ways."

Tam Binh scrunches up her nose, looking skeptical. "You think a person can grieve while wearing bright pink and making sample cupcakes with luster dust and sprinkles? And humming *Baby Shark* the whole time?"

"Anything's possible," I say, though even I can tell I don't sound convinced. I've been so focused in on the artists, I don't even know where Rosa was yesterday, or who told her about Hernan's death.

We get about a hundred boxes filled and sealed by the time Logan has information on Arlo's location. He says, "Arlo's car is parked outside of a cake supply store."

Tam Binh and I exchange skeptical, worried glances.

I tell Logan, "He was following up a lead on the case. We need to get over there."

Tam Binh offers to make sure everything is put away, and to hang up my apron. I realize with a start I've taken the apron off, and I'm just holding it limply in my hand.

I accept the offer, grab my purse and head for the door, with Logan right behind me. We move quickly down the alley behind the shop to the lot where Logan parks. We get into Logan's Mustang.

He says, "I'm sure Arlo's fine. He's resourceful."

I nod. "I'm sure he is."

But neither one of us says anything else on the short drive. If I'm this worried – does that mean that I still care about Arlo, more that I've been wanting to admit?

I still can't figure out why I didn't immediately reject Arlo's attempts to renew our relationship, how I let myself get drawn into this complicated love triangle in the first place. But now, I can't imagine life without Arlo in it.

We pull into the parking lot for the cake supply shop, which is a stand-alone building closer to the middle of the island. It is surrounded by oleander and palm trees, with a fence in the back separating it from a small apartment complex. Arlo's car is one of the only ones in the lot. We park next to it, and take a look through the front windows into the store. Nothing seems amiss in there. There's a flash of motion in the bushes at the edge of the lot, as a figure starts moving at the edge of the foliage, running towards the fence.

"Hey!" Logan shouts, rushing forward.

The figure is wearing an oversized sweatshirt. It is possibly the same person who snatched my purse.

"He's probably armed," I shout, warning Logan, who hesitates and scrambles back behind his car. The figure seems more interested in making it to the fence than whatever Logan might be doing. The person doesn't even look back.

I move out to where Logan is crouching. He's got a gun in his hands, but it's pointed at the ground, since he wouldn't shoot at someone who's running away.

"You said he," Logan says. "But that person runs like a girl."

"Kaylee thought it was a guy, when she gave chase after my purse got snatched." I gesture towards the fence, where whoever it is has disappeared onto the other side. "But she was flooded with adrenaline and is hardly an investigator."

Logan holsters the gun and moves towards the spot in the bushes where the figure had been. I follow. As we get closer, I spot a pair of shiny shoes and the bottom part of suit pants peeking out from the foliage. Something queasy balls up in my stomach, like an oily lump of cookie dough. Arlo wears shiny shoes like that.

I don't even realize I'm moving, but somehow I find myself down on my knees, pulling at the shoes to get the guy attached to them out where we can see him. It *is* Arlo. And that queasy feeling jumps up into my throat. There's an odd feeling of déjà vu – I had felt just like this when I'd first been notified about Kevin's accident.

Arlo kept making those tasteless jokes about me finding dead bodies. I won't be able to take it, if right now I am finding his.

But then Arlo groans, and I jump, startled and relieved and falling to bits.

"You're okay," I blurt.

Arlo opens his eyes. "Mostly. I just feel stupid."

His head is bleeding, but he doesn't appear to be injured anywhere else. He brings his hand to the injured spot. I reach out and grasp his forearm, to stop him from touching it. "We need to get you checked out."

Logan asks, "What happened?" He's standing a few paces behind me, his hands in his pockets.

Arlo says, "I fell for one of the stupidest setups in the book. It sounded like there was a kitten stuck up in one of the palm trees. I was about to call you back, since I didn't want to answer the phone in the middle of a suspect interview. But I heard this supposed cat, and I came over to take a look, and I got hit from behind, and the phone yanked out of my hand. And then you showed up."

He's still bleeding, but the wound looks superficial. Logan grabs a small towel out of his car, and I get Arlo to hold pressure on it, to try and stop the bleeding. Scalp wounds tend to bleed a lot, so the blood is no indication he's in trouble.

Logan says, "Whoever hit Jonah hasn't changed their M.O."

"Was there an interval where you were unconscious??" I ask Arlo.

If he lost consciousness, the head injury could be more serious.

"I don't think so," Arlo says. "I closed my eyes because the sun hurt, but I'm sure I was lying there for only a minute or so after the person who hit me ran away."

"You said you were going to call me back," I say, as I help him sit up. "Did you get a chance to look at the text message I sent earlier?"

Arlo looks at me like it's an odd question and says, "The thing about the sculpture? Yeah, I got that."

"You didn't happen to send the photos on to someone, or save them somewhere?"

Arlo shakes his head, then tries to bring his hand up to the injury again. I stop him, suddenly realizing how close I am to him, how warm and alive he is. How kissable.

Which is a completely inappropriate thought given the situation. And the fact that Logan is standing right there – looking equally kissable, come to think of it. I clear my throat and release Arlo's arm.

Arlo says, "You think I just got assaulted to make a photo of an old ship's bell disappear?"

"Probably," I say. "But it seems like a big risk, since the person who attacked you couldn't know for sure that you hadn't saved the photos somewhere other than the Cloud."

Logan says, "A risk a desperate person would feel is worth taking."

"But why?" I ask. "What connects the ship sculpture to the murders?"

Logan says, "Not necessarily anything. We could be talking about two separate crimes."

Arlo says, "But that seems like a bit too much coincidence."

Logan says, "I still think it is possible that someone killed Amálie because of the grant competition, or for reasons of personal dislike, and that someone else killed Audrey during the theft. It is possible for two crimes to take place at the same time and be unrelated. And poor Hernan just got caught in the middle."

Arlo makes a dissatisfied noise and turns back towards the cake shop. "I still say that the most direct reasoning is always the most likely. Hernan was the one who got shot, and Amálie was the one who wasn't supposed to be there. So this has to all be over something Hernan was involved in. I think I need to talk to Hernan's widow again."

"No," Logan says. "What you need is to see a doctor. I already called an ambulance."

Arlo says, "Is there any way we can skip all that? It's already going to be beyond embarrassing, for a cop to have to fill out a police report about getting phone-jacked by a girl. I'm never going to live it down at the station."

Logan says, "Fine. Cancel the ambulance. I'll drive you to the hospital and keep things more low-key. But we're taking your car. I'm not about to have you bleed all over the Mustang."

So according to Arlo, the phone thief really was a girl. But it couldn't have been Rosa–since she's still inside her store. I say, "You two go. I think I'm going to pop into the cake supply shop. Seeing as we're here already."

Logan arches an eyebrow at me. "You think you can get more information?"

I nod. "I'll start by asking for some supplies for the sculpture."

Logan asks, "We're spending more money on this?"

Arlo asks, "What if the killer is still in the vicinity?"

Logan gestures at the fence. "I highly doubt that. Especially if she has your phone, and it's mission accomplished."

Arlo says, "Killers always make a mistake. It's just a matter of catching it."

Logan says, "You watch a lot of cop shows on TV, don't you?"

He helps Arlo up and gets him into Arlo's car. Then he tosses me the keys to his Mustang. Logan has never offered to let me drive it before. It makes me feel special, and I'm sure I'm grinning like an idiot.

I wave as I watch the two men drive away, then I pocket the keys and head into the store.

Rosa is standing near a display of cupcakes, which each show a different frosting technique. I'm guessing the cake underneath is actually floral foam. Rosa is wearing a neon pink tunic top that emphasizes her baby bump. She is talking to a co-worker. They are both laughing.

I can see what Tam Binh was saying. Rosa doesn't look like someone who just lost a loved one.

I walk over to Rosa and say, "I'm Felicity Koerber, from over at Greetings and Felicitations."

"I know who you are," Rosa says. "Carmen comes in here all the time. She says you're a good boss and a good friend."

I can't help but smile. It's nice that Carmen thinks of me as a friend. We've been through a lot together, more than an employer-employee should ever have to.

I say, "I know she was just here. But I wanted to swing by and get that isomalt after all."

Rosa looks at me, wide eyed. "But I thought the sugar artist who wanted to work with it was killed."

"I'm going to give it a go myself," I say. I'm improvising, but as I say it, I realize it's something I might really want to do. It's a technique the sculpture really needs.

"Let me get it for you," the other staff member says. She grabs a dolly and heads to the back of the store.

I tell Rosa, "I just wanted to say I'm sorry for your loss."

Rosa's smile fades. "Thank you. It was unexpected."

"How are you holding up?" I ask.

Rosa looks at me levelly. "You don't think I look sad enough, no? Maybe that's true. Hernan was a difficult man to love. He always had to be in the right. And when he got an idea it turned into an obsession."

"But you did love him," I say. It's more of a question. I can't imagine a relationship more different from the marriage I had had, the loss of which had devastated me. How is this really affecting her? Assuming that the phone thief is someone separate, is it possible that I'm looking at Hernan's killer?

Rosa says, "I do love him, despite how he could be. I don't think it's really registered yet that he's gone. And it will be hard, raising a child and not being able to share the big events with her father. But at the same time – I feel relieved that my life has gotten less complicated. I guess that makes me a horrible person."

I put a hand on her arm. "Don't judge yourself for how you feel. Grief has stages, and a lot of them aren't logical. And when the relationship was complicated—it may be even less straightforward to deal with the loss."

Sudden tears are glittering in her eyes. "I know you've been through this. Coming from you, that means a lot."

I ask, "You said Hernan went through a series of obsessions. Did any of them have to do with local history?"

Rosa looks surprised. "How did you know that?"

I shrug and say, "Just a hunch."

Rosa picks up a jar of edible glitter, holding it up to the light. "He kept saying that he'd stumbled across something that could revolutionize the understanding of a chapter in Galveston's history. When I asked him to explain what he meant, he said he didn't want to say anything until he had more details. But I found several books in his study relating to shipwrecks in the Gulf, and a whole stack about Galveston history. I'm guessing it had to do with the Civil War, or World War II. Then one day, those books were gone. But Hernan was like that. He didn't find whatever he was looking for, so he moved on to something else. A few weeks later, he had a whole stack of books dealing with model trains."

"I'm not sure he really moved on," I say. "Is it possible he took those books to work?"

"I guess," Rosa says. "He had a locker there."

The police already opened the lockers at the museum. I wasn't allowed to be there, but I'm sure that Arlo would have mentioned if there were a stack of books relating directly to the pictures I'd sent him. But apparently Hernan had worked in the library at the art museum. Maybe he'd stashed the books there. Or they'd been taken – potentially by whoever killed him.

I ask, "What were you doing yesterday?"

Rosa doesn't hesitate when she says, "You mean at the same time when Hernan was killed? Like I told the police, I was at the knitting circle at Sonya Popescue's yarn shop. I go every Wednesday."

Since Sonya is one of my closest friends, it shouldn't be difficult to verify when Rosa arrived and when she left. And if Sonya doesn't remember, I can always ask Miles, who usually goes to the circle with his mom. It isn't likely that Rosa is the murderer, if she's offering that solid of an alibi. But she might know more than she realizes.

"Was there anybody else – maybe someone he worked with, or a friend – who might have been interested in shipwrecks or treasure diving too?"

"Treasure diving?" Rosa says, incredulous. "Hernan never learned how to swim, let alone dive."

Which certainly puts a different perspective on things, if Hernan cared about the ship's bell – and even that is still a supposition – but didn't want to get into the water. Maybe he wasn't looking for the wreck's location after all, but something else entirely.

Rosa says, "When they first started working together at the museum, Tracie kept trying to get him to join the dive club she's a part of. He complained about how persistent she was, and I always thought he got upset because she was being just as stubborn as he was. But then they both went up for the same grant, and she stopped trying to be friends with him."

"And those two girls came into her life, so Tracie probably didn't have as much time to participate in the dive club herself, anyway."

Rosa nods. "I'm sure that's true."

"Who else belongs to that dive club?"

Rosa says, "No idea. I never went. But Hernan's ex-girlfriend was an avid diver. She would just go if someone invited her, even if they had something else planned. It's one of the things they fought about, and part of the reason they broke up."

I thought Hernan had dumped Violet because he had met Rosa, but I keep that thought to myself. It wouldn't make anyone look good to say that out loud, and I'm not looking to speak ill of the dead. Neither Violet nor Tracie have an airtight alibi for the time of Audrey's death, and they were both present in the room where Hernan and Amálie had died in the dark. I still can't see either one being a murderer, but someone has to have done it.

Rosa says, "I think Syed Patel does some sort of watersports. He was one of Hernan's good friends, and Hernan went to watch him once in some kind of competition."

The only competitions I've heard about on Galveston are for surfing, but that doesn't mean that someone who surfs doesn't dive too. And if Syed was Hernan's friend – I really need to go talk to him and see how he fits into all of this.

"One more question," I tell Rosa. "Did Hernan ever mention the name Culliver?"

Rosa squints at me. "I don't think so. Is that someone who works at the museum?"

Well, that feels like a dead end.

Chapter Fifteen

I look it up. Syed lives in a 3-story beach house right on the water. It's on the North end of Galveston Island – where the real estate prices come at a premium.

I text Logan, asking if he cares if I drive the Mustang over there.

He replies, *Pick me up at the hospital first, if you don't mind. I'd love to see the inside of that house.*

He also has a protective streak, having been both a cop and a bodyguard in former iterations of his career. My guess is that he really just doesn't want me to go alone to a murder suspect's home. Especially a suspect that neither of us have met.

It's Logan's car, so I shouldn't leave him stranded at the hospital if he's ready to leave anyway.

I text again, asking *How's Arlo?*

Logan texts back, *He seems fine, but they want to keep him in for observation. Our thief really clocked him one.*

Arlo has never been a good patient. I'd been responsible for him hurting himself when he was a teenager – long story involved me driving a car without a license – and I'd gone with him to his physical therapy, to try and make up for it. He hadn't liked sitting still, even back then. And now, getting sidelined like that in the middle of a case has got to be absolutely killing him.

When I get to the hospital, Logan is waiting outside.

I ask him, "Is another detective going to take over the case?"

Logan says, "Arlo can maintain his status as lead on the case if he gets out of the hospital soon. But I'm sure there's someone still working on it without him."

I say, "The observation period is going to be at least four hours at the hospital. They might let him go home after that, if someone agrees to observe him there. It costs him or his insurance a lot less if he goes home."

"That makes sense." Logan puts the address for Syed's house into his GPS.

He doesn't say anything about switching drivers, so I drive us over to the beach.

There's not a ton of homes in that Northernmost corner of the island. Some of the houses over here are impressive, multi-million-dollar beach house showpieces. Syed's place looks like one of those. It's painted crisp white, with arched architecture and teal trim. The bottom floor has a three-car garage facing the street, but looks deep enough to have a first-floor room or two, too.

I tell Logan, "If Syed can afford to live here, he doesn't really need to find pirate treasure. Or win a grant."

"True," Logan says, "but logic doesn't always reign when treasure is involved. People can get caught up in the romantic notions of it all."

"You act like you've seen it happen," I say

Logan crosses his arms over his chest. He says, "Europe has a lot of history."

I know he'd spent several years in Europe, before coming back to take the bodyguard gig. He's never really wanted to talk about that time. And that enigmatic statement leaves me with even more questions. But I don't push him for details.

Instead, we get out of the car and go up the staircase to the main front door of the house. Logan rings the doorbell.

At first, it doesn't seem like anyone is home. I've given up and turned back to the stairs when a guy in his late twenties opens the door. He has light brown skin, thick black eyebrows and even thicker black-rimmed glasses. Behind the glasses, his eyes are red-rimmed, like he may have been crying recently. He's wearing a teal tee-shirt and teal-and-black patterned board shorts, which almost look calculated to match the house.

Logan says, "We're looking for Syed Patel."

"That's me," Syed says. He gestures for us to come inside the house. "You two were there at the studio yesterday. I was in the middle of a delicate stage of my sculpture when you came in, or I would have come over and introduced myself. But if you don't breathe life into a piece when it is ready, it dies in your arms."

"Like what literally happened to two people yesterday," Logan says.

Syed nods, missing Logan's implied criticism. "Exactly. So tragic."

I say, "Hernan's wife says you were one of his close friends."

"I was," Syed says. "He was one of the few people who liked me for me, and not my parents or my money. It's hard when you're trying to make a name on your own, and not get drawn into the family practice."

I say, "I get the idea that Hernan was big on integrity."

"That's true," Syed says. "Except when it came to women. He was dating a girl when he met Rosa, and he didn't tell either one of them about the other for months. It was the one time I saw him compromise. He asked me to cover for him once when he wanted to cancel on one girl to go to an event with the other, and I said no."

"That must have been hard to do," I say.

Syed sighs. "It's always hard to see a friend going down the wrong path. But then he proposed to Rosa, so it seemed like he'd sorted out what he wanted out of life. I was happy for him. And now this-" He gestures with his hands, flipping his palms up then letting them collapse to his sides. "It's such a waste."

Logan asks, "Were you competing with Hernan and the others for the grant?"

Syed snorts a laugh and gestures around him at the open, airy living room with its ratan furniture and oak flooring. It's lush with green plants, neutral fabrics, natural materials. Aspects of it remind me a little of Logan's apartment, which is on the other side of the island. Syed says, "Does it look like I need a grant?"

"There's need – and there's wanting to build credits on your resume," Logan says.

Syed says, "I wouldn't take a grant away from someone who needs it."

I ask Syed, "Do you still do surfing competitions?"

Syed says, "I do. I've never won one, but they're a ton of fun. You should come out to one of the local ones. Even if you don't compete, you can catch some rays and listen to local music." He sounds genuinely excited, but his eyes still look sad.

I make a noncommittal noise. I mean, it could be fun. But first, I need to figure out what happened at the museum. I ask, "What about other water sports? Do you sail or ski? Or maybe dive?"

I'm trying to make what I'm really asking less obvious, but it feels awkward coming out of my mouth, and I'm sure Syed is going to notice.

He doesn't seem to, though. He says, "All of the above. I don't water ski so much anymore – I prefer to snow ski in the winter. But I dive a lot." Syed's eyes widen, as though he's remembering something. "You know what? Hernan started asking me questions about diving, over the past couple of months. I thought it was odd, because he never learned how to swim. But he wanted to know about dive tables and nautical charts. I told him about a couple of apps, like the one from NOAA. I assumed he was just being supportive, since he knows I don't have a lot of friends I can talk about that kind of stuff with." Syed hesitates. "You don't think that had something to do with what happened to Audrey? I heard she had a diving accident and died."

"That's not exactly what happened," I say.

At the same time, Logan asks, "Who told you that?"

Syed shrugs. "I read it somewhere. Maybe Twitter? I could have gotten it wrong. Mainly, I just read the headlines. Otherwise, the news gets too depressing."

I ask, "What about when you were there? Did you see anything unusual before Hernan got shot? Or maybe someone acting odd afterwards?"

Syed pauses to really think about this. He says, "I saw Gently have a little melt-down because Amálie threatened to shave his cat. She's always complaining about the cat hair."

I've already decided that Gently probably wouldn't kill someone for not liking cats. And he has an alibi for one of the murders.

"Anything else?" I prompt.

Syed says, "Destiny had a fight with Hernan over something. I wasn't close enough to hear the details. But they're both usually easy-going, so whatever they were fighting over, it was odd."

Logan asks, "Did you spend a lot of time at the studio?"

"Recently, yes," Syed says. "I'm working on an exhibition – but don't tell Delores. She'll flip, because it's at a museum across town."

"You call her Delores?" Logan asks. "I thought she wanted the artists to call her Mrs. Cook."

Syed gestures around again. "Delores is easily impressed by money. I never asked for special treatment. She just offered it."

So technically, Delores could have committed the first murders. I guess I need to verify that she really is hours away with her family – which would mean that she couldn't have killed Audrey.

Logan asks Syed, "Do you happen to own a boat?"

Syed nods. "A beautiful catamaran. It's right here at the yacht marina. So much more convenient to have a boat on this side of the island."

"Right," Logan says. He gives me a significant look. Having a boat is the most direct connection we have between any of the artists and what happened to Audrey.

Syed says, "I meant to go sailing this morning, in fact, but at the last minute, I got a spot in an online technique class. Violet was supposed to go, but she decided to come help you all instead."

"Then Violet knew your boat was there, ready to go," Logan says.

"I guess," Syed says. "I don't see why that matters, though."

Logan shrugs. "Just trying to piece things together."

Syed says, "If you're going to see Rosa, I have a bunch of stuff that Hernan left over here. I can box it up real quick, if you want to bring it to her."

"We can help you," Logan says.

"Thanks," Syed says. He stops in at a small room that is obviously an office and slides a package of unassembled banker's boxes out from behind the desk. "This house is so big, I like to entertain as often as I can. My friends know there's an open door for them to stay if they want to spend the weekend by the beach. Hernan liked to come here sometimes and work where the big windows face the ocean."

We go down the hall to a glassed-in sunroom. There's a half-finished wood sculpture in here that has swoops and arcs that remind me of the ocean waves. I can't decide if the sculpture itself is evoking feelings of sadness in me – or if I am just sad because it will never be finished.

Logan goes over to the window and I follow. Looking down, there's a stretch of narrow road and muddy soil before you get to the beach, but the water is right there, and it is clear to see Hernan's inspiration. My parents used to own a house with a view like this – before they moved closer to Houston, after a hurricane damaged it.

There's a table with some chisels and hand tools. Syed assembles one of the bankers' boxes and starts putting the tools into it. He gestures at a stack of books on a shelf in the corner. He says, "All that belongs to Hernan too."

Logan and I bring another box and move over to the books. I start flipping through each one as I put it in the box, trying to get more of a feel for who Hernan was. These are books of artists he was probably inspired by. Some of it is paintings by Augustus Renoir and Alfredo Ramos Martinez. And some drawings by M.C. Escher. But a number of them art books about sculptors, most of whom I know nothing about. And there are a few technique craft books.

I start to open a detailed art anatomy book, with color-coded musculature on the cover, when a thick sheaf of folded paper slides out from between the cover and the dust jacket. I put the book down and unfold the paper.

It's photocopies of pages from a journal, with dated entries written in neat cursive. Each one is signed at the end with ~*Terry Culliver*.

I puzzle over that. What kind of guy feels the need to sign each entry in his own journal? It's so oddly formal.

"What do you have there?" Syed asks.

I show him the pages. "I think this is part of Culliver's diary."

Logan asks, "Who's diary?"

I explain about what Renoir the cockatoo had said, about finding Culliver's diary, and that Terry Culliver was a dive instructor who may have been a treasure diver. I start reading through the pages. It soon becomes clear. I say, "Make that Terry *is for sure* a treasure diver, and he was looking for historic wrecks in the Gulf. These diary entries are dated last year."

"Did he find anything?" Syed asks, peering curiously at the papers.

I flip through to the last couple of entries, trying not to look excited and shocked as I read through the details. The edge of the last page is ripped, but I'll deal with that when I come to it. I say, "He did. And he salvaged the bell, and an old sextant. Only, there was some kind of seismic activity between the date the wreck went down and when he found it. According to him, there's rock debris in on top of the rest of it. Culliver says here that he saw what he believed to be iron chests through a gap in the debris, and he has a list of pieces of equipment he felt he needed for the return trip, to excavate the rest of the wreck."

"But that trip obviously never happened," Logan says. "So what kept Mr. Culliver from finishing what he started?"

Syed takes out his phone. "What dates are we talking about?" I give him details, and he does a few searches, then he says, "Culliver got in a car wreck a few months after he got back to Florida. This article claims he was T-boned by a drunk driver."

The tragedy of that hits me in a way that reminds me of Hernan's unfinished sculpture. So many plans cut short by incident and accident.

"I wouldn't have waited that long to go back," Logan says. "But if the location of the wreck was extremely remote, maybe Culliver believed that it was unlikely that anyone would stumble on the location before he could get back to it."

I flip to the last page. Part of the text here is in French. This has to be the rest of the page from the ripped strip of paper the purse snatcher dropped. I take that paper out of my purse, where I had tucked it.

Logan raises an eyebrow. "You didn't feel the need to give that to the police?"

I match up the text, saying, "I will when I'm done with it. But look, this is talking about the location of the wreck. It sounds like he found it based on some information in some French documents relating to the failure of the plan for Lafitte to save Napoleon. Tell me I'm not the only one who had no idea that was a thing."

Both Logan and Syed give me puzzled looks.

Syed asks, "Jean Lafitte was alive at the same time as Napoleon?"

"Apparently?" I say. "I never really thought about the way Texas history overlaps history elsewhere."

Logan takes both pieces of the paper from me. "I think this needs to be examined more thoroughly using proper channels."

But I get the feeling that he just doesn't want me to say the location of the wreck in front of Syed. Which I guess makes sense. Syed does have a boat and a dive certification, after all. There's no way we can rule him out one-hundred percent as the killer – you can probably fake attendance at an online class if you are tech savvy enough. It is possible that he killed Hernan over these papers – not realizing Hernan had hidden them inside Syed's own house.

That feels unlikely, though.

"So obviously, the person who snatched my purse must have been fighting Hernan for this paper at some point, and it ripped," I say.

"That's a possibility," Logan says. "But don't limit yourself to that idea. Someone else could have had these papers, and Hernan later stole them, or found them. We don't know for sure."

"But it explains the theft of the equipment from the rig this morning, right?" I say. "It's the kind of thing someone could use to move debris in deep water. It's all connected together after all."

"Maybe," Logan says. "It's still possible Amálie was the intended victim. It's so poetic to make her another step in the Rube Goldberg machine, and so many people had a motive. Hernan and all this treasure stuff could be something separate."

Syed is staring at us, eyes wide. "You think my friend got killed by mistake?"

"It's possible. Not exactly a mistake, but as part of a bigger plan," I say. But then I realize what he's said. "I take it that you and Amálie weren't friends?"

Syed makes a so-so gesture with his hand. "Amálie kept to herself. She was . . . particular about how other people talked to her. She could get poetic sometimes, and I liked that. I'm a poet myself. But she had no sense of humor. Hernan and I made the mistake of pranking her with silly string, as a welcome to the studio. I don't think we were ever going to be friends after that."

We go to leave, and it looks like Syed is going to follow us out, like he wants to come with us. It feels like everybody I talk to these days is catching the detecting bug. I'm about to find a tactful way to make it clear that we don't need any help, when Syed says, "Want to see my boat? She's a beautiful craft."

"Sure," Logan says. "I've always got time for a beautiful boat. Just for a minute, though."

We follow Syed for the short drive from his house to the yacht marina. Then Syed leads us out to the docks. As we get closer to the boat slip he pointed out, he slows down. Finally he stops and says, "What the heck?"

"What's wrong?" Logan asks.

Syed points over at the deck of the boat. "That tarp. And whatever's under it. It wasn't there when Violet called me this morning."

"Stay there," Logan says to both me and Syed.

He jumps up onto the boat and unsecures the bungees holding down the tarp. He pulls the tarp back – and there on the deck is a big yellow industrial-looking piece of equipment with mechanical arms on the front. My guess would be that this is the missing ROV.

The side of the boat is damaged where the obviously heavy piece of equipment was awkwardly moved aboard. If Audrey had been on this boat with the thief – which seems probable – she probably helped get this piece of equipment on board before she wound up going into the water.

Chapter Sixteen

Once we leave the marina and get back into the Mustang, I call Delores.

She answers almost immediately. "Felicity. Please tell me nothing else has gone wrong."

I don't know how much she knows, so I'm not sure what to say. I start with, "There was another murder."

Delores gasps. "At the museum?"

"No," I say. "But it was one of the artists who works from the studio. Audrey."

"Oh, that silly girl," Delores says. "I told her she needed to work on her attitude. She probably upset someone very much. Or she asked too many blunt questions in the wrong places."

I clear my throat. That is more likely to be something that would happen to me than to have happened to Audrey. I say, "We're still trying to figure out what happened. But I do have some good news. I just got off the phone with the police." Actually, Arlo had called me from the hospital. He's still working on the case from there. "They're releasing the crime scene. That means that tomorrow morning, we can get back into the studio to start assembling the sculpture. Now that we've got some extra hands working on it, it's coming along well."

"Interesting," Delores says noncommittally.

Well, at least if she does pull the plug on the event once the sculpture is coming together, I'll have a much better chance in court if I have to fight her for the fee she is supposed to pay me.

I ask, "When will you be coming back? Or are you back already?"

"It will be a couple of days," Delores says. "I – that is, Mom and I decided to take advantage of the museum being closed. We flew to Mexico early this morning."

"Mexico?" I say, startled. "That's – far." And puts her far out of the frame for Audrey's murder. Just to make sure I say, "Text me a selfie. I'd love to see where you are."

As soon as we hang up the call, my phone dings with a text and a batch of nineteen photos. And yes, according to the picture data, Delores is exactly where she said she is: Monterrey, Mexico. Factor in airport time, and she couldn't possibly have been on a boat in the Gulf this morning.

I tell Logan, "At least we're narrowing down through the people who didn't do it."

Logan snorts a laugh. "That's one way of looking at it."

I tell him, "I have one more thing to check. So far, we're taking Marissa's word that she was doing maintenance all day. I want to get her boss to verify that."

I call the charter company listed on the business card, and the guy who answers says, "My office is at the end of the dock, and I have a window looking out towards the boats. Marissa got here early this morning – and I'd have seen her walk past me if she left."

We discuss the time when he actually did see her leave, and the general timing lines up. She probably went directly to the dive shop right after she got done with work. So she couldn't have killed Audrey – even if she did have a discernable motive. Which she doesn't.

Logan gestures at the envelope in the seat behind us, which Syed had helpfully given us to hold the photocopied pages from Culliver's diary and the page with the supposed location of the wreck. He asks, "So where is the location of the wreck, anyway?"

I say, "You have to keep in mind that my French is rusty. I took it in high school, and a few semesters in college – and then haven't used it since. But as far as I can tell, it says the wreck is North of the flower garden, and the map is a reference point from that. But I don't know which flower garden he could be talking about. I mean, there's Moody Gardens, but that's not where you'd launch a boat from, is it?"

Logan says, "Culliver wasn't talking about a literal garden on the island. He was talking about Flower Garden Banks. It's the only national marine sanctuary in the Gulf of Mexico. There are a bunch of underwater salt domes out there, which forms a huge reef system."

I say, "I always think more about reefs being in places like Hawaii or the Caribbean. I never thought about there being reefs in the Gulf, but I guess there have to be. We have so many different kinds of fish, and sharks, and all those dolphins."

Logan says, "It's a fascinating place to dive." He cuts a glance over at me. "Assuming you'd even want to dive again, after everything that happened today."

"I'd be willing to give it another go," I say. "It was fun right up until everything went wrong."

Logan's face shifts through relief, to a slightly goofy grin. He really is happy about the diving thing. He leans towards me and wraps me in a tight hug. He says, "The Flower Gardens aren't beginner dives. But with a bit of practice, we can get you the skills you need to see them. They're one of the most spectacular places you'll ever visit."

He lets go, and a feel a vague disappointment at the loss of contact. It had felt really nice being in his arms.

"So how far is this reef system from the shore?" I ask. After all, I am confused. "Everything we've learned says Lafitte's flagship ran aground. But you're making it sound like it's out in the middle of the Gulf."

"See that's the problem with all of this," Logan says. "The marine sanctuary is over a hundred miles out to sea. And it's not small. The whole thing encompasses about 150 square miles, and Culliver claimed he found the wreck far enough out from the coast that nobody just stumbled across it. So the idea of Lafitte's ship running aground – which most people seem to take as fact –

has to be wrong. Maybe it's just something somebody said to keep people from looking in the right place. I'm hoping your page has more details on it than just North of the Flower Garden, because it's hard enough to find anything in the water when you have a precise location. You wind up making a grid and swimming it until you find what you're looking for. Imagine trying to grid out hundreds of miles."

"No wonder Culliver wasn't worried about someone stealing his find," I quip.

Logan sighs. "We'll look at it in detail when we get to Arlo. It's only fair."

I don't tell Logan that Arlo sort-of proposed. That he's not interested in things being fair, but in seizing life in the moment. Kind of like Logan had done with his impulsive hug.

When we get to the hospital, Arlo is on his phone, with a laptop open on the rolling table that should be holding hospital food. We had stopped and grabbed some sandwiches on our way over. Logan puts one of the paper bags on the table next to Arlo's computer.

Arlo tilts the phone away from his face for a moment to whisper, "Thanks."

He finishes his call – which seems to be with someone who has lab results. He doesn't seem happy with what he's hearing. When he hangs up, he grimaces. At this point, I know better than to ask what he learned on the phone – he'll likely just say something about police evidence. But I get the idea that someone had a mild sedative in their system. Assuming that the call was even about the same case, I can only imagine that he was discussing Audrey. A little something to slow her reactions would have made it easier to chain her to something and throw her overboard.

Logan takes a seat in one of the small chairs near this room's solitary window. He takes out his sandwich – his is a quarter muffuletta, since no one I know can reasonably eat a whole one. They're made on a full-sized loaf of round bread, spread with spicy olive salad and layered with ham and provolone cheese. I like them, but I wasn't in the mood for one today.

I assumed that Arlo still likes a good Reuben – it had been his favorite sandwich when we were younger – so we'd gotten one of those each for me and him.

I hand Arlo the envelope. "You might want to take a look at this before your hands get messy."

"Oh?" Arlo takes the envelope and pulls out the papers. I explain what he's looking at.

Then I sit down on a long bench and take out my sandwich. I'd opted for the Cajun version of the Reuben, with spicy remoulade and minced jalapenos added to the traditional ingredients. The bread is still crunchy and the sandwich warm, and the spice works with the tang of the sauerkraut rather than against it.

By the time I'm done, Arlo has read enough to look intrigued. He is holding the paper with the French text, peering curiously at the map. He says, "There has to be a nautical chart he was using during his last expedition. He would have wanted a record, so he could find the location exactly. If we could find that, it would give context to this information."

Logan moves over to peer at the paper, and the two men study it for a while. Then Logan uses an app and the camera on his phone to do some auto translation.

Finally, Logan says, "This is describing a formation in East Flower Garden Bank. It's still not as precise as a chart, but you could use that as a starting point and wind up with a reasonable search area."

Arlo says, "Wouldn't you love to be able to go do that? Just put an expedition together and go look for history?"

"You can't even leave this hospital," Logan points out.

"True," Arlo says. "But I have been streaming video. Check this out. This was recorded from one of her livestreams. I'd have taken it down, if it was me, but apparently it got her a ton of views."

Arlo turns his laptop. And there's Destiny, doing live art carving. The name of her YouTube Channel – and the way she signs her art – is *It was Destiny*!

Apparently, she can see the comments coming in as she works, and at some point she starts feeling the need to respond to someone who is criticizing her technique. At first it's just her turning to the camera and saying, "Chad L2D2, remember that art is in the eye of the beholder. Just because you don't like a technique doesn't mean it doesn't have value," but it quickly escalates to, "Come on L2D2, I'd like to see you do any better. Why don't you come on down here?" And after that, she starts yelling at him to stop commenting. And eventually, she grabs an apple from a fruit bowl at the edge of the shot and stabs her chisel through it.

I haven't had a ton of negative comments on any of my own social media – I mean, who is going to hate on chocolate? But even I know that the only way to respond to haters is by either ignoring them, or by deleting the comments and if necessary blocking the commentor. Destiny is losing it – which is probably just egging Chad L2D2 on.

I gesture towards the screen. "It looks like Destiny has a temper. But that doesn't make her a great candidate for our killer. After all, the murders all seem to have been meticulously planned, rather than impulsive."

Logan frowns down at the computer. "I don't know. Look at the art piece behind her. That kind of detailed carving would take forever. She has to have patience to do that. And not just once – but pretty much every piece of hers that I've seen has that level of intricacy."

"Fair," I say. "I signed up for an art class she's teaching later tonight, and now I'm a bit intimidated."

Arlo looks like he's about to tell me to cancel, since he knows I'm only going to snoop. And we both know he thinks this case is too dangerous for me to be poking around in – with the fact that he's in the hospital right now to prove his point. But he hesitates. Maybe it's because I never answered his proposal, and he's afraid of pushing me away at a crucial moment. Or maybe it's because he is tired and hurting, and it takes effort to fight the inevitable. But in a small voice, he asks, "What kind of class is it?"

"It's one of those wine and painting things. We're doing a painting of a cow."

"A cow," Logan repeats. "Why?"

I say, "I don't know. I guess cows make people think of Texas?"

"Fair," Logan says. "That's one of the things I thought before I moved here. And you can't get very far inland on the Bolivar side of the mainland without passing huge pastures full of them."

Logan is originally from Minnesota. It's often interesting to see his perspective on my hometown. But right now, I'm thinking about how ridiculous it all feels, looking for a killer at a place people go for date night. And I'm going by myself. Obviously, I'm not about to ask either of these guys to come with me, and I don't want to put any of my friends in an awkward position when I go asking questions.

I say, "What we're painting is irrelevant."

"That's right," Arlo says. "Just – be careful. I can still loan you that stun gun"

Logan says, "The class will be in public. Just don't criticize her teaching style, and you should be fine."

Arlo looks like he wants to say something else about safety. Instead, he changes the subject. "The doctor says I can leave after four hours, if I can have someone vouch that they'll make sure I'm not alone tonight. Lis, I was wondering if I could stay at the hotel. I know you have enough rooms ready to put up a few people."

Logan says quickly, "You need someone to actually keep an eye on you. I usually don't sleep right anyway. You can stay at my place."

I'm not about to get into the middle of that, so I try to look suddenly interested in the comments section of Destiny's video.

They make the arrangements for Logan to come back to the hospital later to pick Arlo up. And then Logan drives me back to the shop, so I can get my catering van and head home to change into clothes I don't mind getting paint all over.

When I get there, Stewart and the girls are in the kitchen, making soup.

"That smells amazing," I say. "I can't really place it, though."

Stewart says, "It's our own take on Thai Tom Kha Gai. But we're using catfish in place of the chicken, and we added in some pineapple. I know it sounds weird, but it works."

"I'll have to try it when it's done," I say.

Charlotte beams up at me. "Or you can have some of mine. It has durian instead of meat."

"Maybe," I say, forcing myself to smile back. Durian is used as a substitute for chicken in a number of vegetarian dishes. But durian has a unique funk—something like turpentine crossed with onions. It's actually banned on public transportation and in hotels in certain countries, because of the way the smell permeates. Many people consider it a delicacy. I've tried it twice, and wasn't a fan. I don't usually like funk—hence my aversion to bleu cheese. But what's going on here actually smells good.

Charlotte seems satisfied. She says, "I wanted to feed your bird, but Daddy said we had to wait for you to get home. But he's really lonely in that room. It makes me sad to hear him."

"I'll go check on him now," I say. I grab a bunch of grapes out of the fridge and pull some off the stem. Delores said grapes are Renoir's favorite treat. I want him to be as happy here as possible—even if I had to lock him in the office for his own safety. It's not his fault his home is a crime scene.

Charlotte follows me through the hotel's dining room and into the hall.

My Aunt Naomi is home today. She's sitting with her laptop in one of the chairs in the lobby. She sees me turn the corner and waves, calling, "How was your dive?"

She must have talked to Uncle Greg. I hadn't thought to call him back and update him about the murder that had taken place not far from the rig. I guess the Coast Guard didn't question everyone in the rig, or he would have called Aunt Naomi back with an update.

But I don't want to talk murder in front of Charlotte. Sure she seems mature for her age, but she's still a child. So I call back to Naomi, "Let's talk about it later. Charlotte and I need to check in on the cockatoo."

Aunt Naomi gives me a questioning look. She looks a bit like me, with similar long brown hair and brown eyes. She's not even that much older than me. I gesture with my chin towards Charlotte – trying to mime that I'll talk when she's not there – but Aunt Naomi just looks more confused.

As Charlotte and I get closer to the office, I hear fluttering as Renoir senses us coming. When I get to the door, he's flying around the room.

I tell him, "You be a good boy. We're coming in."

Renoir says, "I love you! You!"

"Me? Really?" I say, teasing the bird, even though Delores told me he doesn't understand what he's saying.

But Renoir replies, "Really, really." He lands on his cage and considers me.

I hesitate. Maybe he does understand. I wonder if someone spent time teaching him that response. I can't imagine he's spent his whole life in the museum. And there's bound to be a story behind how he wound up there.

Charlotte asks, "Can I feed him?"

I consider the potential danger in a beak as big as Renoir's. There's a toy in his cage made out of a coconut that has been cut and then chained back together. Since yesterday, he's managed to break one of the chain links with that powerful beak.

I tell her, "I think it's better if we put the dish on the desk and let him help himself."

I give her the dish, though, so she can feel like she is participating. Renoir watches the progress that dish is making across the room. I quickly move close to Charlotte, just in case he decides to dive-bomb her to get his treat. But he waits like a gentleman, for Charlotte to put the dish down on the desk and move away. Then he glides over and lands close to the grapes. I notice that he pooped on the desk at some point. I'm going to have to do some serious cleaning in here once he's gone. And I can't help but imagine that whoever has to clean the museum must really hate this bird.

Renoir picks up one of the grapes with his foot and holds it up where he can easily reach it with his beak. He nibbles at it delicately.

"You can see why birds are the best," Charlotte says. "They're like gentle dinosaurs."

I'm not sure I would describe Renoir as gentle. But I get what she's trying to say. I tell her, "Birds are pretty great. But I still like bunnies the best. But I may be biased, since Knightley saved my life once."

"Really?" Charlotte asks skeptically. I get why she would think that. Bunnies are often timid.

I feel like I need to explain, but I don't want to make her feel unsafe. I say, "Knightley distracted a bad guy one time, because that guy thought bunnies were shy. But rabbits are group animals, and they will defend members of their colony." I don't want to go into any more detail than that. So I smile and say, "Plus, a group of bunnies is called a fluffle. I don't think anything is cuter than that."

"Cuteness, fine, bunnies win." Charlotte gestures at Renoir, who is now on his third grape. "But for defense – a bird's beak is a serious weapon. A macaw could break the bad guy's finger. I bet a rabbit bite doesn't even hurt."

I laugh, then make a face. "Actually they hurt quite a bit. Knightley was a rescue bunny. He was really skittish when we brought him home from the shelter, so he would bite if you moved close to him too fast."

Her eyes go wide. "Poor bunny."

Renoir has had enough of not being the center of attention. He squawks, "Josephine!"

I tell Charlotte, "I think he's talking to you."

"Are you?" Charlotte asks the bird. She makes a helpless gesture. "I can't come pick you up. My mom says I'm too young."

Renoir squawks and starts dancing. I have to admit, he's pretty cute when he does that. Then he says, "Audrey said she would do it."

"What?" I say, startled. The bit about Culliver's diary – and now what Renoir just said about Audrey. The bird has to be repeating things he heard at the museum. I assumed at least part of what he's been saying has to be from watching pirate movies on TV. But what if it's not? What if somebody actually said, *If you do that, I'll kill you*? And then someone else said, *Audrey said she would do it*? And now Audrey's actually dead?

I move closer to Renoir, bend down a little closer to his level. "What about Audrey? What did you hear?"

Renoir says, "Audrey's a pretty girl. Audrey's a pretty girl."

I'm guessing that Audrey herself taught him that one. I repeat what the bird said earlier, slowly. "Audrey said she would do it. Do what?"

Renoir says, "If you do that, I'll kill you."

And here we are, back where we started.

Charlotte asks, "Who's Audrey?"

Renoir says, "Audrey's a pretty girl."

"She was a pretty girl," I say miserably. "But now she's gone." And there's no way to explain that to a bird.

Charlotte asks, "What's going on right now, Miss Felicity?"

I tell her, "I think this bird overheard a fight at the museum that might explain why people got hurt He already said something about Culliver's diary, which turned out to be a real book a treasure hunter had."

"Share Culliver!" Renoir announces.

"Who wants to share Culliver," I ask, hoping for the astronomical chance that I'll get a straight answer.

Renoir says, "Napoleon and Josephine."

Okay. That was too much to ask for. Still, I'm trying to piece it together. It must have been more than one conversation that Renoir overheard. At one point, someone announced that they had found Culliver's diary. Maybe whoever this person was had seen the bell from the *Pride* on the sculpture and had managed to track down where it came from. Having the diary meant a treasure dive could commence, but it was obviously too big of a job for one person.

Audrey was involved – and had said that she would do something. Participate in the theft from the rig, maybe. Or maybe just keep her mouth shut about what was going on. Because someone else wanted to, *share Culliver*. I'm guessing that means to make the diary or the shipwreck's location public, or share it with someone the person who found it didn't approve of. Unless the person who found it was also the one who wanted to share it, and someone else didn't want it shared. And whoever didn't want it shared had possibly been the one to say, *If you do that I'll kill you.*

Of course, I could have everything lined up wrong. Maybe the snatches of conversation didn't happen together at all, and someone was being overdramatic about something, like borrowing paint or tools. In that case, Amálie would likely have been the speaker, as she's the one people said didn't have a sense of humor. Could someone have committed a double murder just to shut her up?

I sigh. Trying to solve a case based on the ramblings of a bird could be leading me down a completely wrong path.

As if to emphasize the randomness, Renoir says, "Behind the green flowerpot! I love you!" But somehow he seems so troubled. I feel like whatever he witnessed must have traumatized him.

Chapter Seventeen

There's something I need to do before the painting class starts. Audrey had said that Amálie's husband had gotten her fired from her previous job, implying that she had uncovered something untoward at the firm. And considering Audrey's dead, I should talk to Amálie's husband about what really happened. Not that he's likely to tell me much, if he is guilty of something. But maybe I can figure it out.

It isn't hard to find the address for his office. So I get in my catering truck and drive over there. I don't even know if he will be at work, given everything that has happened, but if not maybe I can find out where he is. It's a big building, and I have to check in at the front, but when the receptionist tells Roger who I am, he has her send me up. So I take the elevator up to the third floor and I find his office. I knock on the door.

Roger answers it himself. He doesn't seem to have an assistant, or anyone working in the same space with him. His eyes are red-rimmed, and he looks a little rumpled, but he smiles at me as he says, "I was wondering when you were going to show up."

"Pardon?" I ask. I never even heard of Roger Timbers before two days ago. So why would he be expecting me to visit his workplace?

Roger gestures at me. "You're the chocolate detective, right? You knew my wife. So you must be investigating the case. And the spouse is always extra suspicious."

I feel my mouth dropping open without my permission. I say, "It never occurred to me that you might have had anything to do with your wife's death. Otherwise, I would hardly have come here alone." I hesitate. I'm not getting a dangerous vibe from this guy. But he just told me himself that he is suspicious. I ask, "I'm not going to regret coming here alone, am I?"

"Of course not," he says. "But if you don't think I did it, then why are you here?"

I say, "I want to talk about Audrey Scruggs."

Roger grimaces. "Now that's another matter entirely. But you should have called first. I'm in the middle of a conference Zoom. It will be half an hour, at the most. You can wait if you like." He gestures to a side room inside the office, with a sofa and a television. There's a Keurig machine and a little fridge with bottles of water.

"Sure," I say. "Why not? It would take me that long to get home and back here later anyway."

I go into the side room, but I can still see Roger sitting down at his desk. He plucks a tissue from a box and blows his nose loudly. Then he straightens his tie and puts headphones into his ears. He must have muted the Zoom and turned his camera off. He pastes a smile on his face. I assume that means he's turned the camera on again.

I help myself to a bottle of water from the fridge. Then I plop down on the sofa. Ignoring the television, I take out my tablet and start looking a few things up about people I think seem a lot more suspicious than Roger Timbers. If Roger were to have killed Hernan to cause-and-effect murder Amálie, he would have to have been cruel and sociopathic. And first impression, Roger isn't that type. Though sometimes sociopaths hide behind charm – so I should still be careful.

I start my search with a few basics. Each of the artists working at the studio that night has a website. They're all making money off their art, one way or another.

Destiny has her teaching and podcasting, and she has pieces for sale as well as virtual art. There's nothing in her web presence that shows her being into diving, but she is in the group photo for the bookstore's History Book Club. She's sitting right next to Hernan in the pic. She obviously knew him in more than

one context, and that video I watched proves she has a temper, so
if this is about the art grant, or Hernan's attitude towards other
artists, she's definitely a prime suspect. If it's about the treasure
wreck – I'm less sure. But from the casual way she's leaning
towards Hernan for the photo, if she was a mastermind suddenly
in possession of a secret diary, I can see Hernan being one of the
people she might approach to see if he wanted in on a treasure
hunt. A Google search reveals, among other things, reviews of
Destiny's work. People seem to think she's either an innovative
genius who marries the present to the past seamlessly, or an
absurdist with no connection to human emotion. Which kind of
sounds like her critics are describing a sociopath. And her social
media feeds are almost entirely pictures of her car, parked in
different scenic locations, with a marked absence of people. It's
that and her uncontrolled temper that bumped her to the top of my
suspect list. But I haven't really talked to her yet, so who knows.

Tracie's the most obvious suspect – but she just seems
too obvious. I already know a bit about her, so I'm not surprised
that her social media feeds heavily feature her twin nieces.
There's pictures of them in snorkel gear, in hiking boots, carrying
disc golf discs. Basically, if it is an outdoor sport, they do it. Her
art has predominantly positive reviews, and she offers services to
create custom art for websites, and hand-drawn caricatures for
parties. The caricature samples on her site are adorable. There's
clear intelligence and a sense of humor in all her work. I know
Tracie's a member of both a dive club and of the same history
book club as Hernan. She works at the museum and is a history
buff, so if anybody was going to notice something about Amálie's
sculpture, she was in the perfect position to do so, and she would
have been at an advantage to commit the break-in too. It was her
machine that was used as the murder weapon. It all lines up. And
still – I don't think she did it.

And then there's Violet. I really hope she's not the killer,
because that might break Carmen. But I think she might have
done it. Violet takes chances with her art. Sometimes they pay off
for her – as evidenced by articles about her and award wins – and

sometimes they flop. If her social media is to be believed, she takes it all in stride, saying repeatedly that you can't take risks if you aren't willing to fail. And if you don't take risks you can't innovate. She's the edgiest artist of the ones I've been looking at, with paintings featuring riotous colors and sharp angles, and her sculptures are larger than life and somehow give me all the feels. But there's something calculated in that edginess. And she has the strongest motive, as Hernan's ex–who had had to watch him marry the girl he'd broken up with her to be with.

The others all have alibis for at least one of the murders. Some of those alibis are weak – like Syed's claim that he'd been taking a digital class from the comfort of his home, and Jonah and Gently vouching for each other as not having left the shop all day, when both were clearly focused on working – but they make it a lot less likely that any of them could have done it. Still, I'm kind of hoping someone faked an alibi, because that means that Violet didn't do it after all.

Of course, there's still the possibility that the murderer isn't any of the people I know are connected to the incidents. It is possible that whoever set up that Rube Goldberg scenario counted on the door being open and snuck in, then snuck back out, well before that slamming sound sent Logan running out into the night. If that's the case, I have no hope of figuring out who the killer was, and I can just sit back and hope the police uncover more solid information, with all their access to forensics.

I hear Roger say, "No, I'll be taking some time off. My wife just died, and I need to process things. Emotionally. Someone else will have to take over with Sydney."

I'm not sure who or what Sydney is, but it sounds like Roger is genuinely grieving, a lot more than Rosa was. I've been in a similar situation, so I get what Roger is going through. I feel a great deal if empathy for him. I hope I can keep that from clouding my judgement when I finally get to talk to him.

I try to consider anything I've might have missed about the case. Going back through the suspects, I remember Tracie asking me for the copy of *Treasure Island*. She'd seemed terribly invested in the book and had seemed more upset than anybody when we thought it had been stolen. I hadn't been able to find out anything unusual about the book itself, but it would make sense that somebody interested in an actual pirate ship wreck might feel a connection to a fictional story about pirates. The story itself is about good versus corruption, and about the relationship of Jim, the innocent kid who wound up being given the pirate map, and the mutinous pirate Silver, who used to have the same idealism as Jim, before life got to him. It's such a complex piece. And in some ways, it reminds me of everything that's happened. Because one way or another, this is all about greed and money.

I still have the donation slip, which I took out of the book well before Stewart Jr. had borrowed it. I have no idea who J. Mills might be, or what relationship this person has to the museum or anyone who works there. I do a few random Google searches with the name plus the name of the museum, then the names of all the artists. At first I don't get much, but when I put in J. Mills plus Marissa Reid, I get an article about a salvage operation three years ago off the coast of Louisiana. Apparently, the operation was financed by Joan Mills, of Galveston, Texas, working with her sister Marissa, who actually did the diving. Joan had been obsessed by all things pirate related – which means she is probably the same person who donated the book to the museum.

In the article, Marissa talks about her mother, who was an artist, and who encouraged her to pursue her dreams, and her father, a marine biologist who instilled her a respect for the life in the ocean. She had that brief moment of fame after finding the wreck of a battleship more or less accidentally. But there's not much about either of them after that. I look up more information, and realize I haven't gotten to know much about Marissa at all. Her social media feed is gossipy, snarky and filled with sarcastic memes. She's been talking about the murders on her feeds with a kind of horrified fascination. And there's a GoFundMe Marissa set up for her sister – who needs some kind of operation. Honestly, she makes a much better suspect than Violet or Tracie. Well, except for the fact that Marissa is literally the only one of the artists with a verified alibi.

I sigh. Of course it couldn't be that easy.

Roger Timbers finally gets off his conference call. He comes and sits in the side room in a little chair opposite me. He says, "So what do you want to know?"

I say, "I do have a few questions about your wife, if that's okay, before we talk about Audrey."

"That's fine," Roger says. His eyes look sad and his voice sounds tired. I get it. He must be exhausted.

"Can you think of anyone who had a reason to dislike her? Or who might have wanted to hurt her?"

Roger runs both of his hands over his eyes. He says, "Amálie was blunt, to a fault. She often rubbed people the wrong way. But she had a good heart, and if she came across as criticizing or trying to correct you, she really was just trying to help. So yes, I could probably name a dozen people in the local art community who disliked her enough to say negative things to her face. But I don't think any of them would have hurt her."

I say, "I heard Amálie had intense work habits."

Roger says, "That's just the way her brain was wired. She was like that with everything. When she was in the planning stages of a project, she wouldn't be able to slow her mind down enough to sleep. She would work like crazy for multiple days, and then she would just crash. It used to worry me when we were first married, but eventually I realized that that was just her. But it was something else people didn't understand. It bothered Amálie that she had a reputation for being calculatedly eccentric. They assumed that she had this whole whimsical artist-poet thing going on for the sole purpose of getting attention. But that wasn't it at all."

I say, "It sounds like your wife was a special person."

Roger says, "She was. I really don't think anyone meant to intentionally hurt her. I believe someone wanted to kill Hernan, and Amálie was just in the wrong place at the wrong moment."

He's probably right. But I still want to explore the possibility that Amálie was the killer's target. I say carefully, "At least one of the artists I spoke to felt betrayed, because Amálie downvoted an entry for a competition."

Roger nods. "Amálie told me about that. She regretted having to do that, but she didn't believe in showing favoritism to friends. She felt that people getting a pass when their work wasn't up to par yet would never grow to reach their full potential."

"That's fair," I say. But I think he underestimates the effect his wife had on people. Amálie was a passionate person, intense and poetic. I can't help but think about how jealous I'd gotten over some of the complements Amálie had given Logan. If that was her genuinely encouraging someone to pursue their art – well, the potential for misunderstandings is great.

But trying to point that out would only hurt Roger even more than the loss of his wife already has. So I switch subjects. I say, "I talked to Audrey before she died. She claimed that you got her fired because she uncovered irregularities."

Roger reflexively looks at his office door, to make sure it is shut. His lips narrow into a hard line. He says, "I did no such thing."

"Okay," I say slowly. "Then why did she believe you did?"

Roger says, "Audrey had a big imagination. At one point she believed that I was in love with her – but I've always been loyal to my wife. After that, she decided she was in the middle of a John Grisham novel. She used to talk about having met Grisham once. Audrey got fired for photocopying confidential client files. And I had nothing to do with it."

I study his face. He has earnest gray-blue eyes with crow's feet at the edges, salt-and-pepper hair and a slight weakness to his chin. He doesn't look diabolical. But either he's the world's best liar – or else Audrey was crazy. I ask, "If you had nothing to do with Audrey, why didn't you seem surprised that I wanted to talk about her?

Roger gives me an ironic grin. "I assumed that you knew my wife intercepted the letters Audrey kept sending me during her love-struck phase. It was Amálie and her bluntness that finally brought the truth home to Audrey. But then Audrey slashed Amálie's tires. There's a police report about that and everything. I thought you were going to propose that Audrey was still holding a grudge. But she wasn't. We'd all finally made our peace."

I don't know what to say to that. But Arlo's comment that Audrey could have been the one who killed Hernan and Amálie suddenly makes more sense. It's possible – but is it really likely?

I'm pretty sure that Roger couldn't have been the one who shot Hernan. A complicated Rube Goldberg machine doesn't exactly seem his style. But what if he found out that Audrey had killed his wife? Or if he just assumed she had? After already feeling that Audrey had been persecuting him, could it be possible that he had snapped and killed her?

Audrey isn't here to defend herself. There's no way I can tell whether Roger is telling the truth about any of it. He could have concocted the elaborate story to destroy Audrey's credibility, if she really did report Roger for corrupt business practices. Or maybe Audrey really had uncovered corruption – and Roger hadn't believed her. Or the truth could be anything in between.

Still, if he's not lying his perspective could be valuable. I ask, "So if somebody told Audrey there's pirate treasure and if she kept a big secret she could have part of it?"

Without hesitation, Roger replies, "She would have believed it."

Chapter Eighteen

When I walk into the building where the painting class is being held, there's pop music playing, and people are shuffle-dancing their way around the room as they set up their supplies. It doesn't look like I'm the only one to come alone, which makes me feel a bit better. I brought a bottle of cabernet – which for me is way too much to *drink* alone, though. There's a wine glass at each spot. Hopefully someone will sit next to me who likes a nice Chilean red.

I can't believe it when Kaylee walks in. I wave her over, and find she's also carrying a bottle of cab – though hers is Tuscan.

I guess we do have some things in common after all.

Kaylee settles into her spot, then she says, "I had no idea you liked to paint."

I pick up the paintbrush that is closest to my wine glass. "Usually the only thing I paint is chocolate molds. But this class seemed like it might be enlightening, for other reasons."

Kaylee grins conspiratorially, then says more softly, "So it's a recon mission."

"Something like that," I say.

Kaylee says, "I kept thinking about our conversation, and how this could be about art or about history. I got to wondering where art and history intersect. Did you know there's a history book club that meets at my bookstore?"

"I though you just had a long-running Pokeno game," I say. I hope she realizes I'm trying to be light-hearted, even though said game had apparently been the subject of some controversy in the past.

Kaylee says, "That's after hours. I'm talking about an official store event. And when any group comes in for book club events, I always run a giveaway that encourages attendees to sign up for the store's newsletter. So I get their name and e-mail address. And do you know how many artists show up on that book club's lists?"

"A lot?" I guess.

Kaylee says, "True." Then she drops her voice even more and adds, "But there's three you might be specifically interested in. Hernan was a member. Along with Destiny and Marissa. And two months ago, the book for the meeting was about America's most notorious pirates. Hernan and his wife were both on the list as attending."

"Huh," I say. "When I talked to his wife, she didn't seem to understand his recent obsession with Galveston history. She thought it might have to do with World War II."

"That was the subject of the previous meeting," Kaylee says. "Though I don't think Rosa came to that one."

I glance over at Destiny, who is lining up tiny gift bags along the edge of her table at the front of the room. I'm guessing it's going to be chocolates and business cards. My first instinct is to ask if she'd be interested in ordering chocolate squares from Greetings and Felicitations. But that's not really appropriate – since she's one of the most probable suspects in multiple murders. Especially since Kaylee just said that Destiny was at the book club with Hernan. Why had they chosen to read a book on pirates? Could it be because either she or Hernan had uncovered Culliver's diary?

Just before the class is due to start, the door opens and Tracie rushes in. She says, "Sorry I'm late!"

Destiny smiles at her and says, "Thanks for coming on short notice." Destiny turns to address the class and says, "Since there are so many of you tonight, this place's policy is to have a second instructor, but tragically-" She stops mid-sentence as she gets choked up a bit. She takes in a deep breath then lets it out through pursed lips. When she's able to continue she says, "There's no easy way to say this. Audrey has passed away."

There are several murmurs of distress, and one cry of, "Oh, no!" from the students, many of whom must be returning for the class. I glance around, trying to see if any of them look like they might know anything. They all look either confused – as in *who might this Audrey be* – or distressed.

Outside the window, lit pale by the streetlight, I see a face staring in at us. I squeak, and Kaylee turns to see what I'm looking at.

"Who is that?" she asks.

I blink as recognition dawns. "I think that's Jonah. He's another artist from the studio."

I get up from my seat and go to the door. I open it, and Jonah has started to walk away. I call out, "Hey Jonah!"

He turns and forces a smile. "Wa'sup?"

I ask the obvious. "Are you following me?"

I can see his guilty look, even in this poor light, but he says, "Of course not. I'm here for the class."

I tilt my head, curious to see how far he's going to take this. "You mean the beginner painting class? Where we're painting a cow?"

"Yes?" he says, but it's more of a question.

"Well, come on inside," I say, "It's about to start."

Jonah follows me in. He makes his way over to the other side of the room. I would assume that Tracie would have seen him loitering outside as she made her way in, but from the questioning look she gives him, maybe she was too focused on getting here.

Destiny, on the other hand, looks amused at seeing Jonah. The two exchange a long moment of eye contact. Destiny looks away, addresses the entire class when she says, "This is Tracie's first time as an instructor here at Pottery and Paint, so let's give her a round of applause."

Tracie smiles, but it looks forced, as all attention turns towards her. She says, "I hope you will all be kind."

I wonder how Tracie feels about replacing Audrey. That has to be at least somewhat creepy. And it is unexpected how genuinely upset Destiny sounds over Audrey's death. If she really is the one who killed Audrey, she's one heck of an actress.

The art class starts out being a lot of fun, which makes me wish that I wasn't going to have to approach Destiny and ask uncomfortable questions afterwards. I need to figure out what Destiny was fighting with Hernan over. But I can't exactly ask that in the middle of her mini-lecture on the proportion between a figure's head and its body. I get the idea that we're getting more actual information on art than you generally would in this kind of class.

And Destiny is funny. She has all these stories about different artists and stupid things that happened to them, and even though a lot of people seemed upset about Audrey's death, Destiny gets the class laughing.

We start work on the first stage of our project – sketching out the basic shapes that are going to become our cow. Tracie comes around to the table I'm sharing with Kaylee and two others, checking on our work. After checking in on the other tables on this side of the room, she comes back to ours.

Tracie says, "I wanted to thank you for taking care of Renoir. I would have taken him, only at home I have neither the space nor the time to care for him properly, what with the girls."

"I didn't realize you had a special attachment to him," I say.

Tracie pauses to correct a line on Kaylee's canvas, tracing where it ought to go with the back of a paintbrush. Then she says, "I'd be sure to spend a little time with Renoir every time I come into the studio, talking to him and making sure he had treats. And I always wind up cleaning up for him a bit. That bird can be a total mess, but I've always felt a little sorry for him, after hearing his story."

"Oh?" I prompt. I had a feeling that the cockatoo hadn't always been at the museum. Now I'm hoping I'll hear where he was before, and if that might explain some of his random words. Like the thing about the green flowerpot.

Tracie says, "Renoir was a companion pet for an elderly lady who lived in an apartment over by the hospital. She had to evacuate from Hurricane Ike, and the folks she rode with wouldn't let her take a cockatoo in the car, since they had a dog. Renoir spent four days alone in a flooded apartment before a rescue crew was able to get to him. And then after that, the old lady's family decided she needed to move into assisted care, so he probably never saw her again. He was in a shelter for a while, until someone who worked there talked to Delores at a party or something."

"But Hurricane Ike was more than a decade and a half ago," I say.

Tracie nods. "Yeah. Long enough for all of the museum's surfaces to be bird-proofed, and all the staff to know his routines. There are poop guards over most of the art. And he usually stays in the same gallery with his cage, unless he's followed someone through the door."

So I guess Renoir wasn't really supposed to be perched on that sculpture the day I'd met him.

"How old is Renoir?" I ask. I had assumed he was relatively young, simply because he is so mischievous and in need of attention.

Tracie says, "He's forty-one. Sulphur-Crested cockatoos can live to about eighty years in captivity, so he's barely middle aged."

I say, "It's weird to think that a bird is older than I am."

Tracie moves around to the other side of the table to check the other students' progress. She says, "A bird like that is a serious commitment. In some cases, people have to think about who they're going to leave their bird to in their wills."

If Renoir has been at the museum for that long, it probably means the phrases he's been using are things he's heard at the museum. Except – what about when someone leaves – or threatens to leave – and he says, *I don't love you*? Could that somehow relate to his experience of being abandoned? I resolve to bring him some grapes the minute I get home. And maybe sit with him and watch a movie or something.

We finish our sketching and move onto the actual painting. Destiny gives us another mini-lecture on mixing paint and brush technique. Afterwards, we get started painting and Tracie goes over to talk to Destiny. At first it sounds like they're discussing teaching technique. Tracie obviously wants to do a good job – with the most enthusiasm I've seen her display for any job yet. Maybe she was meant to be a teacher.

But then Destiny says something about the way Hernan used to choose brushes when painting a sculpture.

Tracie says, "You didn't appreciate that on his Rube Goldberg entry."

Destiny says something sharp in response, but I can't make out the words. They argue back and forth in hushed tones until finally Destiny squeaks out, "You aren't suggesting I might have killed him to get rid of the competition?"

Tracie says, "You were the one who helped me store my Rube Goldberg. Who else would have known where to find it?"

"Anybody," Destiny says. "Your garage isn't exactly Fort Knox. And you can't think I would have hurt Audrey. She was my best friend."

"Or so you say," Tracie says.

Destiny throws a paintbrush at Tracie, leaving a long blue streak down the front of Tracie's blouse. She says loudly, "Now you're just being stupid. Check our social media feeds. We were always there for each other."

The whole class has stopped painting. We're just staring at the meltdown going on between our two instructors. I have more context for what's happening than most of the rest of the class, so I can only imagine what the others must be thinking.

But Jonah heads over and takes Destiny's hand. He squeezes it and says, "Don't let her get to you, Babe. You know you didn't do anything wrong. It doesn't matter what anyone else says. Especially someone with the exact same motive." Jonah gives Tracie a look that implies, *maybe you protest too much.*

Kaylee and I exchange a glance. Apparently she's surprised too, at finding out that Jonah and Destiny are a couple. But it's more than that. Destiny and Tracie – two of the people high on my suspects list – basically just accused each other of committing the murders. Something you usually only do if you're *not* the one who did it.

"It's not the same at all," Tracie says. "I had no reason to kill Hernan. I got eliminated from the competition."

"By Amálie's recommendation," Jonah points out.

"Then why would I have wanted to kill Audrey?" Tracie protests. "It had to be one of you."

They clearly believe that this is all about the grant competition – and not the pirate ship. Which is still a possibility. But if it is about the grant, it doesn't really narrow down the suspects. Tracie and Destiny were involved in the competition true – but so were Jonah and Violet. I really hope the killer isn't Violet. Carmen has already had one roommate wind up in prison for murder. I'm not sure if she will be able to take it if that happens again.

The door to the classroom opens, and there's Detective Beckman and two uniformed officers filing into the room. Detective Beckman has gobs of curly black hair pulled back into a low ponytail. She's worked with Arlo on previous cases. She must be assisting with this one while Arlo is stuck being under observation.

The class is already frozen from the argument between the instructors. Nobody says a word as Detective Beckman walks over to Tracie. Tracie's eyes are wide, and she looks frozen.

It's a little bit surreal when Detective Beckman says, "Tracie Boudreaux, you are under arrest for the murder of Hernan Núñez and the manslaughter of Amálie Timbers."

"This is crazy," Tracie says. "I didn't hurt anybody."

Detective Beckman starts informing Tracie that she can remain silent. But after Detective Beckman finishes reciting the

Miranda rights, Tracie demands, "Why do you think I did this? If I was going to kill someone, do you think I would be stupid enough to do it with one of my own art projects?"

Detective Beckman shrugs. She says, "Apparently? Or maybe you thought it would make you look too obvious as a suspect. We obtained a warrant to search your house, and were let in by the neighbor watching your nieces. We found a bottle of the sedative used to drug Audrey Scruggs. And we found bullets of the same caliber as the one that killed Hernan Núñez."

Tracie says, "Those bullets were for an ironic anti-violence sculpture I did last year. It was exhibited in a gallery in California. You can check. I don't even own a gun."

Detective Beckman says, "Hernan wasn't killed with a gun."

Tracie turns to me. "You know I couldn't have done this. Tell them. I was talking to you right before Hernan got shot."

I hesitate, then I shake my head. "I'm sorry. I went back to working. I lost track of where everyone was by the time the lights went out. And there was a lag between the power going down and the shot in the dark. Personally, I don't think you killed anybody, but I can't vouch for it."

Tracie looks absolutely betrayed. And the expression in her eyes is going to haunt me if I don't figure out who the actual murderer is. She doesn't say anything else as the cops lead her out.

Class is a bust, with half-finished cow paintings at every station. For some reason, that doesn't affect me in the same way as Hernan's incomplete ocean sculpture.

Kaylee asks me, "If they found the sedative in her house, why didn't they charge her with Audrey's murder too?"

I look down at my sketched-out cow. I say, "I guess that sedative must not be that hard to get. It wasn't enough of a direct link."

Kaylee says, "I agree with you. I don't think Tracie did this."

I say, "Obviously, whoever took the Rube Goldberg machine from Tracie's place took the bullet and the sedative while they were already there."

I thought Arlo was still in charge of the investigation. I didn't think he'd be this hasty in making an arrest. I blame the head injury. Either he's been sidelined entirely from the case, or he's trying to lead it remotely, and he isn't getting all the information. Which means I need to take this even more seriously.

I still need to find out what Destiny and Hernan fought about. And at this point, I'm prepared to just ask.

Destiny tells everyone, "I think we should adjourn class. I'll talk to Deanna, and we will either get you a refund or a rescheduled class. I'll be honest, I'm not in any condition to teach."

A couple of the students hug Destiny on their way out, more offering condolences or saying they understand how impossible it can be to focus in the face of grief. And I agree . . . if that grief is genuine.

I wait until the room has emptied, then I approach Destiny and ask her, "Can I speak to you for a minute?" I give Jonah a significant look.

Jonah says, "I'm not going anywhere. I still think you killed people, and I'm not leaving my girlfriend alone with you."

I sigh. "Fine. Destiny, I was told that you had a fight with Hernan shortly before he was killed. I'd like to know what that fight was about."

Destiny cuts a glance at Jonah. Whatever she's about to say, she isn't excited for him to hear. Yet she says, "Hernan just got hired to do an art column for a local webzine. His first column was going to include a roundup of current exhibitions, with his reviews. And you met Hernan. He was arrogant and condescending. There was no way that his reviews were going to be positive, unless something was absolutely perfect. Right now, Jonah has an exhibition of outdoor neon installed in a local park as part of a civic project. Hernan couldn't resist hinting that he had called the exhibit pedestrian and dull, involving clever puns about the park paths and the fact that the exhibit was made of lights. Like traffic lights. I *thought* Hernan and I were friends. So I asked him to reconsider. He impolitely declined."

Jonah asks, "Since when did Hernan get an art column?"

His shock and dismay look genuine. Which means that he didn't know about the bad review, so it couldn't have given him a motive.

Destiny, on the other hand, could have wanted to shut Hernan up and to protect her boyfriend so badly that she could have snapped and killed him. Maybe she'd taken the Rube Goldberg already from Tracie's place and stashed it upstairs for some other reason. She could somehow have put the other elements in place while we were all working on our own projects. It would have been bold, acting without being really seen.

But I have no proof. And at the moment, I have no way to get proof.

Destiny obviously sees the suspicion in the way I'm looking at her, because she says, "I didn't kill anybody. But I can tell you how the killer timed it."

Before I can say anything, Jonah asks, "How's that?"

Destiny says, "Hernan's sneakers were meant for night running. That green webbing glows in the dark. I noticed it when the lights went out. Hernan's feet were one of the few things I could still see. So the killer knew when to trigger the Rube Goldberg based on where Hernan was standing, and their plan assumed he wasn't likely to move too much on narrow scaffolding in the dark in the time it took to trigger the device. So you're looking for someone who knew Hernan was into night running. And someone willing to take chances with a risky plan."

And if the intent was to kill both Hernan and Amálie, the odds of something going wrong were that much greater.

Jonah says, "I knew Hernan was a runner. He used running analogies all the time, and he wore those shoes pretty much every time he worked in the studio."

I tell Jonah, "Well, I couldn't possibly have known that. The first time I saw him in the studio was the day he died."

Jonah taps at his chin. "I admit, thinking about it, you aren't likely to have known about Tracie's Rube Goldberg Machine either. So maybe you didn't do it."

Destiny says, "But maybe she really can figure out who did."

Jonah says, "If I don't beat her to it." He leans in close to Destiny and asks, "You don't think my exhibition is pedestrian, do you?"

When I go downstairs the next morning at the hotel, Carmen and Violet are sitting in the lobby, waiting for me. Carmen's boyfriend Paul is there too, slouched against the wall, doing something with his phone. He still looks a bit disreputable, with the notched eyebrow and neck tattoos. But I've gotten to know him well enough to realize he's really trying to turn his life around, and that deep down, he's not a bad guy.

I stifle a yawn. I say, "Good morning," but what I mean is *What are you all doing here instead of at the shop*?

I can hear Tam Binh's kids chatting excitedly from somewhere in the hallway that leads to the dining room.

Charlotte comes running up and tugs at my sleeve, saying, "Miss Felicity, are we going to hang out with the bird again?"

We'd spent a good amount of time with Renoir last night, letting him fly around the business center's big conference room, while Naomi and Tam Binh's family and I all watched a movie on the giant wall monitor meant for showing PowerPoints. With the amount of detail my Aunt Naomi and my friend Tiff are putting into this place, I'm beginning to wonder if Naomi's going to be able to bring herself to flip it when the time comes. I don't think she's cut out to be a hotel manager, though, so she's going to have to.

Charlotte looks so hopeful for another TV day that I hate to deny her, but I shake my head. "Your dad tells me you guys are going fishing again. He booked another charter."

Charlotte sighs dramatically. "We already did that."

"But this time it's going to be a bigger boat. You'll get to go out much farther in the ocean." I try to sound encouraging. "It has a balcony up top where you can watch for dolphins." Which I'd found out when I'd looked at the website listed on the business card Marissa had given me. I'd passed the card on to Stewart when he'd asked about more things to do.

"Can't I just stay here with you?" Charlotte asks. Her voice is whiney, reminding me that as mature as she tries to act, she really is just a kid.

"I'm not staying here," I say. I give Carmen a questioning look, trying to ask, *I'm not, right? There's nothing wrong at the shop*?

Carmen says, "There are people already lined up outside Felicitations. We're getting the usual lookie-loos curious about what's going on since there's been another murder. As we were leaving, I saw a bus low-key cruising down the Strand that had the words True Crime Tours on the side."

"How is this different from what happened yesterday?" I ask. "You had plenty of baked goods, and everything ran smoothly."

Violet says, "Yesterday, you didn't have a partially assembled sculpture taking up all the table space in your café. And first thing this morning, there was an incident with the tempering machine. The bad news is that there's a film of chocolate across most of the floor. The good news is that it seems like it's going to come off without doing any real damage."

I groan. "That's not exactly how I wanted to start this morning."

Carmen says, "I made extra baked goods, but I have no way to sell them. And there's more people than even I expected. Apparently, there was a mystery book convention going on this weekend in Houston. According to one guy I talked to this morning, we're an official stop on their local interest spots for the pre-conference events."

I say, "I'm guessing Ash's articles have had something to do with that."

In addition to what he'd already said about the murders, Ash had made a new post to his blog this morning. I had checked it before even coming downstairs. Ash had made me look like I'm at the center of the investigation, uncovering clues that have baffled the police. And he had implied that the wrong suspect had been arrested yesterday. I agree with him, but it feels like he's still making big statements in print – statements that could upset the real killer. I hope he's at least being careful.

Violet says, "You have artists working in view of the windows, and there's already been a couple of minor crisis points. Having people staring in at us waiting for the shop to open is breaking everyone's concentration. Gently is practically catatonic."

It's still over an hour before opening. I hadn't expected Violet and the others to get such an early start. But apparently these artists have embraced the project and are taking ownership – despite the chaos surrounding the events that happened at the museum.

"Gently's there?" I ask. "That means Ruffles is too." I was already worried about possible complaints about there being a cat in the shop. Though no one had said anything yesterday, and I get the idea Ruffles is registered as an emotional support animal, there's no guarantee that everyone will be cool about him hanging out. But now all I can picture is a floor covered with chocolate and cat hair. I don't want customers seeing that. And more importantly, chocolate is toxic to pets.

Violet says, "You don't have to worry. Ruffles won't get into anything. We know cats can't have chocolate. It was the first thing Carmen told us after the tempering machine fell over. Gently has a soft carrier for him."

That giant tempering machine got knocked over? It's potentially broken, and it is one of the more expensive pieces of equipment in the shop. It's so heavy – how could that even happen? I look over at Carmen. "It fell over?"

She looks a bit evasive. "It fell away from the bookcases, so none of the stock got messed up. And Gently said he could fix the spout, so it should be working again soon."

Logan had told me we were wasting money when I'd done the sculpture of Knightley. Both the expense and the scale of that project are nothing compared to what I've gotten us into with this museum contract. And if we lose equipment and stock in the process – we could actually lose money on this, even if Delores honors the payment in the contract. Logan trusts my judgement. But maybe he won't after this.

I groan and say, "I haven't even had coffee yet."

"My mom's making coffee," Charlotte says. "I can bring you one, then we can check on Renoir."

I can't help but laugh at her obvious ulterior motive. But I'm not saying no to another Vietnamese-style coffee. I say, "Sounds like a deal."

Charlotte rushes off, shouting, "Mom! Mom!"

Renoir hears her from inside the office, and shouts back, "I love you! Josephine!"

I feel awful that we're going to leave him here all day. But I have to get work done. And I am still hoping to find a way to get the person who cares about him the most out of jail. It would be awful if he lost another caregiver without even getting a chance to say goodbye.

Charlotte delivers the promised coffee. I sip the strong brew as I call Logan to ask what he suggests we do about the problem at the shop.

Logan sounds groggy when he answers. I suspect he really did stay up last night – or at least set alarms to get up periodically – to check on Arlo. Logan says, "Just stay closed. Put paper in the windows or something."

"I could do that," I say. But the caffeine is kicking in and I get a better idea. "But it's cool enough outside now, we could probably take a couple of tables onto the sidewalk and sell chocolate and baked goods without anything melting. It'd have to be cash only, but with all these artists on site, someone should be able to make a big sign that says that."

"You do that then," Logan says. "I'm going to drop Arlo off at the police station, since that's where they took his car, then

I'm coming back here and crashing out for a couple of hours. I have a flight later today, and I'll try to see you before that, but I need some sleep."

I tell him, "I don't blame you there. You be careful driving. And flying."

He hesitates. Then he says, "You too. I love you."

I don't know what to say. I do care about Logan. But I'm so conflicted right now, I'm not sure what's the appropriate response.

He says, "I'm sorry. You don't need to say it back. I promised I wasn't going to pressure you. I'm just so tired."

"It's okay," I say. But I think I do love him. And I'd *wanted* to say it back.

After I hang up, I brief Carmen and Violet on the plan, and they're both on board with doing tables outside. Violet says she has an app on her phone that allows her to take payments on the go, and offers to help Carmen set up something similar.

Paul says, "I want to help too. I don't have class this morning, and my kid is with my ex. I don't cook at all, but I can man a table. It would give me a chance to spend time with Carmen today."

I hesitate, trying to decide if I should trust someone with a criminal record to handle a cash box. But really, I claim to be all about second chances and looking for the best in people. I shouldn't even be thinking about saying no. So I tell Paul, "That would really help. I'd like to go check on Arlo at some point today, and Miles is finishing up the immersive photo presentation for the exhibit. So we're going to be busy yet shorthanded."

Carmen tells Paul, "She's also likely to get distracted and go off to investigate some clue. Especially with what happened to Audrey, I wouldn't be surprised if she wound up over by the yacht marina."

I feel so called out by that, but I can't really argue. "That's accurate," I say. "If Audrey wound up on a boat, maybe somebody saw something."

Paul says, "I saw Audrey's car yesterday morning, but it was over on the wrong end of the island for what you're talking about. The car was somewhere off Broadway, on the other side of I-45. She was pulled into a parking lot, but not near any particular building."

"Was she in the car?" I ask.

Paul says, "I dunno. I didn't stop to look."

"So how are you sure it was her car?"

Paul looks insulted. He says, "I used to be a car thief. I think I'd recognize when somebody drives an Audi with personalized plates. Her plates say NACHOS, as in it's my fancy sports car, not yours."

"I guess it would be hard to mistake that," I say. Though I have to wonder how Audrey could afford an Audi, if she was working inputting oral history projects for the library. Maybe her art was doing well on the side? Or maybe she'd been bribed to keep her mouth shut about something? I ask Paul, "What time did you see the car?"

Paul says, "Maybe eight thirty, nine in the morning."

Neither Ash's blog nor the standard news had said anything about Audrey's car being abandoned. Surely that's a detail that would have been hard to miss.

Ash walks in the hotel's front door. He's wearing a ridiculous floppy hat and his nose has a visible line of zinc sunscreen. I ask, "What's up with you?"

Ash says, "Stewart invited me to go on the fishing charter. I've never been deep sea fishing, and he seems to think it would make a great article, to get local perspective on some of the boats and their captains."

I say, "Well, you got here just in time. I need to ask you something."

"Oh?" Ash says. I guess he's still not used to me actually being happy to see him.

I ask, "Do you know where they found Audrey's car?"

"At her house, I'm pretty sure," Ash says. "One of her neighbors said how shocked she was to find out Audrey had died, since she thought she was home working. She didn't say what gave her the impression Audrey was working – in retrospect, I should have asked."

I say, "It seems a lot easier to narrow down the details of what happened to Audrey, than to figure out what was going on with Hernan and Amálie."

Ash says, "I wanted to float something by you. I'm thinking about starting a true crime podcast. I'm looking for a couple of co-hosts. And since you've been involved in some of the cases I want to cover, and you have an upbeat yet persuasive speaking style, I think you'd be a perfect addition. It would give you the chance to give your perspective on all of these events, and to share life lessons from having become a mega murder magnet. You could make money directly from the podcast, and it would be excellent advertising for your store."

I tell Ash, "We may be friends now, but there are some things we're still not going to agree on. I don't want to make money off people's pain, and I don't think my perspective on events would comfort anybody involved in any of them. What I want is for life to go back to normal."

Ash adjusts his ridiculous hat. "I know you, Felicity. If that happened, you'd be bored so fast. The notoriety may not be your favorite part, but there's worse things that could happen. Look at how people treated Jessica Fletcher. She was the original murder magnet, and people invited her to all the best parties. She's beloved by millions."

"Ash," I say slowly. "Jessica Fletcher is a work of fiction. Nobody really had to live in Cabot Cove. In a town that small, with a murder rate that high – people would have to be insane not to move."

Ash says, "Life is what it is, and people can adjust to any circumstance. Cabot Cove-rs probably didn't think anything was odd about it. I still think doing the podcast would help you process everything you've been through."

"I have enough with Tam Bin asking me to be a guest on a couple of cooking podcasts. I'm only doing that to support Carmen. The *Greeting and Felicitation's Cookbook* is hers, but she needs me saying how awesome it is."

"Really?" Ash says. "I'll have to ask Tam Binh about the whole project. She's a big deal in the blogger world, and I'm pretty sure she still doesn't like me. Maybe if I help Carmen too, it might change her mind."

"Tam Binh's in the kitchen right now," I say, gesturing down the hallway to the hotel's dining room, with its kitchen on the far side. "Compliment her coffee, and I'm sure that will get you off on the right foot."

I leave Ash to it, since I need to finish getting ready, so I can help handle the crisis at the shop. But I hope he and Tam Binh can sort things out, the way I've sorted things out with Kaylee. Sometimes people can be awesome inside, but for one reason or another you just don't mesh. Until one day you do.

As I'm heading in to check on the bird, with Charlotte appearing from around the corner as soon as I head for the door, I tell Ash, "If you and Imogen are looking for someone to do your wedding cake, Carmen's here too. That would be a huge way to show your support."

Charlotte must have been waiting for me on the staircase. I tell her, "I found out yesterday that Renoir is over forty years old. Can you believe that?"

Charlotte says, "He must have seen everything."

Yeah, I think, and too bad he can't really tell us about it.

Violet's been busy texting, so by the time I walk into the back of the shop and then through to where the tables are, there's already paper plastered over the windows. The inside of the paper is speckled with chocolate smudges and fingerprints. There are two guys I don't recognize mopping the floor, which looks gray with residual chocolate. I don't even bother asking who they are. Despite the mess, I can see the progress the artists have made on the sculpture. The white paper still allows light through, giving everything a calm, diffused feel. And the chaos I was afraid I was going to find seems to have calmed down.

Gently is working hard, and there are already two detailed panels for the sculpture sitting on a nearby table that he's programmed in and 3-D printed. One of them resembles a figurehead carving that has been sliced in half to allow it to lie flat in profile against the body of the sculpture. It is a large piece depicting a parrot, with immense detail in the feathers. If Destiny were here trying to hand carve it, it would have taken forever. I've seen eagles as figureheads before – but never a parrot. I wish I could have seen the original piece, before Amálie cut it. It might well have come from a pirate ship too.

Gently's cat is lying across his feet – which feels like progress, honestly. He seems to relax, at least a little bit, when he gets into his work.

But Destiny isn't here – and today, neither is Jonah – despite what he promised me yesterday. He probably decided that since I'm not a likely suspect for having killed Hernan and the others, he should pursue clues elsewhere. Marissa is here, though, which I didn't expect.

I say, "Thanks for coming in. I thought you had a charter you were supposed to be on this morning."

She gestures at a pair of crutches propped against the bookcase, and she gingerly moves her legs around from under the table to show off a neon pink wrap on her foot and ankle. She says, "This is what I get for being in a hurry. I literally fell off a curb with my hands full from the grocery store. My boss wasn't about to let me sail if I can't even stand on a boat reliably."

I make a sympathetic noise. I move closer and look at her hand carving work. I'm having a hard time telling what part of the ship she's supposed to be working on. I ask, "What's that?"

She says, "This is the roll that's supposed to be the base of the sails."

"Oh," I say. I look at it again, but I still can't see it. It looks more like she's making a lightning bolt. I think I'm starting to understand what she was saying about people not getting her art.

The real surprise is that Sonya, my friend who owns the yarn shop, is there helping with detail work. She's brought a couple of ladies I've seen hanging out at the yarn shop to help her.

Sonya says, "You should have let me know sooner you needed help. If somebody's going to sculpt knotwork, you can rely on knitters to know what it should look like."

The two women nod. And I have to admit, their work is a lot more realistic than what Marissa is doing. I hope Sonya isn't upset that I'd discounted her as an artist with a capital A by not calling her. People can get touchy about things like that. But Sonya is one of the most laid-back people I've ever met.

I tell Sonya, "I never realized you were into sculpture. I thought you worked exclusively in yarn."

Sonya says, "I took some generalized art classes when I was in college. I think even then a part of me knew that I wasn't cut out for the corporate world."

I look at her in surprise. Sonya and I haven't known each other for a super long time. Basically, just since I moved back to Galveston, about a year or so ago. But still, I thought I understood who she is. I say, "All the time we've spent hanging out, you never told me you had a corporate job."

Sonya says, "I don't talk about it because it isn't relevant. The coursework bored me to tears. But I was stubborn. And I wanted my parents to see me as a success. I got my MBA, tried to rise to the top, but just burned myself out. I rebuilt myself from the ground up, and knitting basically saved my sanity – and my life. And then when my sister wanted to move here for the job she'd been offered at the hospital, I decided to at least put part of that business knowledge to use when I opened up the shop."

I'm choked up with sudden, unexpected emotion. "I never realized we have so much in common."

After all, Sonya knows that I was a physical therapist with a thriving practice in Seattle, until my husband died and I felt the need to re-invent myself too.

Sonya says, "And when you found chocolate, you just knew you could be happy doing it, right? Without having to second guess?"

"Absolutely," I say. "Except for this morning." I gesture at the remnants of the choco- mess still on the floor. I ask Sonya, "How did that tempering machine get knocked over anyway?"

Sonya says, "Ruffles got up on the bookshelf. Gently was trying to get him to come down, so he was between the tempering machine and the shelf. One of those guys came over to try to help-" She gestures at the guys with the mops. "I'm not sure exactly what happened after that, but the machine tipped over, and Gently and the cat landed on top of it in a heap."

"Wow," I say. "I'm glad no one got hurt."

In part because I'm not sure what my shop's insurance would cover in a situation like that.

Violet comes out from the back. She takes a look at what Marissa is doing and says, "Great job." Her enthusiasm looks genuine. Which I hope means she has a way to blend Marissa's style with what everyone else is doing. Violet turns to me and says, "It looks like everything is under control here. Now that we can get back into the museum, I think I'm going to go back up there and start re-pouring some of the large slabs that got shattered."

"Do you need someone to go with you?" I ask. "That sounds like a lot for one person."

"Nah," Violet says. "I'll be fine." She gestures at the other artists and says, "They're all in their grooves. I don't want to mess with that."

There's something tense in her face, an anxiety in her eyes that I can't tie to anything specific. And I wonder if she has another reason for wanting to go back inside the museum by herself. She's one of the people with no solid alibi for any of the murders. What if she is the killer – and she wants to get rid of something left behind inside the museum? But even thinking that feels a bit paranoid. The police have been all over the museum.

What could she want to remove that they wouldn't have already seen? I force a smile and say, "Have fun, and call if you need anything."

Gently flags me down. He says, "Can I talk to you for a minute?"

"Sure," I say.

Gently picks up his cat and gestures me into the hall. I'm still a bit leery about going alone with anyone into that hallway. I'd once been trapped in my own office – which is at the end of that hall – with a killer. Gently isn't an intimidating person, but my nervous system is still sending fight or flight signals, in part because he's so much taller than me.

"What's up?" I ask as cheerfully as I can.

Gently pets his cat for a second, looking down at the black fur before responding. He says, "I saw something. Not the day the murders happened, but about a week before. The police asked me if I knew anything, and I didn't tell them. When I get anxious, it's easier just to shut down. But Violet trusts you. I'm hoping you can tell them."

"Of course," I say. "I'm going to see Detective Romero later today. I can pass along whatever you want me to say."

Gently takes a steadying breath. "Good. Thank you."

"What happened?" I prompt. "What did you see?"

It takes Gently a bit to get ready to speak. I can't help but wonder what happened to him. Anxiety disorder that severe usually has its roots in trauma of some sort. What he's experiencing is probably a stronger version of the fight or flight response I have from coming back to this hallway with a guy who's taller than me. I can empathize, even though I have no idea what he's been through.

Gently says, "You know how in the studio there's all that junk upstairs in the loft? Well, the policy is that if it's up there you can use it, so sometimes I re-use other people's old canvases. It's a time-honored tradition. Even Van Gogh used to re-use canvases, since he was always broke. If the painting wasn't good enough, or if the commission fell through, there was no reason to keep it."

"That's interesting," I say. And it is. But I have a feeling that's not the point.

Gently says, "I was up there, trying to find a canvas I could partially paint over. I wanted to leave some of the original art, for a contrast in style. And so I was focused. And quiet. But the acoustics in the loft are weird, so I heard Hernan and Audrey talking from downstairs. I could see them, partway across the studio, and they were talking to someone else, but I couldn't see that person. Or people. There could have been more than one. I couldn't hear everything, but Hernan kept saying things like, 'It belongs in a museum,' and, 'There's only going to be one.' And Audrey kept trying to convince him to do the project with them. I think she wanted him to work with her to make a piece for a competition or an exhibit, and, well, Hernan thought very highly of his own work. He probably presumed that his contribution to a joint project would have been so much greater than hers that it would be pointless. Maybe-" He makes a shruggy-rolling gesture, unable to go on.

But I can piece together what he wants to say. I say, "Maybe whoever the unidentified person was, they could have been so disappointed at the lack of cooperation that they decided to kill."

"Do you think that's what happened?" Gently asks.

And I suppose that's possible. It could have been about an art opportunity, since both reputation and jobs are prime sources for motive in a murder.

But so is greed. And it is possible – just possible – that Hernan was actually being the noble one in the scenario. If you put together Hernan saying, *It belongs in a museum,* together with Renoir mimicking someone having said, *It's for the history, not the glory!* – then maybe they were talking about the pirate wreck. What if Hernan was part of a small group that discovered the origin of the bell on Amálie's sculpture – only he decided that privately salvaging a wreck with that much historic meaning was wrong? His opinion would have been at odds with the others, including Audrey. But if he hadn't said anything to the police or to the news or to the museum, then what would the murderer's motive be to actually kill him? And if Audrey had been a willing part of the salvage plan, then what would have been the motive for killing her?

Gently is looking at me, waiting for me to say something.

I tell him, "I think this is something the police are definitely going to want to know. Thank you for telling me all of that."

Ruffles meows. I think for a second Gently must have been squeezing him too tight. Gently says, "It's nice to have someone believe what you say. Without second-guessing it, you know?"

I nod, wondering if there was a time in his past when he hadn't been believed about something important. Or if someone hadn't believed him over a long term about relatively insignificant things. But I can't ask without breaking this fragile friendship that we've just achieved. And talking about the specifics probably wouldn't help anyways. I say, "It's important to listen, don't you think?"

And I leave it at that.

Chapter Twenty

I've gotten to the point where I need to start working with the isomalt, and I've watched as many instructional videos as I can justify. Rosa had sold me some new silicone molds to quickly shape the molten isomalt. The polycarbonate molds we use for working with chocolate might be a bit problematic when you can't crack out the finished pieces by whacking them on the counter. Silicone, on the other hand, is flexible enough that you can turn each cavity in the mold inside out to press out a fragile piece.

Rosa also recommended thermal gloves, since working with isomalt or sugar is a lot like working with tempered chocolate, except for the fact that while chocolate tempers at close to body temperature, isomalt has to be hot enough that it will potentially cause serious burns. I'd also sprung for a couple of silicone mats meant specifically for sugar work. I probably could have used something we already had, but I'm a sucker for new kitchen equipment.

I get some of the isomalt crystals into a pot and add a bit of distilled water. While it's cooking down, I lay out all my molds and grease them. I get out a brulee torch from the cabinet, along with a couple of small knives. I'm going to tint the isomalt and use it to mold seashells and make filagree pieces. I'm going to use clear isomalt poured out onto the silicon mats and cut into circles and shaped to fill in the empty spaces in the portholes and light fixtures. I prepare a bowl of ice water to shock the hot liquid once it's done. It doesn't take long to get the isomalt melted down, then shocked and ready to work.

I get the molds filled, and pop the bubbles, so that I will wind up with pieces that really do resemble glass. I pour out more isomalt onto the mats and let it partially set, then I cut out free-hand circles. By that point, my seashells are ready to unmold. I lay them out on a separate mat, and hit them briefly with the torch, to give them more clarity and shine. A lot of it feels the same as what I do in working with chocolate – but the heat element and the torch make it feel like a whole new craft. Some of the videos I'd looked at had talked about working with pulled or blown sugar, and I can see how those elements would help the sculpture too – though I doubt I'd have time to master the much more difficult techniques I'd need to make sugar globes for buoys or the bodies of fish before the Gala.

I really am feeling like an artist today, and I think it might be fun to go a little more artistic with some of the products we sell in general. I'll need to brainstorm on that later. I take pictures of my isomalt work and add text to share on my social media. While I'm using my phone, I see that I got an e-mail from Miles. He's finished the presentation for the immersive cacao tree exhibit. When I follow the link he's given me, it's a 2-D preview that gives a hint of what the eventual project will feel like, and the images of the trees are beautiful even rendered on a flat screen. It's odd that I've never considered myself an artist, when really art is in much of what I do.

I send Miles a thank-you reply. He's really put in a lot of work to make me look good. I'm grateful to him – and to the artists currently working in the front of my shop.

I put all the equipment I've been working with away. Eventually Carmen is going to come back into this kitchen, and I don't want to leave her a mess. I carefully move the formed isomalt pieces out into the main area of the shop, where the artists can incorporate them into the chocolate pieces that they are working on.

I love the air of creativity in the room, and I wonder if there will be ways to keep that after this project is finished. Since the beginning, I've wanted my shop to be a gathering place in the community, where people feel comfortable staying a while to play the board games or read the books. I've done a couple of classes on chocolate molding and panning, as well as educational classes about appreciating craft chocolate, or even making it. Maybe I can figure out ways to expand that.

Gently stretches, then turns back to his laptop. Ruffles starts batting at his owner's shoelace, obviously wanting to play, but Gently doesn't seem to notice. "Guys," he says. "They just made an announcement about the grant. The winner is right here in this room."

"Who is it?" Violet asks, moving over to stand next to Gently's chair.

It has to be her. Unless one of the two guys currently mopping happens to be a gifted sculptor, or one of the knitter ladies, Violet is the only one here who is entered in the competition.

Gently smiles up at Violet. "It's you, of course. You've worked so hard. You deserve it."

Violet lets out a little squeak of happiness, literally bouncing on the balls of her feet. Her work is amazing, so she probably does deserve this win. But the fact that two of her competitors have died, and another one is in jail, has to take the shine off the victory. And Amálie had exercised some kind of influence on the competition too. I know it's a lot more compelling to believe that the murders were over pirate treasure, instead of over a grant – but when you really look at it, Violet does make a strong suspect.

After Violet's moment of excitement fades, there's sadness in her eyes, too. Which is what makes me doubt that she's actually a killer.

And if this really is about the grant, Violet is really the only one suspect who makes sense. Otherwise, if someone was bumping off the strongest competition – why kill Audrey, who seems to have been more of an underdog in the competition, but not Violet?

And why go through all the trouble of framing Tracie, who got eliminated early in the competition? I mean, Tracie probably was the logical person to frame, considering she had her own potential motives. But the way the killer had gone into her house, taken the project Tracie had been proud of – it seems like framing her was personal.

Marissa gives Violet a tight smile. "Congratulations."

"Thanks," Violet says. "You have no idea what this means to me."

"I have some idea," Marissa says, and there's a note of bitterness in her voice. "But honestly, those contests are all rigged for a certain art style."

Violet says, "Way to downplay my talent."

Marissa looks back down at her chocolate work, with the stylized take on the pirate sails. "That's not what I meant."

Violet says, "I'm sorry. I'm just touchy. Things have been stressful."

The tense moment passes, and they all get back to work. But Violet is humming a happy little song. And Marissa still looks unhappy.

I go into my office – the only place I know nobody in the building will hear me. It's probably because I just don't want Violet to turn out to be a killer, but I find myself questioning Marissa's negative attitude. Of course, her feelings are probably justified, to a degree. Marissa obviously isn't at the same level of artistic skill as the others. If she entered contests and was repeatedly rejected, it would make sense that she'd be frustrated when someone who works in the same studio gets accolades and recognition. It's a big jump from that to thinking she'd kill someone over it, though.

Still, it couldn't hurt to double-check her alibi. I call the tour company and wind up speaking to the same guy. I say, "I was afraid you'd be out with the charter trip today."

He replies, "I have captains to do that."

We chat for a bit about how the charter business works, where his passion for fishing came from, why he's operating out of Galveston. Turns out, he grew up land-locked in Oklahoma, and moved here a decade ago, because it's close enough to still get home if he needs to.

I say, "I know we already talked about this, but I just wanted to make sure. Is there any way Marissa could have gotten off that dock yesterday without you seeing her? You didn't get distracted or go to the bathroom?"

He says, "I didn't leave this counter. And after we talked yesterday, I started second-guessing myself, so I reviewed video from the security camera that faces out from the building. There's a clear view across the dock. Six hours of video, and nothing out of the ordinary."

I say, "I feel bad that I put you through all that trouble for nothing." I try and think of any other possibilities. "There's no way she could have taken one of the boats? Or gotten onto a skiff or something?"

"I would have noticed that," he says. "Our boats are big, but not big enough to require their own lifeboats, or anything she could have launched. And you can hear other crafts approaching."

"Fair enough," I say. "Can I ask you though? What do you think of Marissa as a person?"

He says, "She's a hard worker, and she really loves sailing. She seems to have a lot of friends, and there's always somebody calling saying she recommended us."

Which hardly sounds like somebody who's a multiple murderer.

"How long has she been working for you?"

He says, "On and off? Since she was in high school. Sometimes she leaves for dive trips, or to help her sister, but she always comes back. Honestly, she's always been a good kid."

I let him go, no closer to figuring out who killed Hernan and the others.

I go out front to where Carmen and Paul are selling chocolate bars and baked goods to the line of people. I spot the honeycomb cake that I missed last time, so I grab a piece off the table for myself. It's a gorgeous cake, with an airy interior full of holes and a waxy texture from the tapioca that really does make it look like a honeycomb. And I can smell the spiced coffee flavoring that Carmen has added, in place of the more traditional pandan. She's drizzled melted chocolate over the top – and this time it is my Peru chocolate. I take a bite. It's both chewy and fluffy, full of coffee flavor and spices without being overly sweet.

Carmen says, "You look happy."

I say, "This is so good. I have such talented friends, and when they work together, it's magic."

The next customer tells Paul, "I want to try that too."

The guy after that waves at me. "Felicity! Say death by chocolate, so I can record it for a ringtone on my phone."

I give him a tight smile. People have been trying to make that my catchphrase ever since the death at my shop's grand opening party. Ash had even used it in one of his first, less than flattering, articles. Emotionally, I have a hard time dealing with this type of customer. They have no tact or understanding of the reality of grief and loss. I say, "No one has actually been killed by eating chocolate in my vicinity. But you should be careful with chocolate around your pets. Dogs and cats should not eat anything with chocolate in it." I think about Renoir and add, "Or birds. Chocolate can be toxic to birds too."

There's no way he's going to turn that into a ringtone. So I win. I guess that thought is a bit passive-aggressive, but I'm dealing with a lot this morning. And I am not ready for dealing with this line of people, at least not on a one-on-one basis. As for the whole crowd at once, I wave generally at all of them, and I say, "Thank you for coming! Please make sure to attend the exhibition to see the finished sculpture and a mini-exhibit all about chocolate. The museum can use all of your support. And so can we."

There's a smattering of laughter from the folks in line. I'm starting to recognize some of them, and I feel happy to see the ones who ask intelligent questions and post good pictures of my chocolate.

The fact that this is starting to feel routine is not a good thing. For most people, having one murderer show up in their lives would be unthinkable. When I hit two, Ash called me a murder magnet in an article on his blog, because who has something like that happen to them? Especially going all their lives fairly far removed from violence. And now I'm up to four – in a single year. Which can't be good for my mental health. And now, my first instinct is to ask people questions, about their motives and their lives and their fears. And people, like the ones who keep making the trip out here, are starting to ask *me* for answers.

I pull Carmen away from the table for a moment and ask her, "What do you know about Marissa? Does she get along with Violet?"

Carmen raises her hand in a so-so gesture. She says, "Sometimes people's personalities just don't mesh. I don't think it was either one's fault. Violet likes to cultivate this whole edgy persona for her art and her online presence, but she's really a marshmallow inside. Marissa's genuinely edgy. She's snarky, and she's said things about Violet online before. You wouldn't think something like that would hurt someone like Violet, but at one point, it had her eating Blue Bell ice cream on the sofa while binge watching *Forged in Fire*. Which for Violet, is comfort viewing."

Interesting that Carmen doesn't see comfort-watching a show where they test out if knives and swords will kill as edgy. But I get what she's trying to say.

"Was the clash just between the two of them? Or did they not get along with the others either."

"I don't know about Marissa," Carmen says. "I only know what Violet told me about her. From Violet's comments, I don't think she's really close to anyone in the art community. Violet gets along with most people. But she had some problems with Tracie. Apparently, Tracie gets jealous really easily. But I'm not really part of the art community myself. I'm just a good roommate."

"I understand that." Carmen is also a good chef, and her baked goods are selling out quickly. She keeps glancing back at Paul and the giant line of hungry folks. She's going to have to go back inside soon to get more treats to re-stock the tables. I should let her get back to it.

I turn around and head back inside the shop. I gather up some get-well chocolates to bring to Arlo and check one more time to make sure everything is going to keep moving forward while I'm gone. Gently is the only one who pays me any real attention. He waves and shows off a chocolate take on the wooden fish that had been on the original sculpture. I give him a thumbs up.

Then I grab my purse and head out the back door. I drive over to Arlo's place. He lives on the other end of the island, past the entrance onto the bridge for I-45 but before you get to the State Park. The neighborhoods over there are named things like Pirate's Cove and Campeche Cove – more evidence of the influence Lafitte had on the island's history. Campeche was the name of Lafitte's short-lived settlement, and it had been peopled with rogues and criminals. From then till now, what good has ever come of pirates and the legends surrounding them? And yet somehow I can't seem to get away from the whole pirate myth right now.

The neighborhood is familiar. Arlo lives down the street from his mother. There's a logic to that that is very much in keeping with the younger version of him I had been in love with. Arlo has always had a huge heart, and a soft spot for family, so if he moved back home, obviously he would want to be near his mom, in order to help take care of her. But he's had a wildly independent streak, ever since he was a kid. He wouldn't want to move back in with her. His house is one of the smaller ones, more of a cottage, really, in a neighborhood of houses with grand beach-view patios. His place doesn't even face the water. Which shows his frugal nature.

I get out of my catering van and go knock on the door. Arlo's mother answers.

She looks surprised to see me. She says, "Dios mio, Felicity."

Which about sums it up.

"Hi, Mrs. Romero," I say cheerfully, like I didn't ever break her son's heart and then skip town for about a decade. "Can I come in?"

Reluctantly, she backs out of the doorway and gestures me inside. She says, "Arlo's in the kitchen, with a bag of peas on his head." The look she gives me says that she somehow suspects that that is my fault too. "I came over today to baby him a little while he's hurt. We're about to have some ropa vieja and plátanos."

"Oh, wow, that sounds delicious," I say, even though technically she hasn't asked me to join them. She turns to go back into the kitchen. Before she can, I say, "Mrs. Romero?"

She looks at me, questioningly.

I say, "I'm sorry, about everything that happened between Arlo and me when we were kids. And I was sorry to hear about your mom."

I can't read her expression, and she doesn't respond. She goes into the kitchen, and I follow. Arlo is sitting at a little wooden dining table that has been pushed up against the wall. When he sees me, he smiles. His mom gives me a questioning look.

Arlo says, "Mom, can you give use a minute?"

"Sure," she says, going over to stir the contents of a big pot on the stove.

Arlo gets up and leads me into the living room. He sits down on the overstuffed brown leather sofa and says, "I can only assume you're here to talk about what I said on the boat yesterday. Otherwise, you could have just called."

I sit down next to him on the sofa. "Did you get a new phone already?"

He says, "Actually, my phone turned up at the police station. It was turned in anonymously. Which makes the whole incident even more embarrassing."

I say, "At least you're alive. And safe. The doctor said you got hit with a branch or something. I can't help but feel like it was partially my fault for sharing those photos with you."

Arlo says, "You can't blame yourself because a crazy person tried to kill me. But you can be careful. That's all I ask."

I look him in the eye. "You think there's still a killer out there, too, don't you? Then why the heck did they arrest Tracie last night?"

Arlo looks embarrassed. "I wasn't there, or I would have tried to get them to wait. I'm still on the case, but I was obviously out of the loop for a bit, so at this point I'm just deferring to the detectives on site. You have to admit, their logic chain for arresting Tracie really is strong."

"It is," I say. "She is the obvious suspect. I can't prove it, but I know she didn't do it."

"Maybe it's for the best that she's been arrested," Arlo says. "It could help put the real killer off their guard."

"Maybe," I admit. "So much happened yesterday, it's hard to know what will help."

"Tell me about it." Arlo shifts the bag of peas to a slightly different part of his head. "So much indeed. Logan told me last night that he's actually going to be in your friend's wedding."

I knew Arlo wasn't going to take that well. I can't think of anything meaningful to say, so I settle for, "Yeah."

Arlo says, "I can't say that I'm happy about it. I told Logan that I had proposed to you, but hadn't received an answer. He took it better than I would have."

I put a hand on Arlo's arm. He catches my hand and draws me to him, and suddenly he's kissing me, right there in the open with his mom in the other room. And I find myself melting into the kiss. My hand is on his chest now, and I can feel his heartbeat quicken as his hand comes up to tangle in my hair. Forget the consequences. I close my eyes and just enjoy the kiss.

When we finally break apart, his eyes are glittering with emotion. He says, "Should I take that as a yes?"

"Arlo," I say. "I just – I just don't know. Things have gotten so complicated. And there's something we haven't talked about."

I feel his body language go tight against me. He says, "Oh?"

I nod, telling myself that what I'm about to say isn't going to be a big deal. Though I know it is. I tell him, "I know you're all about family. And you would make a great dad. Kevin and I – we were never able to have kids. So that probably wouldn't be part of the picture."

Arlo says, "I just want to be with you – whatever dynamic that looks like."

It's a big thing, him saying that. And looking into his earnest face – I can tell that he means it. Sudden tears blur my eyes, threatening to fall.

"Marry me," he says. "Please."

Part of me wants to say yes and kiss him again. But then a thought of Logan sitting comfortably next to me on that boat pops into my head. And I can't get past how much I'd miss that, too. But with Arlo, that kiss felt like going home. And in my confusion, those tears escape, dripping down my cheeks. I say, "Please. I'm not saying no. But I'm not ready to say yes."

Arlo says, "I don't understand. We know each other so well, and the spark's obviously still there. If we both want to be together, why deliberate?"

"Look," I say, pulling back both physically and emotionally as best I can. I shouldn't have kissed him like that. It wasn't fair. I try to explain myself. "I'm not ready to make a decision that is going to push one of the people I love to the side of my life. I care deeply about both you and Logan. And if you push me for an answer right now, I'm going to have to say no."

"That's not what I'm trying to do," Arlo says. "I know the position I've put you in is awkward, since you were already getting close to Logan when I realized my feelings for you were more than just nostalgia, and the timing makes it worse. I'm not trying to say you're wishy-washy or careless of other people's feelings because you haven't figured out what you want. But the uncertainty is driving me crazy. I can't just relax and let myself fall back in love with you, because it's going to hurt too much if you choose my friend over me. And at the same time, I can't give up hope that you're going to choose me, despite all of my mistakes. And somehow the hope is the part that hurts worse than the headache I had all evening yesterday in the hospital."

I laugh. Did he really just compare being in love with me to being hit on the back of the head with a tree branch? I tell him, "Give me until Autumn's wedding. I'll figure out what I want by then. I promise."

Having given myself a deadline immediately makes me feel somewhat better about the whole situation. I'm not floundering. I'm considering. And that feels completely different. Now, I don't know how I'll feel when the deadline to actually make the decision gets closer. But for right now, I feel more in control and less like I'm abusing either guy's affections.

I'll have to tell Logan what I'm thinking – it's only fair, and he's all about being fair, after all. But I'm not going to tell Autumn. I don't want to take away from her big day, or make her feel like it might be derailed into conflict.

Arlo takes in a deep breath, and I can see both hope and pain in his eyes. He says, "Don't be surprised if I do everything in my power between now and then to woo your answer in my favor. I've never been a big romantic like Kevin was, but I know what you like. So expect peonies and dahlias."

I play-shove his shoulder. "Arlo, you're allergic to flowers."

I didn't push him hard, but he brings a hand to his forehead. Apparently, he still has a headache and me jostling him just made it worse. I feel like that has killed the mood. I get a bit more serious and change the subject to everything I've uncovered about the artists.

Gently had specifically said he wanted me to share what he'd overhead with the cops, so I tell Arlo about the confrontation that Hernan and Audrey had with the mystery person Gently couldn't see. I say, "I think whoever they were talking to misjudged Hernan. I don't know whether Hernan is the one who figured out what the bell meant on that sculpture and he went looking for Culliver's diary, or if the killer had the diary and was looking to recruit him to help find the wreck. Or maybe Gently's right and this really was about putting together a team for an art project. Either way, the few times I met him, Hernan came across as arrogant and self-centered, so the killer probably thought that he'd be easily swayed by money. But he wasn't – and for some reason, that made him a liability. Tracie worked with Hernan, and actually seemed on good terms with him. So I don't think she would have made that mistake."

"Lis," Arlo says. "You know that logic isn't going to be enough to get Tracie released. Especially if Gently won't tell what he told you directly to the police. The case against Tracie is circumstantial, but it's strong. You need to be patient. I'm working on gathering other evidence."

"No you're not," I protest. "You're here, having ropa vieja with your mom."

Arlo laughs. "You should totally get in on that. I know you always used to appreciate my mom's cooking."

"I might have a little bit," I say, feigning reluctance. Because it is true. Mrs. Romero is an amazing cook. Unfortunately, she taught very little of that skill to her son.

Arlo says, "I'm waiting for a warrant to search Violet's place. Traffic cameras place her car about a block away from Audrey's house on the morning Audrey died. So, you see, I really am working on the case. And do hope that this time, you'll wait and let me do my job. I'm not second guessing you, but I do want to protect the woman I love."

I say, "Arlo. I'm not trying to get in the way of the cops, I promise."

Arlo looks a little skeptical. "I shouldn't even have told you about the warrant, except I think I'm still drunk on your kiss. Plus, the pain medication."

I wish he hadn't told me. Because ethically, I can't share that information with anybody, not even Carmen. And it's Carmen's home, too, that's about to get turned upside down.

Chapter Twenty-One

I stop in at the bookstore on my way back to my shop. Kaylee sent me a text saying she wants to show me something. When I get there, I don't see Kaylee at first. But after a moment, I spot her at the back of the store, folding up chairs and storing them in an oversized closet. Her bookstore has a tiny café area, but these chairs must have been for a somewhat larger event.

I grab a chair and start helping. I ask, "What's up?"

Kaylee says, "Possibly nothing. But I keep plastic tubs for each type of event we hold here at the store. Mostly it's just sign holders and tablecloths. I had a book club meeting in here, so I pulled out the tub with all the clipboards and stuff, and at the bottom, I found this."

Kaylee reaches into her pocket and pulls out one of Destiny's business cards. With a thick Sharpie, someone has written the words $100,000 Firm across the image on the back.

"Now that's interesting," I say. "Any idea what it relates too?"

"No idea," Kaylee says. "Maybe she's selling maritime salvage, and she killed Hernan for underselling her."

I say, "That's a stretch."

Kaylee says, "I wasn't being serious."

I say, "I know. But if we want to know what's going on, in this case, the only way is to ask."

I call the number on the front of the card. Destiny doesn't answer. Which isn't a complete surprise. I don't answer calls from numbers I don't recognize. I text her, *Hi this is Felicity. I have a couple of questions if you can call at your convenience.*

Almost immediately my phone rings. Destiny says, "What can I help you with?"

I explain about finding her card. I say, "A hundred thousand dollars is a lot of money. I just want to know what you're selling. Or buying."

Destiny says, "Selling, definitely. I'm liquidating my mom's collection of Beanie Babies because she's tired of them. She knew they were worth serious money, but she had no idea how to go about it."

"What's the top baby of the collection?" Kaylee asks loudly in my phone's direction.

Destiny must have heard her, because she says, "Believe it or not, my grandmother is a huge fan of Princess Diana. She actually bought my mom a Princess Bear."

Kaylee gasps. "A genuine one? Not the ones from China?"

"It's genuine," Destiny says.

I pull the phone away from my ear and put it on speaker phone. They might as well talk to each other directly. After they're done talking about the plush bear – which Kaylee is now considering buying – I say, "So if you're firm on the prices of these Beanie Babies, I take it you're not in need of money right now."

Destiny laughs, which sounds flat through the speakerphone. She says, "I do alright. I'm not crazy loaded like Syed. But Mom and I are comfortable."

I ask, "Have you heard the results of the grant?"

"Yeah." Destiny sounds disappointed, but not upset. She says, "I came in second. Which means gift cards to like a coffee shop and an art supply store. I'm not sure yet what else." She gasps, and her tone completely changes as she realizes what I'm really asking. "Are you saying you think somebody killed three people over grant money? And you thought it might have been *me*?"

"I didn't say that," I say soothingly. "I'm just considering all the possibilities."

Destiny says, "There's a reason they arrested Tracie yesterday. It's because she's the one would benefit most from a grant, isn't it?"

"That may be part of it. But there are other possibilities." I ask, "Have you ever sold any marine salvage? Like the kind of stuff Amálie used in the ship sculpture?"

"Me personally?" Destiny asks. "No. But if there's something you're looking for, I can help you find it. I don't mind. I help my mom with computer stuff all the time."

I tell her, "I'm not actually in the market to buy anything. I'm just trying to figure out if anyone who knew Amálie deals with wrecked ships."

Destiny says, "You should ask Marissa about that. She said something to me once about going treasure diving. But that's not really my thing."

And . . . the problem with that is that Marissa still has an alibi for Audrey's murder.

I say, "Okay, I'll do that." After all, it could prove enlightening. I add, "But I do have one thing that I didn't want to ask you yesterday in front of Jonah."

"Okay, shoot," Destiny says. It doesn't sound like she recognizes the irony of her word choice.

I say, "Someone told me that there are rumors that you dated Hernan after he broke up with Violet, but before he got together with Rosa? Is there any truth to that? Somebody else said that he broke up with Violet because he started dating Rosa. I'm looking for a timeline."

"That's not true at all," Destiny says. "I dated Hernan while he was still seeing Violet. I had no idea. When I found out he already had a girlfriend, I dumped his sorry butt."

I say, "So it's fair to say that you held a grudge against Hernan for the way he treated you."

Destiny says, "I know you know I have a temper. And yes, sometimes I do things I later regret. But I get mad, and then I get over it. I don't think it would be fair to say that I had a grudge against anybody. If he'd been dead immediately, it might have been me. Though I'd have poisoned him with snake venom. But if

I hadn't broken up with Hernan, then I wouldn't have gotten together with Jonah. So really, it worked out for the best."

A few minutes later, I hang up the phone, still confused about what kind of person Destiny is. Apparently, after her break-up with Hernan, Destiny had thought about killing Hernan, to the point of considering an ironic weapon. But she hadn't done anything, not then, at least. I don't know that she has a very strong motive now.

The door to the bookstore opens, and Autumn walks in. She sees me standing there, and she breaks into a grin. "What are you doing here, Mrs. Matron of Honor?"

"You know." I shrug. "Just hanging out with Kaylee."

Autumn gives me a nod. I think she's proud of me for solving the conflict on my own. Maybe I really am getting better at dealing with people.

"This is perfect timing." Autumn reaches into her bag and pulls out a dog-eared bridal magazine. "I wanted to get your opinion about the wedding favors. Drake thinks we should do gift bags for the guests, like they do at celebrity weddings, but make it all about reading and books, since books brought us together in the first place."

"That sounds intriguing," Kaylee says. "I have some adorable metal bookmarks, in the shape of a heart. And you can give people reading snacks, too."

"As long as you're not giving out any rare books, I'm in," I say.

Kaylee looks confused, but Autumn laughs. I think Autumn knows what I'm talking about. I don't need any new murder books to add to my collection.

This is confirmed when she says, "We wouldn't want to invite any unusual happenings, now, would we."

We spend a little while brainstorming about the best snacks to go with a book, and it's nice to have something simple and normal and fun to think about for a minute. I, of course, offer to do some limited-edition truffles to go in the bags.

I ask, "Which of the cake flavors are y'all going with? All of Carmen's samples looked amazing. I could echo the flavors from the cake in the truffles."

"We're going to do the lavender frosting on part of the cake, and a traditional almond on the rest," Autumn says.

Kaylee says, "If I ever get married, it will be to a guy who's happy with doughnuts." She sees the look on our faces and quickly adds, "And some really good coffee, of course. The guests would deserve that."

"Obviously," Autumn says.

My phone rings. It's my Uncle Greg. When I answer the call, he's laughing, talking to someone on the other end of the line.

I say, "Hello?" hoping he'll hear me and focus. After all, he's the one who just called me.

Uncle Greg says, "Felicity? Tell me you're safe. I just talked to the Coast Guard, and they told me you found a dead body on your dive yesterday. They seemed to think it was a huge coincidence that we know each other, which they found suspicious."

I move a few steps away from Autumn and Kaylee, not wanting to bring down the wedding planning buzz. I tell Uncle Greg, "That's true. Except for the suspicious part. But I'm fine."

"You're not fine," Uncle Greg says. "I can tell from the tone of your voice that you're getting all involved with something again. Killers are dangerous people. You've almost died now what, three times?"

I don't have a rebuttal for that. I say, "I'm being careful. But I don't know enough to put everything together yet. I think part of it had to do with the equipment theft aboard the rig. So, if you have any more information about that, I'd be grateful."

Uncle Greg says, "The Coast Guard recovered the stolen ROV late last night. Apparently, it had been hauled aboard some rich guy's catamaran. When the thief realized the police had staked out the boat, the thief tried to operate the ROV and get it to crawl overboard. Those things aren't meant to move on land, so it was dragging itself along, damaging the propeller in the process. It punched a hole in the side of the boat and did some serious damage on its way down. It's a wonder the whole catamaran didn't sink."

I say, "Poor Syed. I know the guy who owns that boat. He just got it, and he was so proud of it."

"How do you know it was his boat?" Uncle Greg asks.

"Long story," I say. "Let's just say that he's not the thief."

Whoever *is* the thief – and likely also a multiple murderer – is still out there. Uncle Greg doesn't seem happy about that, but there's not much he can do from aboard an offshore drilling platform. In the end, he agrees to keep an ear out for useful information, if I will in exchange give a giant hug on his behalf to my Aunt Naomi.

I've barely hung up when my phone buzzes with a text. Kaylee says, "Everyone seems to need to talk to you today."

I say, "Some days are just like that."

I check the text. It's from Logan, who has finally woken up from his nap. He, Carmen and Tam Binh are wanting to go for a late lunch before he has to leave for his flight, and they're wondering if I'm almost back at the shop. I assume that Paul and Stewart Jr. are also included in that count.

I ate a bit at Arlo's house, but I could still snack. I'm not going to turn down a chance to go out with friends on a day as stressful as today. I show the text to Autumn and Kaylee and ask, "Anybody in the mood for lunch?"

Autumn says, "Sure."

Kaylee says, "I'm a bit tired today. I think putting those chairs away really wore me out. Used to be, I wouldn't have to think twice about something like that."

Autumn says, "I'll bring you something back."

Logan, Carmen, Aunt Naomi, Tam Binh, Stewart Jr., Autumn and I all arrive at the same time at the Lemony Olive, a casual dining Greek place over on the Seawall side of the island. It's the kind of place where you order from a menu board, but they bring the food to you once you find a table. It smells amazing in here.

I'm about to order my go-to Spanakopita and a side salad when Stewart Jr. taps my arm. He stage whispers, "You need to get out of the shot."

"What, sweetie?" I ask, not sure what he's talking about.

Stewart Jr. gestures vaguely behind us. "There's another food blogger. We're blocking his shot of the menu board. Well, you are. I'm short."

I turn, just in time to see someone holding a camera with a giant lens step behind a pillar. Cold fear spikes through me, but I act like I didn't notice anything. I don't think this is the same person as the purse snatcher, but this guy is also wearing a mask. He's also got a hat pulled down low, shading his face.

I tell Stewart Jr. that it will be okay for the nonexistent blogger to wait for just a few minutes, and then I place my order while casually texting Logan to watch for someone trying to follow me outside. The guy taking my order gives me a dirty look for disrespectful texting, but there's not much I can do about that. People have already gotten hurt over whatever this is all about. I need to get this guy away from these innocent people – every one of whom I care about. I pay for my food, then I tell Autumn, "I need some air." I turn and head outside.

Carmen follows me. She asks, "Are you okay? You don't need your inhaler, do you? There's an old one you left in my car."

"It's not that," I whisper. I gesture vaguely up the street. "Walk with me. Quickly."

Carmen looks confused, but she doesn't ask questions. I guess she can see from the urgency on my face that something is amiss. I can see in the reflection from the nearby shop windows that hat guy has exited the restaurant not long after us.

The street is crowded with tourists and beachgoers, and the seawall is just across from us. Crossing over to it would leave us in the open, which I feel like is a mistake. Carmen and I stay on our side of the street. We turn, as soon as we can, onto a side street, then again onto a street parallel to the seawall and make our way up, back towards the restaurant.

It quickly becomes obvious that someone is following us.

Carman squeaks, "Is that the killer?"

"I don't know," I reply. "Hopefully we won't have to find out."

We start moving faster, and the guy starts moving faster, though he's trailing us at a slight distance. We're nearly running when we pass a house that has been converted into some kind of business. It has a big porch and oleander bushes.

When the guy passes the bushes, Logan jumps out and tackles him. Hat guy cries out, and there's something vaguely familiar about his voice.

I turn back. "Jonah?"

Logan pulls off the guy's hat and mask, and sure enough it's Jonah. He must have hit the street hard, because he's cradling his camera more carefully than he's holding himself.

"Hi, Felicity," Jonah says miserably. He looks up at Logan and asks, "Do you think you could get off my legs."

Logan stands up. Jonah starts to get up too, much more slowly.

"Why are you doing . . . this." I circle my hand, encompassing his hat, his camera, his bleeding elbow. "I thought I convinced you I couldn't be the murderer."

Jonah says, "You did. I wasn't following you. I was following her." He points at Carmen.

"Excuse me, what now?" Carmen says. She looks irritated.

Jonah says, "I was trying to figure out whether you knew anything. Your roommate has all these secret meet-ups with Hernan, and then Hernan winds up dead. All this feels too complicated for just one person to have committed these crimes alone. You're the logical choice for an accomplice."

"You could have just asked me," Carmen says. "Instead of scaring me half to death. There's laws against stalking, you know."

"Go back," I say. "What secret meetings?"

Jonah pulls out his phone. He's taken photos of sign-in logs at one of those co-working-rent-an-office places – over on the mainland, in Friendswood. There are Hernan and Violet's names, one after another in the logs, on a dozen different dates.

"How did you even find this information?" Logan asks.

Jonah pockets his phone. "A detective never reveals his secrets."

Carmen says, "I'm pretty sure that's a magician."

I don't care how Jonah got his information. I just want to know what it means. I would expect clandestine meetings to take place at seedy hotels or back alleys. But the location of a meeting always depends on its purpose. What exactly was Hernan doing meeting his ex-girlfriend away from the prying eyes of the island – in a computer cubicle?

Chapter Twenty-Two

We head back to the restaurant. Logan grabs his go bag out of the catering truck, and then I use some of the contents to patch up Jonah's elbow.

I tell him, "There's no way Carmen was involved in any schemes or murders."

Jonah looks skeptical. "How can you possibly know that?"

I feel heat flaming into my cheeks. "Before I knew her better, I accused her of murder once myself."

Jonah says, "Because that's a sentence a normal person would say."

I give him an ironic look.

He says, "That's not the kind of logic that makes sense anyway. If Carmen was suspicious once, she is still suspicious."

I look over at Carmen, who is talking to Logan just outside the doorway of the restaurant. I say, "You don't know Carmen. I trust her with my life."

Carmen's phone rings. She says something to Logan and steps away to answer it. At first she's laughing – but then she's listening to whoever is on the other end of the line, getting more and more upset.

I move over to where she's standing.

Carmen hangs up the phone. She says, "The police just searched my house. They had a warrant to look through Violet's things, but how are they supposed to separate my things from hers?"

"Did they find anything?" I ask.

Carmen gives me a reproachful look. "I have nothing to hide."

"Not you," I say. I hesitate, but I have to tell her, "I think it's possible Violet's involved in these murders. You don't happen to know why she's been meeting her ex-boyfriend, do you?"

"No," Carmen admits. "But Violet's not a violent person. And she's direct. She would be more likely to tell you why you made her mad, and to make your life miserable over it, than she would be to hurt you for revenge."

"So don't cross Violet," I say. "Good to know."

But if Violet's the kind to get even, and to potentially hold grudges – how can Carmen be sure of where she'll draw the line?

"Why was she even home?" I ask. "Wasn't she at the shop earlier, supervising work on the sculpture. Or on her way to the museum to work there?"

"I asked her to go by and check on Bruno," Carmen says. "She told me she was going to take a nap and then head to the museum. All of this has been stressful for her. She was probably asleep when the cops showed up."

"So did they find anything?" I ask again.

"Oh, come on!" Carmen says.

I'm not sure what there'd even be to find. The murder weapons were both at the scenes, and the bullets and the sedative were both taken from containers at Tracie's house. There haven't been fingerprints – at least not any Arlo has been willing to talk about – but just owning a pair of gloves wouldn't be enough to make Violet suspicious. Maybe the cops think she has the original book of Culliver's diary, or that she might have kept the ship's bell. I suppose when you're looking for evidence, you don't always know what it will be until you find it.

We all still have work to do, and Jonah doesn't seem to have any other unexpected insights, so after lunch, Logan and I head for the museum. I promise Carmen and Tam Binh that I'll only be there for about an hour, then I'll head over to Felicitations to record the podcasts.

Logan is driving the catering truck, so on the way to the museum, I call Rosa. When she picks up, it sounds like she is at the cake shop. In the background, someone is asking for tips on the best way to level cake layers. Rosa sounds neutral – she's probably not excited to hear from me, in case I want to talk about her husband's murder, but I'm also a customer, so I might be calling to place a giant order. I try to think how I can tactfully broach what could potentially be a painful subject.

I ask, "I was just wondering, did Hernan keep an office anywhere? Artists have to do business too, right?"

Rosa sounds confused. She says, "Why would he need an office outside the house? He had an office at home. The police searched it. They took his computer and his files, but you're welcome to take a look at the rest of it, if it helps."

I say, "That probably won't be necessary. I just want to know if he had anywhere else besides the studio that he would go to work. Maybe somebody's office he visited regularly."

"What an odd question," Rosa says. "He worked mainly from home, unless he was physically making art. Then he went to the studio." After a moment, she adds, "Oh, well, sometimes he went to his friend Syed's house. There was some kind of ocean project he was working on there."

Which is something I already knew. I make a noncommittal noise. The main thing I've learned here is that whatever Hernan and Violet were doing, Rosa had no idea about it.

I tell Logan, "It's a bit overwhelming how many different directions all of this could have gone. I've narrowed it down to about three people who potentially had reasons to kill all three victims. But there's no proof."

Logan says, "Sometimes you just have to trust your instincts. Pick the path that feels most logical, and if it turns into a dead end, try something else."

So take a shot in the dark.

I say, "I'm afraid the most logical path ends with Violet being arrested for murder. Though I don't have a clear picture of why she did it."

"I'm afraid of that too," Logan says.

We ride in silence until we get to the museum, and when we park around back there's a couple of cars already parked in the lot. I recognize Violet's Subaru. And Gently's truck. I wasn't sure Violet would really be here, after her place got searched. But apparently the cops really didn't find anything.

We go inside. I can see Logan loosening his jacket, to make it easier to get to the gun I know he's carrying, should he need it.

"Is that really necessary?" I ask Logan.

He says softly, "You just said you think Violet's a killer."

Logan knows I'm uncomfortable with violence and with guns in general.

I say, "I'm just planning to talk to her." I gesture around the studio. There are a couple of people working here today, different artists that I haven't yet met. "And it's not exactly like we're alone here."

Logan says, "I'm here to follow your lead. You have an outside the box way of solving things that I like to watch. But I'm not about to let anything happen to you."

I lead the way into the studio. Violet and Gently are working in the open area in the middle of the room, where we were doing the preliminary assembly of the sculpture. Violet is up on the scaffolding, which gives me a moment of déjà vu. Gently is being a lot more careful about working down below than Amálie had been. Ruffles is on a leash, and tied to a workbench, which the cat is gleefully scratching on to sharpen his claws.

Revisiting this scene, with Violet out in the center of everything, it occurs to me again how bold the killer must have been. There aren't any security cameras in the studio, and people are always carrying in cases and bags of supplies. So there's not a definable record of how Tracie's Rube Goldberg components got in the building. But the killer had to get up to the loft and set things up, and attach the other pieces of the machine either in front of other people working in the space, or with the potential of someone walking in at any moment. And nobody had noticed.

According to Tracie, people sometimes work on their projects all night. But the door between the studio and the museum is always supposed to be locked. Which means the real question is how somebody got into the museum to deface Amálie's original sculpture in the first place. It had to be either someone who belonged in the museum, or someone who walked in past the camera at the entrance and signed in.

I tell Logan, "We should take a look at the entrance sheet for the day of the break in. Maybe we're missing something."

"Not a problem," Logan says. "I can get us through that door, when there's a quiet moment."

Violet and Gently get the slabs of chocolate lined up, and the supports in place. Once it's all stable, Gently gives Violet a thumbs up. Violet sees us and waves. Then she starts to descend the scaffolding.

"Hey," she says. "I didn't think you were coming here today. Don't you have all those podcasts to record?"

I tell her, "We just wanted to get a few things started printing on the plastic 3-D printer, so they can be covered in chocolate at the shop. And I want to preview my presentation for the immersive cacao tree exhibit before I send the file to Delo – I mean Mrs. Cook."

Violet says, "The museum is closed on Friday. I don't think you'll be able to get in."

"Don't worry about that," Logan says. "If we need to, we can get in."

Violet gives him a questioning look, but she lets it go. She says, "I'd like to see the preview of your immersive photography. I know how to operate the computer to get it started."

"That would be great," I say.

Gently says, "We brought the small tempering machine from the shop, so we could pour more of the chocolate slabs for the other side of the boat. I'll bring it back later, so you can do your bonbons."

"That's very thoughtful," I say.

Logan walks over to the door separating this space from the museum. He tries turning the handle but nothing happens. He stands squarely in front of the door, and after about thirty seconds, it opens. Gently gives me a questioning look. I gesture that he should go through. Gently starts to say something, but he thinks better of it and instead goes and unties Ruffles. He leads the cat on the leash through the door into the museum with him.

Violet follows. Once we have the door closed and locked behind us, she says, "I think we're making good progress on the main body of the sculpture. This is a really cool project, and I'm happy to be a part of it, despite the tragedy. I still can't believe Hernan and Audrey are gone."

I notice that she didn't mention Amálie. Logan gives me a significant look. He noticed too.

Logan tells Violet, "Let's get the presentation queued up."

Violet heads for a door on the other side of the gallery we've found ourselves in. Logan and Gently both follow her. I make my way through the galleries to the front, to the stand where the sign-in sheets are kept. The lighting in here is dim, giving everything an eerie quality. I pass a picture of the beach, with swimmers in old-fashioned dress and the figures seem to be laughing at me.

But this is the same cheerful place I had been not long ago, when I'd first met Renoir. I shake off the creeps, and I pull the clipboard with the sign-in sheets out of the stand. I guess there are a lot of places that still require paper signatures, and on this sheet, there's a place to give the museum an email address and a phone number – likely for event updates and donation requests.

I flip back through the papers until I get to the day I'd first arrived. I find my own signature on the sheet. I scan down the list of names. There's only one I recognize: Audrey Scruggs came in about an hour before the break-in. It wouldn't have seemed odd to anyone. She's an artist who's here frequently to work in the studio. And with so few cameras, it would have been easy for her to get past them, and slip into the closet that holds the breaker box. It's mostly a hunch, but I'm certain she's the one who messed with the power, allowing the sculpture to be damaged. She likely came and left, installing something that would control the power, well before the actual break-in.

If I'm right, that means that Audrey was working with the killer, at least initially. It's possible that whatever she did to the power during the break-in is what allowed the killer to shut off the power in the studio later. Maybe she wasn't working in the studio that night because she was somewhere remotely shutting off the lights. Or maybe the killer chose the time of the murder specifically because Audrey wasn't there. I choose to believe it was the latter, unless proven otherwise.

I make my way back to gallery with Amálie's ship sculpture, arriving just in time to see the area off to the side light up with what looks like a cacao plantation. I walk into the space, to get the full effect. Miles did an amazing job, adding text from the captions I had put on my Instagram feed, building transitions that make me feel like I'm really traveling, adding in images of people I've met – farmers and chocolate makers – along the way. It's beautiful and personal – and suddenly there are tears running down my cheeks. I started this whole chocolate making journey to honor my late husband, and dreams we'd had together. Looking at this – I think he would have been proud. And that gives me a profound sense of peace.

I sense movement as Violet, Logan and Gently join me. Logan obviously isn't going to let Violet go anywhere without shadowing her. But honestly, even if she is a killer, I don't think she's stupid enough to try anything when it would be so obvious that she would be the only one who could have done it.

We stand there as the rest of the presentation runs through. It's about fifteen minutes worth of material. When it ends, the room fills with white light, making all of us stand out against the shadows outside this small alcove.

Violet says, "I forgot to click the button that would have this loop. During the actual exhibit, it will run continuously, with the opening and ending slides signaling people when it's time to enter and exit."

I look over at Logan. He's wiping at his eyes. Did he cry a little in the dark? Does he care about me that much?

He doesn't look like the kind of guy who cries over anything, and he's done both strong and terrible things. Right now, I don't know what to think. Especially not after the passion I'd felt when I'd kissed Arlo. Logan is sexy too, in a more controlled and self-assured way. And apparently his emotions run just as deep, even if he's trying hard not to share them.

But right now is not the time to focus on my personal life. I'm here with someone who may well have killed three people. I need to be asking the right questions, trying to find justice – and making sure this exhibition actually gets to happen, for Amálie's legacy, and more selfishly for my own business.

But I'm still not convinced for sure that Violet is guilty. And if she's not, I don't want to add stress to her relationship with Gently unnecessarily.

I know Logan's not going to like it, but I ask Violet, "Can I speak to you alone for a moment?"

Violet looks up at me in the bright lights, and I swear she looks frightened. She says, "I'm not sure I want to do that. Not here, anyway. Anything you want to say to me, you can say in front of Gently."

Of course. When does anyone ever actually let me talk to them alone?

"Okay," I say slowly. "We found out that you and Hernan met up secretly multiple times at a co-working space in Friendswood. What were you doing, and why were you hiding it?"

Violet casts a distressed look at Gently. I bet she wishes she had gone for the option of talking to me alone. But it's too late for that now.

Gently says, "Violet? Hun?"

Violet takes a steadying breath. "It's not what you think. We were working on art for a video game."

Gently asks, "Why would you hide that?"

Logan asks, "Are you even qualified to do that?"

Violet answers Logan. "I took a couple of classes. But Hernan didn't think Rosa would understand him spending that much time with his ex. We weren't hiding what we were doing, we were hiding the fact that we were working on it together."

Gently says, "I'm not sure how I feel about *you* spending that much time with *your* ex."

Violet says, "Well, he's dead now, so it's a moot point."

Gently's face registers shock, which I'm sure is what Violet had been going for. Gently's not the kind of guy who wants to be seen as callous, or jealous of someone who got murdered. Gently picks up the cat and starts petting it, perhaps a little too hard. Ruffles sinks his freshly sharpened claws into Gently's arm. Gently drops him and Ruffles runs off, trailing his leash behind him.

Gently follows after Ruffles. Violet follows after him, calling, "Babe. I'm sorry."

Logan and I look at each other. Logan says, "If she and Hernan were working together, there's not much motive in killing him."

I add, "Especially before they finished the project." I gesture off into the shadows the couple had headed into. "And obviously Gently didn't know anything about it. So it's not like jealousy would give him a credible motive either."

Logan starts heading in the direction Gently had gone, so I follow. I quickly tell him what I found out about Audrey and her visit to the museum.

Logan says, "That means she was either killed because she was a loose end, or because she decided the killer had gone too far, and she tried to change sides."

I say, "It's driving me crazy that I can't figure out which."

Suddenly, all the lights in the museum flip on. Gently shouts, "Hey, look at this."

We rush over to where the door is now open to the closet holding the breaker box.

Logan stares at the breaker box, studying it critically. Finally, he says, "What exactly am I looking at?"

Gently, who is now holding firmly onto Ruffles' leash, points at a tiny green rectangle at the top corner of the box. He says, "This came off Violet's Rube Goldberg machine entry. Her remote for it still works."

Logan turns towards Violet and arches an eyebrow. Because she might not actually have much motive – but she's collecting almost as much circumstantial evidence as Tracie had.

Violet says, "On my machine, it allows you to change the colors of the LEDs and set off the drone that holds the glitter storm. But I haven't looked at it since I got it back after the demos for the grant competition."

Logan says, "But you have the remote."

Violet holds up a set of keys, with a futuristic-looking chrome oval. "I made a couple of remotes as I was working out the design. This one is a keychain. I thought it looked cool, so I left it on my keyring."

Whoever killed Hernan and the others obviously attended the demos Violet's talking about, which explains how that person knew about both Tracie and Violet's designs. I can't decide whether that means we're looking for someone innovative, seeing new applications for the machines, or someone who just steals someone else's work.

I ask Violet, "What about what you said about Hernan being arrogant and annoying? You said it was to the point that Rosa might want out of their relationship. So why would you work with him?"

Violet says, "Hernan was arrogant and annoying. But he was also brilliant and funny and loyal. He was about to have a kid, and he wanted to be able to buy all the things that kid was going to want. I'm still saving for my trip to France. So when the video game project came up, we agreed it would solve both of our problems. And when you're not dating Hernan, the annoying things about him don't seem as annoying. Because there's distance, you know?"

"I can see that," I say. I tell Logan, "There's one more thing I want to check on while we're here."

I go through the galleries that lead to the hall that will get me into the library. Logan had said I should trust my hunches, and I'd had a hunch that Hernan might have hidden some of his research materials in plain sight. And sure enough, on one of the shelves in the library, I find the books on treasure wrecks that Rosa had said Hernan had had in his study. I flip through them, but nothing falls out, and there don't seem to be any hand-written notes. I suppose that not all the books that show up in my life are going to have clues. But the question is why Hernan would have bothered hiding them?

Violet watches me searching the books. She asks, "Anything there I can help you look for?"

"Nothing specific," I say.

Gently asks Violet, "Did you still love Hernan? Be honest. I can take it. Because what you just said kind of sounds like you did."

Violet puts a hand on Hernan's cheek. She says, "On some level, you always love someone you gave your heart to without reservation. And I was glad that that love had turned into something that let us work together seamlessly. But it was friendship love. I promise. It was nothing like the way I love you."

Gently says, "Just – trust me to understand, in the future. I don't do well when people lie." That must be a reference to whatever trauma has shaded Gently's past.

"I know," Violet says. "And I'm sorry."

So much of this keeps coming back to Violet, though, and I remember another reason I'd thought of Violet as suspicious: someone had to know that Syed was taking Violet's place in that class, and that presumably his boat wasn't going to be missed. Of course, whoever took the catamaran hadn't planned on damaging it while getting the ROV on board, or on me and Logan finding the ROV before the thief had a chance to move it.

I ask Violet, "Did you tell anyone you were planning on giving up the spot in that class to Syed? I mean before that morning, when you showed up at my shop."

Violet says, "I told Carmen, when she asked me to help with the sculpture project. And then I called everyone Logan had invited, to see who was coming."

So absolutely everybody knew. Curse Violet's organization skills.

Chapter Twenty-Three

Carmen and Tam Binh have set up three fancy microphones in the kitchen at Felicitations. We would probably get better sound quality in a smaller, more padded space, but Carmen is convinced that the ambiance we'll get from being in the kitchen is worth any loss in acoustics.

We're pre-recording several sessions, so we're going to be in here for a while. Logan is out doing his other job –he's flying a client to Houston – but he should be back for at least one of the sessions. The artists out in the main part of the shop have been coming and going throughout the day. There's a few of them out there now, but they're working quietly as the energy winds down towards quitting time.

We start the first recording. Tam Binh talks about Greetings and Felicitations, giving a brief history of the shop, and asking me to add in more details. Then she interviews Carmen about where she got her ideas for the cookbook, and why she has such a specific philosophy about flavor – and how the need to pair everything she's been making with craft chocolate has affected the way she adds herbs and spices into the recipes.

But soon the conversation turns more casual, with each of us sharing stories about the food-related adventures we've had. I talk about how I'd spent a day on one of the cacao farms I'd visited helping harvest cacao pods with a machete, and how nice everyone had been about it when I'd had an asthma attack. Which of course leads to me explaining about the treatments I've undergone, and how my asthma symptoms have all but disappeared.

Carmen starts talking about visiting her extended family in Mexico, and making tamales in bulk, with women who insisted on grinding the corn for the masa from scratch. She explains the process of nixtamalization, which uses slaked lime to soften the kernels. Then she moves on to talking about the uncle that took her wildcrafting for herbs and cactus paddles, and how hard it is to prepare nopales without getting at least a few cactus spines in your hand.

Tam Binh pauses to consider what story to tell from all her culinary world travels. She says, "It wasn't as delicious as your experiences, but there was this one time Stewart and I ate barnacles right off the boat we were traveling in. They were tiny, because it wasn't the gooseneck barnacles most people consider a delicacy, but we were on this sustainability tour, and they were proving a point about thinking outside the box when it comes to food."

Carmen says, "I didn't even know barnacles were edible. All I've heard is that they increase fuel consumption in boats because they increase drag."

Tam Binh says, "Barnacles are actually related to lobster. In Portugal and Spain, the gooseneck ones are harvested off rocks that are repeatedly hit by the ocean. It's quite dangerous, as the people get pounded by waves. What we did was tame by comparison. Our tour guide hooked us up with a diving hookah – which is a surface-supplied air setup – and we got little scrapers and mesh bags and we went under the boat."

I feel like what she's saying is trying to make a connection in my brain, but I'm so nervous trying to think of what I'm going to say next, that I can't decide to what. And the fact that that connection refuses to be made is making me more anxious.

While Carmen and Tam Binh are talking, I scroll through my Instagram feed, looking for a bunny pic or maybe even video clips of Ash's cavorting kitten to calm my mind. Instead, I find that Ash has posted a set of pics from the charter boat, probably a few preliminary shots he took in case he can use any of them for his blog article. There's a dining room inside the boat, set up for maybe twenty people, with a bar off to one side. There's a closer-in shot of a bored-looking bartender. And at the edge of the photo, there's a fake palm tree in an oversized green pot. And behind the pot, there's a silver panel bolted into the wall. And in my head I hear Renoir saying, *Behind the green flower pot.*

I wouldn't have phrased it that that way, but it is possible that the oversized pot I'm looking at is what the person Renoir picked that phrase up from had been referring to.

And if my guess is right, that person may well be in my shop right now, so I don't want to be overheard.

"Excuse me," I whisper to Carmen. "But I need to step outside."

Carmen gives me a panicked look. And I understand that she would like to get this all in one take – but it isn't going out live. Tam Binh is still speaking into the microphone. When Tam Binh pauses, Carmen leans forward and starts talking about the notoriety Greetings and Felicitations has gained, and how she has been able to handle it. She'll be talking for a while, I suspect.

I head out the back door, but it feels a little out-in-the-open standing in the alley. And Logan's not here yet, so nobody has my back. I head down the alley to the lot where I parked my catering truck. I get inside and lock the door. Not that I'm expecting anyone would approach the truck, and I feel a bit silly, but I don't unlock it.

I call Ash. I'm not sure he has phone reception that far out on the water, but I'm hoping that if he is Instagramming, the signal is strong enough to talk. And the call connects. I feel actual elation. When Ash picks up, I ask, "Can you get somewhere alone?"

"I can try," he says, "But this isn't a private charter. There's a lot of people on this boat."

I wait through the noises of Ash moving, and people talking, and then wind blowing. He's probably moved up onto the second-floor deck at the top of the boat.

He says, "What's up?"

I ask, "Did anyone else seem interested in that green flowerpot?"

"What green flowerpot?" Ash asks.

"The one you just posted in your Instagram feed."

"Hold on," Ash says. I get the idea that he's moved the phone away from his ear to get a look at what I'm talking about. After a few moments, he says, "I don't know that anybody noticed the pot, but a couple of people did take pictures with the palm tree. This is something like you crossed a party barge with a serious fishing charter. Half the people on board aren't even planning on fishing. And they're doing a three-course French-style lunch."

"Sounds like a great day," I say. "And I hate to interrupt it. But I'm hoping you can do me a favor. You saw that panel in the picture behind the flowerpot? It's a hunch, but I think there's a clue hidden inside that panel. Is there any chance you could take a look?"

"With that bartender guy just hanging out?" Ash asks. "That sounds complicated."

I'm disappointed, but I try not to sound it when I say, "Oh. Okay. I just thought I'd ask."

"Now wait a minute," Ash says. "I'm not about to pass up the chance to actually be part of the story this time. I'm just saying it sounds complicated. I could try to steal a screwdriver and lock the guy in the bathroom or something."

"How likely do you think that is to work?" I ask.

"Less likely than if I just walk up to the guy and tell him what I'm doing. Most people are curious. If I tell him there might be something in the wall, there's a fifty-fifty chance that he finds me that screwdriver. What do you think is in there?

"I don't know," I admit. "Hopefully something that tells us whether these murders were about an art rivalry, a pirate ship – or something else entirely."

"Dang," Ash says. "If I tell the bartender that, he might go open the wall himself. Seriously, you really should be on the podcast if you can come up with those kinds of turn of phrase off the top of your head. And it would be great if I'm busy and we need things scripted. You could get credit as a writer."

"I'm more of a reader," I say. "But thanks."

"Let me put you on speaker phone. You'll be in my shirt pocket so you can hear what happens." There's noise as he moves the phone, and then I hear him talking to people as he makes his way back downstairs and then inside.

And it turns out that Ash was right. When he tells the bartender what he suspects, the guy says, "Wait here a minute. There's a tool kit in the storage closet." After a few minutes the guy comes back and says, "Let's take a look."

There's the faint noise of metal on metal, then a louder *boing* as the panel moves. And then the guy says, "Dude! What is all that?"

Ash says, "I'm not sure. This looks like a journal." He talks directly to his phone, saying, "Felicity, this claims to be a journal belonging to Terry Culliver. And there's a bunch of rolled up maps of the Gulf. I assume they have a specific purpose that I don't understand."

"They're maritime charts," the bartender supplies helpfully. "With handwritten notes, and a literal x-marks the spot."

I say, "That must be the course of Culliver's previous trip through the Gulf," I say. I don't want to say that x might mark literal pirate treasure. That could put Ash into a complicated situation, if the guy decides to try to take the charts away from him. "Finding that diary in that spot connects some threads I've been trying to pull together."

"Felicity," Ash says. There's something ominous in his voice. "That's not all that's in the space. There's also a phone and a set of keys. And one of the keychains is a cartoon cat that says Audrey."

A flash of cold goes through my chest as that information hits home. "Oh my."

There's only one person who could logically have hidden all of those things on board this particular boat: Marissa Reid.

And if she had gotten stuck with Audrey's keys . . . there's only one thing that makes sense. She had seemed a little odd at the dive shop, when I'd seen her yesterday. That must have been shortly after she'd killed Audrey then snuck back aboard the boat she was doing maintenance on. However she'd actually managed to do that. Maybe she was at the dive shop replacing something that had gotten damaged during the theft – or during Audrey's murder – something that she had to get replaced aboard the ship she was working on, or aboard Syed's ship before it was missed. Marissa had to have dropped off Audrey's car and then taken other transportation back to the marina, only to realize once she got back to the boat that she still had Audrey's keychain. She'd stashed it instead of throwing it overboard, so she must have had some kind of plan for returning the keys that somehow didn't work out, probably because she wasn't able to sail today.

I think about how Paul had mentioned seeing Audrey's car on the wrong end of the island for her to have been getting on Syed's boat, relatively early in the morning. Audrey wouldn't have been far from where the charter Ash is currently aboard had been moored. Not far at all from where Marissa had been doing maintenance alone on her boss's boats – including that vessel.

And then the connection my brain has been trying to make hits home: Tam Binh had just told me that people use hookah diving systems when they go down to scrape boat hulls. So there would have been dive equipment aboard the charter boats or in the marina. There might even have been air tanks in addition to the hookah.

And . . . I feel dumb for not questioning Marissa's alibi more. She's clearly a diver. And the pixie-cut hair I'd taken for slicked back could just have been wet from being in the ocean. There's no reason she couldn't have donned scuba gear and swam underwater away from the dock, to somewhere she couldn't be seen from her boss's office or the video cameras, or noticed by anyone as she was emerging unexpectedly from the bay. And where Paul had seen Audrey's car parked would have been near just such a secluded spot. It would have been a long swim, which is probably why her boss discounted the idea, but for someone as athletic as Marissa, it might have been doable.

Then she could have gotten into Audrey's car and driven to the other marina to hotwire Syed's boat. Assuming that Audrey had indeed helped with the break-in that had allowed Marissa to take the ship's bell from Amálie's sculpture, she would have been complicit in the theft. Audrey would even have wanted to help Marissa create her alibi – never knowing that Marissa has stashed everything needed to murder her aboard Syed's boat in advance.

I ask Ash, "Can you turn on the phone? Is there any chance it might be Amálie's?"

"It goes to a lock screen," Ash says.

The bartender says, "Try 1-2-3-4. That's what a lot of people use."

A second later, Ash says, "Yes, it's hers."

"That means the killer and the purse snatcher really were the same person," I say. And Marissa's short hair and athletic build make it make more sense that in a mask and an oversized sweatshirt, Kaylee had gotten the impression of a guy. And Marissa's twisted ankle makes sense now too. I bet she got it going over the wall after she hit Arlo. Which means that if we hadn't given up chasing her, we probably could have caught her then and there.

I tell Ash, "You need to get this evidence to the Coast Guard or the police."

Ash still has me on speaker phone. I'm not 100% sure he can trust the ship's captain, or even the bartender he's been talking to. But I can't exactly say that out loud. I text him a warning, though. In response, he sends me pictures of everything that was in the locker, CC'd to both Arlo and Logan.

Logan immediately replies, *Did you find the ship's bell?*

Ash says, *No.*

I ask Logan if he's on his way back to the shop, to which he replies, *No.*

Which could be a problem because Marissa is still inside Greetings and Felicitations.

My phone rings. It's Arlo. When I pick up, he asks, "Where are you and what does all this evidence mean?"

I explain everything that has happened, ending with my theories on how Marissa might have faked her alibi by diving from the ship she was supposed to be maintaining.

Arlo says, "Marissa would have to be crazy to try that. People don't dive in the bay, because visibility in the bay is garbage."

"I know," I say. "And that's exactly why she didn't expect anyone to question it."

Arlo says, "Maybe she could have done it, if she stayed near the surface. It wouldn't be safe, but if she was willing to risk of being run over by a boat, it might have worked."

I say, "There's no way Tracie had access to a secret cubby hole on somebody's charter boat. Surely finding Amálie's phone somewhere where she couldn't possibly have put it has to be enough to get Tracie released from jail."

"It should be," Arlo says. "But there's still no real evidence tying Marissa to these crimes. Unless we find her fingerprints on Amálie's phone or something, it's just as circumstantial as what we arrested Tracie on."

I say, "Then we need to get evidence."

Arlo says, "Don't do anything stupid."

"I won't," I promise. But then I get a message from Jonah, saying he's found the missing ship's bell, hidden on a small boat that nobody realized Audrey owned – until he tracked down the tax records. He sends me his location, which is not far. The sun is just going down. It will be dark soon. But if I hurry, I can make it there before we lose daylight.

I text the Arlo-Logan-Ash channel, telling them where I'm going, and asking all available to meet me there. I call Carmen and tell her I'm going to have to take a rain check on recording the podcasts. I tell her, "It should be safe to go see what

Jonah found, since Marissa is in the shop. Tell me immediately if she leaves."

"Hold on," Carmen says. I hear rustling as she moves. Then she says, "There's a problem with that. Marissa already left."

Chapter Twenty-Four

The sensible thing would be to turn around and go back to Greetings and Felicitations. But what if Marissa is on her way to destroy the remaining evidence, the ship's bell? I'm sure she doesn't want to, because it's the main thing she can use to verify that the wreck she's hoping to salvage is indeed Lafitte's flagship. But all she has to do is toss it back in the ocean, and the biggest connection between her and these murders disappears back into the Gulf.

And if Jonah really is on Audrey's boat – he could be in trouble.

Of course, I may be overreacting. Marissa could have just gone home. It's not like she knows Ash found her stash of charts and other evidence. I'm *probably* overreacting, honestly.

Still, I drive a little more quickly than usual and hop out of the catering truck the minute I get to the dock. Audrey's boat is in a small, out of the way place away from the main marina, and there's only a couple of boats out here. The wide pier the boat is moored against is stacked with old crates and rusting machinery. I don't see Jonah. Maybe he's still on the boat. I make my way up the dock, and over to the boat, feeling more and more nervous the farther I get from shore.

I stage whisper, "Jonah."

He pokes his head out from belowdecks. "You have to see this place."

I'd rather just see the bell and get out of here, but he's already turned around and gone back downstairs. I climb onto the boat's deck, with its uneasy rocking, and make my way down into the small space. Audrey was apparently a fan of country music. Every surface in here is plastered with posters and memorabilia.

It's odd to think the owner of such a cheerful space is dead. The ship's bell, still attached to a jagged piece of iron from the sculpture, is sitting on a small table, alongside some rolled-up charts and an empty burger box.

There are boxes stacked against the corner. Jonah gestures to them and says, "I guess we figured out how Audrey could drive an Audi."

I look in the box. It's filled with bootleg video games, which only claim to be available in Japan. Hm. So Audrey was a smuggler. That could well have gotten her killed. The only connection to the other murders is this bell. It's evidence we have to get to the police.

I tell Jonah, "Okay, I've seen it. Now let's get out of here."

Jonah takes out a giant 2-gallon Ziplock bag and proceeds to put the piece from the bell in it – without touching it with his hands. He says, "It would probably be better for the chain of evidence just to leave it here, but I think it would disappear, you know?"

I nod. "We need to-"

There's the sound of something falling over out on the dock.

"Wait here." Jonah rushes up the stairs. After a few minutes there's some noise, farther down the dock. I doubt Jonah got the better end of it.

I grab the piece of the bell. Then I sneak from the boat back onto the dock.

I spot Marissa, between me and the shore. She has Jonah by the shirt collar, and she is holding a gun. Marissa makes eye contact with me. I duck behind a large, rusted out crane. I've got the pepper spray in my purse, but I don't think it has the range needed for this situation.

Logan is probably still too far away, but I've told Arlo everything he needs to find me. I need to stall until the authorities get here, or else somehow get that gun away from Marissa. In theory, this pier is wide enough that I could sneak around her, but that would leave Jonah trapped.

Marissa jerks hard on Jonah's collar. "Come on out, Felicity. I've read all the articles about you. I know how you are about justice and innocence. I'll happily trade this guy for you and the bell."

"No you won't," I say, staying where I am, trusting on the sound quality here to mask where my voice is coming from. I put my phone on speaker, and start recording an audio note. My hands are trembling, but I manage to hold onto the phone. "You'll just kill us both."

Because what else is she going to do, if she hopes to get away with this? She says, "You're impossible to negotiate with. You're just like my sister was."

Was? I didn't realize her sister was gone. In that article I had read, her pirate-obsessed sister had been the one to finance Marissa's successful treasure dive. I ask, "What happened to your sister? I thought you put up a GoFundMe?"

Marissa says, "She's not dead. She's just gone. She got sick, while I was away in Florida. Culliver had been trying to put together a crew for a larger scale dive trip. He kept the details about it hushed up, but there were rumors. The dive community is a small world, and it got around that Culliver had found Lafitte's treasure ship. I tried to get in as part of that crew, but before we were supposed to go, Culliver died. That's when I started looking for his diary. Because I knew that if I could just find the treasure, then my sister would get better."

"How did you even know he had a diary?" I ask. I move to a different piece of equipment. Unfortunately, it is farther out over the water.

"It was so tantalizing," Marissa says. She's shifting her head, trying to understand the dynamics of the sound and wind, so she can figure out where I am. "The book was right there, in his hand, in the pictures from every one of his salvage trips. Everyone knew he took meticulous notes."

"So where was the diary?" Jonah asks.

Marissa says, "He kept it in a hidden compartment in his desk. I know that because I turned his entire office upside down. I almost gave up, but then someone came into the room and I had to hide under the desk. And voila – I saw the hinge."

She sounds proud of her theft. Well, I suppose at least she had kept the diary from being lost.

She seems distracted for a moment and Jonah pulls away from her. He makes it to the edge and plunges into the water. She starts to follow him as far as the side of the dock , and if she shoots him from this distance, she's not likely to miss.

"Hey!" I say, stepping into the open.

Marissa levels her gun at me, and I duck partway behind the crane again. Cold fear arcs through my chest, then trickles down my spine. Because if she gets a clear shot, she's not going to hesitate to take it.

I have to keep her talking just a little longer, so I ask, "Why wasn't it enough just to deface the sculpture and take the bell? I get that you needed to get rid of the evidence that the wreck of the *Pride* had been found, so people didn't go looking for the salvage before you could get to it. But why did you have to get rid of Hernan and Amálie too?"

Marissa glares at me, as though I am not seeing something she finds obvious. "Hernan was actually the one who recognized the ship's bell in the first place. I approached him about going in together for the costs of hauling up the treasure, since I had found Culliver's notes. Audrey was there too, and she knew her way around dive equipment, so I offered her the same deal. Hernan turned me down flat. He said that a find like that belonged to the world – and not being sold to line our coffers. Can you believe he actually said that? In those words?"

I say, "I can believe that. I met Hernan a couple of times."

She nods. "At first, he was just all principles, and how everything should be for the glory of history instead of riches. He tried to talk me out of using what I had found in the diary. But later he said that he was going to reveal Culliver's diary at the gala, and that he would reveal the wreck's location to anyone wanting to claim the relics for a museum, instead of selling them on the open market. I couldn't have that. So I killed him – and as a bonus, I got Amálie too. Which saved me so much trouble, because I was going to have to kill her anyway, before she told someone about where she got the pieces that had been defaced. I seriously couldn't believe my luck. She shouldn't have been standing there. No one should. It wasn't a safe zone."

"Was it just because of the photographs on her phone?" I ask, thinking about my own experience with Marissa's thieving ways when she'd taken my phone to destroy my photographs of the sculpture. When that hadn't worked, she had broken into my catering truck to delete the images using my tablet. "Because without that, what did it matter if she talked about some ship's bell? If you wanted her dead – why not me, or Arlo? We had seen the pictures too."

Marissa scoffs. "Amálie was so proud of her talent. She didn't want to help others get better. She's the one who told me to stop entering contests or trying to exhibit since I was never going to get anywhere. She told me to go home and write a play instead." Marissa rolls her eyes. "She wasn't the type of person I could talk to about keeping her mouth shut until we'd completed the salvage. She'd have wanted to tie my find to her own success – when she had been too stupid to recognize the artifact she had uncovered. Can you believe she looked at that bell and just cut it in half?"

"But she didn't deserve to die over that," I point out.

"She did though. She'd have taken my glory – and my money. And my sister's respect for me."

"I thought your sister was gone," I say.

"She is," Marissa says. "She's in a facility up in Dallas. But if I can find the treasure, she'll get better. And she'll come home. I can't let anything get in the way of that." Marissa levels the gun at the crane, like she's about to take a shot through it. Though the crane is metal, and just as likely to ricochet. She sounds tired when she says, "Maybe I should have killed you too, when you chased me after I stole your purse. It would have saved me a lot of trouble having to kill you now."

My heart squeezes with dread. Because if she starts shooting, I'm not likely to make it off this dock. "That's really not necessary."

She laughs. "Keep telling yourself that. But I didn't want to have to kill you or that cop. You didn't know anything at that point. And you both seem like genuinely nice people. Unlike Amálie, who never lets anything go."

"And Audrey?" I ask. "She was your partner for the salvage. She'd even helped you steal an important piece of equipment. Wasn't she nice? And you would need her help once you got out to the location of the wreck. So why throw her overboard?"

Marissa says, "She figured out that I was the one who killed Hernan. Audrey put all the pieces together during the theft. Once we got the ROV up on deck, she tried to pretend that she was still clueless, but I could see the change in her demeanor. I'd been afraid I was going to have to do away with her, so I came prepared."

"You brought one of her own statues?" I ask.

Marissa says, "It was a hideous thing. It deserved to be in the bottom of the ocean."

I see Jonah, soaking wet and dripping, climbing up onto the pier behind Marissa. I need to make sure Marissa's attention is entirely on me. So I dash from that crane over to something that looks like a saucer-style space ship. I think it's one of the life pods from an oil rig. Marissa takes a few shots at me, but they ping off the metal of the pod.

There's a scuffle, and then the gun comes skittering across the pier, straight towards me. I set down the bell and the phone, as both Marissa and Jonah fight each other to get to the gun. My legs feel like jelly, but I dash out from behind the pod and pick up the cold metal. Marissa freezes, and Jonah gets his arms around her. I hate guns, and this one feels heavy and dark in my hands as my heartbeat pounds in my ears. I'm not about to

point a weapon at anyone, even if I don't intend to fire. I throw
the gun off the pier, and hear the satisfying splash of it hitting the
water. There. Threat diffused.

Marissa tries to wrench away from Jonah, and she ducks
out of his grip, but before she gets far, there's the screech of tires
and the wail of sirens as three police cars block off exit for the
pier.

Marissa tries to jump into the water, but between me and
Jonah both grabbing onto her, we keep her from escaping.

Jonah tells me, "I'm glad you threw that gun overboard. I
had no idea what I was going to do with it if I actually beat her to
it."

Marissa glares at him. She says, "This isn't how this is
supposed to end."

Arlo is the one who comes up to slap the cuffs on her. As
he does, he gives me a reproachful look. He says, "I thought you
said you weren't planning to do anything dangerous."

"I never exactly plan it," I say. I gesture over to the pod.
"But the evidence that Marissa and Audrey defaced the sculpture
is over there. And I'm about to send you a recording of her
confession." I feel a little bit sorry for Marissa, now that she's not
pointing a gun at me. I tell Arlo, "She has a little trouble
distinguishing wishful thinking from reality."

Arlo says, "Don't we all, sometimes."

Epilogue

Delores makes good on her promise, so a few days later, we're at the gala. Carmen has taken control of the kitchen, and has servers circulating with all the specialty desserts she and Tam Bin came up with. Tam Binh and her family are still in town, so Charlotte is especially happy with the vegetarian chocolate mousse cake that Carmen made specifically for her.

I go into the kitchen and look at all the gorgeous desserts she's made from my chocolate. I tell her, "This is the most complicated thing Greetings and Felicitations has done so far. Thank you for everything you've done to make it a success."

Carmen says, "I took a lot of notes and did a lot of research. I never really thought about how many food allergies people can have. I have an idea for a second cookbook. I want to do one that will feature sections for gluten free, vegan, diary free, low sugar and egg free recipes. I think it would go a long way towards showing that chocolate can be part of any lifestyle. Unless you're allergic to actual chocolate."

I pretend to shudder. "A fate worse than death."

Tam Binh walks in in the middle of this and says, "Focus on launching the first book first. Ash should be here soon. He's got some ideas he wants to share, and I think most of them are good."

I ask, "You're working together with Ash for a book launch?"

Tam Binh plucks a tiny tart off a nearby tray and says, "People can change. I think Ash has grown up a lot since I last met him."

I'm just glad that he had made it back safely to shore with all the evidence needed to make sure Marissa stays in jail.

I tell Carmen, "Make sure you come out into the gallery soon. Everyone wants to meet the pastry chef responsible for all of this."

I go out to the gallery myself, to take another look at the completed chocolate sculpture. I still think it should count as the world's largest chocolate sculpture, but because there are a number of inedible supports and other parts, it doesn't qualify for that official title – or anything else that says "entirely made out of chocolate." If I had known at the beginning that this sculpture was going to be bigger than anything else anyone else had done, I probably would have said no. But I didn't realize it was a completely ridiculous proposition, and so I undertook it – with the help of an amazing crew of people, most of whom are here tonight.

I especially admire the blown sugar jellyfish that adorn one edge of the sculpture. Jonah had helped me make them, but there are two jellyfish that I completed by myself. In addition to working with neon, I found out that Jonah also blows glass. Blowing glass and blowing sugar aren't that different, and since that night on the pier, Jonah has tried to do all he can to help me get the sculpture done. I guess it is a thank you for saving his life, but the reality is more that we saved each other's lives.

Sonya of yarn shop fame is over near the sculpture, showing her twin sister the detailed knotworks she sculpted. Gently and his cat are standing with Violet as a photographer takes a picture of them with the sculpture in the background. I see Ash sidle up next to the photographer and take the same shot, which is sure to grace an article in Ash's Gulf Coast Happenings. After all, Violet and Gently were the core coordination of the actual art that went into making the sculpture a reality.

Tracie approaches me. She looks nervous. "Mrs. Koerber?"

"Felicity." I interrupt.

"Felicity." Somehow saying that makes Tracie look even more nervous. "I was wondering if you might have any more permanent openings at your business. I've developed a passion for chocolate as a sculpting medium. I think we could do some amazing things."

"I'll have to discuss it with Logan," I say. "I don't know if, after all the trouble we had getting this piece to come together, we have any plans to do any other chocolate art. Well, except for the piece I promised for Autumn's wedding."

Tracie looks disappointed. And I feel a little disappointed too. After all, the artistic part of the project had been fun.

Logan comes over to us. He stands close enough to me that I can feel the body heat coming off him, and I feel a sudden flush in my cheeks when he looks down at me with those intense green eyes. He tells me, "I'm so glad you talked me into doing that sculpture of Knightley. I had no idea some of what we've done here is possible."

I feel vindicated. My business instincts have brought us to a whole other level. But it had come at such a great cost. I gesture at the huge chocolate ship, with masts reaching up towards the arched ceiling. The masts are mostly PVC pipe, but the rigging is all chocolate. I say, "I don't think anybody had an idea some of what we did here was possible. We're finally going to get some real publicity. Positive publicity, this time."

Logan says, "I talked to Delores. She's willing to let us have time on her 3-D printer to do custom work for clients, as long as we put the museum logo on materials advertising the service. I think it's a good idea."

"Oh?" Tracie says.

And just like that, we have a new employee. I tell Logan what Tracie wants to do, and how it could compliment the work Miles is already doing for us. And then I leave it to them to talk terms.

I circulate around the room, saying hi to Autumn and Drake, and to some of the other small business owners who have shops on the Strand. Miles is there, with his girlfriend, the better to show her the project he's been working on all this time. I give him a hug and tell him, "You helped me realize how meaningful this journey has been. Thank you."

Miles says, "I just tried to make it look cool. The meaning was all you."

Kaylee walks into the gallery and does a double take at the pair of sculptures – one a hodgepodge of metal and glass, its twin of chocolate and sugar. She walks up to get a closer look, then comes over to where I'm standing. She says, "The detail work done out of chocolate is impressive. I'd love to have something similar for my shop. Something much smaller, of course."

I tell her that's probably something we can do, and then Kaylee and I start brainstorming ideas for a chocolate sculpture showing figures coming out of an open book, celebrating the imaginative act of reading. It sounds like an exciting project.

But before we can finalize any details, Delores takes me by the arm and leads me into the immersive cacao exhibit. Delores says, "This is my first chance to actually see your photographs. I must say, you have quite an eye."

My first instinct is to reply dismissively, but honestly, I agree with her. I say, "Thank you. If you'd asked me a month ago if I'm an artist, I would probably have said no."

She looks surprised. "Isn't chocolate making an art?"

I nod. "I've realized that it is. And that when I came back to Galveston all broken and grieving, what I wanted – though I didn't know it – was the beauty and hope that art gives. And that sense of belonging and community."

"Good," Delores says. "I'm glad I could help." She laughs a little, but then she adds, "Seriously, though, I'm sorry I ran away. I couldn't have kept everything together here, and solved a murder at the same time. I honestly didn't expect you to try to."

I tell her the same thing I told Arlo. "These things just sort of happen to me."

Rosa shows up, wearing black and looking sadder than she did the day after her husband died. She walks up to me and Delores. After giving Delores a giant hug – they are sisters after all – she turns to me and says, "Thank you. Because of you, I got to see a more noble side to Hernan that I ever realized was there."

She gives me a hug too.

I tell her, "Grief is going to be there with you for a while. If you have a bad day, or just need to talk, I've been through it all. Plus, I have chocolate."

Rosa says, "I may just take you up on that. As long as the chocolate also has peanut butter."

"That can be arranged," I say.

We both laugh. And if Rosa can still laugh, eventually she's going to be okay.

I finally get a chance to talk to Arlo who, as the guy who arrested the woman who murdered three local artists, is finding himself fairly popular tonight.

He takes an appreciative look at my dress and says, "You look beautiful."

I find myself blushing. I reply, "You're not so shabby yourself."

He is after all wearing a green dress shirt and black patterned tie that emphasize his broad shoulders and well-built chest. He gestures over to the copy of *Treasure Island*, which I have on display, under a glass panel, as part of the giant treasure chest that is spilling out bonbons for the guests to take.

Arlo says, "The University is already organizing the group to attempt to recover the wreck."

"I know," I say.

"Well?" he asks. "There's only one way to find out if that ship really was carrying treasure. Or if those chests were filled with bread the fish ate. They're offering an incredible opportunity by saying we can do an observation dive. Do you want to come and see the wreck in person?"

It turns out that me being interested in scuba diving is more important to Arlo than I thought. Probably more than he thought, too.

I say, "I already told them yes, but I'm nervous. This is going to be a big step up from the rig dive."

"We can make sure you get lots of practice first," Arlo says. "They're going to want you to be certified, at the very least."

"Fair," I say. "But while I'm saying yes to things, a couple of days ago, I got an invite to visit a farm collective in Brazil. I know that's where Logan wants to go to visit origin, and to do some diving. I told them I'd be going, and bringing some friends. Are you interested?"

"Absolutely," Arlo says. "As long as I can get off work. Which won't happen if you discover any more murders."

"I'll try my best not to," I say.

I have enough on my plate already, doing more chocolate sculptures and figuring out what I want my future to look like. I've only given myself until Autumn's wedding to do so – and that's not very far away.

Jonah walks over. He takes a bonbon from the display and makes a happy noise. Then he says, "I have been wanting to apologize for putting your life in danger the other night. I should have called the cops immediately, instead of going out on that boat." He turns to Arlo. "I guess I should apologize to you too. I'm not a great private investigator."

Arlo says, "Next time, leave it to the professionals."

I don't think Arlo's including me when he says that, but Jonah looks at me like he is.

Jonah says, "Right."

Tracie comes back from the museum store and hands Jonah a chocolate bar. She says, "Check it out! Felicity made a bar in honor of Renoir."

I grin. I knew Tracie would appreciate my efforts. I say, "It's a limited-edition bar. I chose a chocolate that has a very fruity grape taste to it, since I know that grapes are Renoir's favorite. I added millet, macadamia nut and freeze-dried banana, along with a touch of black pepper. Usually my bars are only two ingredients – cacao and sugar – so this one has a lot of ingredients for me. But they all make me think of Renoir."

"It's too bad he can't eat any," Tracie says.

"Oh, but I have a solution for that," I say. "Wait here."

I go and find Charlotte, and get her to bring the tray I had prepared before the party started. We find Tracie and head over to the closed door, behind which Renoir starts screeching, "I love you! I love you! Josephine!" as he hears us approach.

Tracie opens the door and keeps Renoir from flying out, as we move into the room and get the door shut behind us. On the tray, I've got all the bird-friendly version of the ingredients from the chocolate bar. There's a whole spray of millet, which is easier for a bird Renoir's size to play with or eat than the tiny grains on their own. And fresh grapes, of course, along with a whole banana and a handful of macadamia nuts.

I introduce Tracie and Charlotte to each other, and announce that they're both good friends of Renoir.

Tracie tells Charlotte, "I'm here at the museum a lot, making sure he doesn't get lonely. You should come see him too, next time you're in town."

I say, "I'll come by a bit, too."

Charlotte says, "You'd better. I'll be expecting you to send me pictures, so I don't forget him." She bites at her lip. "You can send pictures of the bunny too, if you want."

"Absolutely," I say. "Let's take a picture right now."

I'm grateful to have friends from around the world, and who travel the world, and friends who are close to me here at home. I hold my phone, and we take a selfie, where we capture Renoir with his beak wide open, in the middle of saying, "I love you."

ACKNOWLEDGEMENTS

Special thanks to Jael Rattigan of French Broad Chocolates in South Carolina, who has consulted extensively on this series. And to Sander Wolf of DallasChocolate.org, who put me in touch with so many experts in the chocolate field.

I'd also like to thank Ryne DeArmond with the Historic Harbor Tour and Dolphin Watch at the Galveston Historic Seaport for giving us a tour so personalized to the research needs for my book, and taking the time to talk to us afterwards. I also want to thank Colton Murphey, Museum Docent and Tour Guide at the Ocean Star Offshore Drilling Rig and Museum. Colton also kindly reviewed portions of the manuscript dealing with rigs and diving. I'd also like to thank Sylvia Beach and her staff at Dive West (Dallas) for additional dive related inspiration and information.

I have to thank Jake, as usual, for reading the manuscript umpteen times, being my biggest fan and cheerleader, and doing all the formatting things to make this thing happen. He always keeps me going, even when things are stressful.

And thanks to my agent, Jennie, for her input on this series, and her encouragement to keep moving forward.

And for this series especially, I'd like to thank my family for giving me a love of the ocean and a curiosity about history. The Cajun side of both mine and Jake's families comes through in Felicity's family in the books. This has given me an excuse to reach out to family members for recipes and inspiration, many of which you can find on the Bean to Bar Bonuses section of my website. Thanks y'all!

Thanks to James and Rachel Knowles for continuing to sharing their knowledge of bunny behavior (as well as videos of their ADORABLE bunny – Yuki pics will always make my day). And to Laurie Laskiwski of Parrots Parrots Parrots Aviary for her information about bird behavior and speaking capabilities. Laurie, I love your bird videos! I'd like to thank Amy Shojai for inspiring Renoir's addition to this book. Your presentation on animal behavior to my Saturday Night Write discussion group proved invaluable to me, and hopefully to the other attendees as well.

I'd also like to thank Cassie, Monica and Tessa, who are my support network in general. I don't know how I would have gotten through these years of social isolation without you three.

Thank you all, dear readers, for spending time in Felicity's world. I hope you enjoyed getting to know her. Her fifth adventure will be available for you soon.

Did Felicity's story make you hungry?

Visit the Bean to Bar Mysteries Bonus Recipes page on Amber's website to find out how to make some of the food mentioned in the book.

AMBER ROYER writes the CHOCOVERSE comic telenovela-style foodie-inspired space opera series (available from Angry Robot Books and Golden Tip Press). She is also co-author of the cookbook There are Herbs in My Chocolate, which combines culinary herbs and chocolate in over 60 sweet and savory recipes, and had a long-running column for Dave's Garden, where she covered gardening and crafting. She blogs about creative writing technique and all things chocolate related over at www.amberroyer.com. She also teaches creative writing in person in North Texas for both UT Arlington Continuing Education and Writing Workshops Dallas. If you are very nice to her, she might make you cupcakes.

www.amberroyer.com Instagram: amberroyerauthor